The Reason for Ann

AND OTHER STORIES

Cluny Classics

ROBERT HUGH BENSON
Come Rack, Come Rope
Dawn of All
The Light Invisible
No Other Gods

ORESTES BROWNSON
Like a Roaring Lion

G.K. CHESTERTON
A Chesterton Reader

GERTRUD VON LE FORT
The Veil of Veronica

NATHANIEL HAWTHORNE
The Shattered Fountain: Selected Tales

DOROTHY L. SAYERS
Whose Body?

GEORGES BERNANOS
Joy
Under the Sun of Satan

MALACHY G. CARROLL
The Stranger

MYLES CONNOLLY
The Bump on Brannigan's Head
Dan England and the Noonday Devil
Mr. Blue
The Reason for Ann & Other Stories

FRANÇOIS MAURIAC
The Dark Angels
The Desert of Love
A Kiss for the Leper
The Lamb
The Unknown Sea
Vipers' Tangle
What Was Lost

SIGRID UNDSET
The Burning Bush
The Wild Orchid

The Reason for Ann

AND OTHER STORIES

Myles Connolly

With an Introduction and Notes by
Stephen Mirarchi, Ph.D.

Preface by
Mary Connolly Breiner

Cluny Classics

Cluny Media edition, 2019

For more information regarding this title
please write to info@clunymedia.com, or to
Cluny Media, P.O. Box 1664, Providence, RI, 02901

VISIT US ONLINE AT WWW.CLUNYMEDIA.COM

ISBN: 978-1949899986

Cover design by Clarke & Clarke
Cover image: Arthur Clifton Goodwin, *Custom House Tower
from the Public Garden, Boston*, c. 1914, pastel on paperboard
Courtesy of Museum of Fine Arts, Boston

For Ann…

Contents

The Six Stories

❃   ❃   ❃

Preface

Through "The Reason for Ann and Other Stories," my father found the perfect way to share what he deeply believed about life, faith, love, family, redemption, good and evil. Both reasoned and passionate about these truths, he brought them to life in the stories summarized here.

The first of the stories, "The Reason for Ann," makes me smile as I imagine the fun my father was having creating O'Sullivan. This rakish and seemingly irredeemable young man thoroughly enjoys the effect he has on young women. In fact, he is having such a good time living life carefree that he is coming close to "using up his mother's prayers," and leaving his soul in serious danger. Could such a life possibly have a reason?

Mr. Somerset from "The Pigeon from St. Bartholomew's," on the other hand, seems to have everything under control. He is striding with absolute confidence toward his goal of "self-sufficiency, the fulfillment of mankind's being, the perfection of mankind on earth." Congratulating himself on every step he takes toward that end, he doesn't stumble even once. But, as we know, God has a sense of humor...

Vinnie is a young girl sent by the courts to "The Big Red House on Hope Street." "Harder, colder, more sure of herself" than the other girls there, Vinnie finds that she is coming up against a young, joyful nun who thinks that she is wonderful and beautiful. The most personal of the stories, this one is based on my aunt, a Good Shepherd Sister. Dad would tell us, with great affection, how she saw all these tough and surly teens as wonderful and beautiful. "Really, Myles! You should take them with you to Hollywood! They are stars, every one!"

The story of "Seminary Hill," in contrast to "The Big Red House on Hope Street," is about a religious institution that inadvertently houses true evil. Hugo, who claims to be a refugee from eastern Poland, has brought his nephew with him to enter the seminary. Although something very dark is going on, the saintly Spiritual Director sees only a good soul in the new seminarian. He, however, detests the priest: "The more I hated him, the more he loved me. I could not endure it." What is this darkness that the uncle and his nephew have brought to "Seminary Hill"?

"Love, Tomi" tells the story of the love a boy has for his father and of his struggle to express it. He remembers his joy when sailing with his Dad, and muses, "I guess I took you for granted, Pop…standing on your shoulders, looking out at the horizon…you were great, Pop. I should have told you." My father knew that it could be hard for a boy to tell his deep feelings to his Dad, and he knew the importance of communicating them while one could.

"Natural Causes" also deals with the efforts of an adolescent to make her love known to her mother and father. As both parents become very involved in seeking their own happiness outside the family, they do not notice their daughter sinking deeper and deeper into her isolation and grief. She tries to communicate this by telling them that "Real loneliness is…wanting to love someone so much, and not being able to." It is the loneliness that too many children know.

We hope that the truths in these stories, and the characters who illustrate them, will touch your heart. This was certainly my father's most devout intention.

~Mary Connolly Breiner
Holy Saturday, 2019

Introduction

Nota bene: This introduction refers freely to the events of the stories within this volume, including their endings. First-time readers may wish to skip the introduction for now and return to it after reading the stories.

Introduction

Myles Connolly was enjoying some of the most productive and illustrious years of his literary life when he decided to collect some of his best "novelettes" in *The Reason for Ann and Other Stories* in 1952. *Mr. Blue*, his little novel from 1928 that had often sold fewer than 100 copies a year to that point, was now selling in the tens of thousands; by 1954, over half a million copies would be in print. The two novels he had published in 1950 and 1951—his first since *Mr. Blue*—were popular and had received fairly good reviews in both the Catholic and secular presses.

This literary success seemed to come out of nowhere—a fact Connolly himself would wrestle with in his silver anniversary introduction to *Mr. Blue* in 1954.[1] For the previous two decades, most of Connolly's artistic efforts had come in his role as a Hollywood writer or producer. He received an Oscar nomination for his original screenplay for 1944's *Music for Millions*, and his work on Frank Capra's critically acclaimed 1948 film *State of the Union* had brought him further praise. Around the time he published *The Reason for Ann*, Connolly had worked on the box office hits *Here Comes the Groom* (1951) and *Hans Christian Andersen* (1952).

Connolly's finely honed sense of cinematographic storytelling was on full display in his 1950 novel *The Bump on Brannigan's Head*, which reads like a screenplay-to-be with nary a wasted word or scene. The selections in this volume exhibit the same expertise. Connolly had many stories to choose from; he had been publishing in the *Saturday Evening Post*, *Ladies' Home Journal*, *The Sign*, and others. He likely selected only those stories that best showcased his aesthetic theory. He explained it cogently in a late 1951 interview: "I am primarily interested in entertaining people and telling them a fundamental truth at the same time and telling them in a hearty, wholesome way—through laughter."[2] This philosophy was in keeping with one of Connolly's greatest influences, G. K. Chesterton, whom Connolly had worked with while editing *Columbia*, the international journal of the Knights of Columbus, and whose work he would continue to cite in his novels.[3]

1.   Myles Connolly, "Introduction," *Mr. Blue* (New York: Macmillan, 1928; Garden City, NY: Image Books, 1954). Citations refer to the Image edition.

2.   Walter V. Carty, "Myles Connolly Sings in His Books the 'Adventure of Catholicism.'" *The Boston Pilot* (8 December 1951), p. 9.

3.   Connolly gives one account of his in-person impressions of Chesterton in "Chesterton's Cap and Bells," *America* (26 August 1922), pp. 439–40.

One story Connolly omitted serves to illustrate his selection criteria. "Are You Anxious?" appeared in *Ladies' Home Journal* magazine in mid-1951 and carried this humorously provocative subtitle: "Johnny's life was pitch-black until he consulted a psychologist. Then it darkened."[4] A straightforward tale of fraud and justice, the story has one comic scene after another, ends on a feel-good note, and imparts an essential truth about healthy self-assertion, as opposed to aggressive arrogance or sniveling self-pity. The story is, in effect, exactly what popular readers would gravitate towards; it has no higher literary or theological aspirations and requires none. Connolly likely thought that the story had served its purpose and need not be reprinted.

The stories that follow, however, all have a higher purpose built in to their very telling and thus bear the joy of retelling.

"The Reason for Ann"

Many readers will immediately compare the volume's title story to Capra's masterpiece *It's a Wonderful Life* (1947), on which Connolly worked even though he remains uncredited. "The Reason for Ann" focuses on the relationship between O'Sullivan, a young man careening through a life of dissipation, and his unlikely bride-to-be, the saintly Ann. Their adventures are told through the ledger-writing of two recording angels: Basil, who like facts, numbers, and charts, and Gerald, who is a bit of

---

4.   Myles Connolly, "Are You Anxious?" *Ladies' Home Journal* 68 (June 1951): pp. 60–61.

a Romantic dreamer. When O'Sullivan is sent to the Korean War, only Ann's prayers save him from his own bravado. That, and a touch of reckless courage on his part, effect one of the surprise endings for which Connolly is celebrated. At the time, the story certainly touched hearts for its spiritualization of the highly sensitive topic of the war in Korea. But the tale also suggests a bold theological idea: without prayer, nothing of any supernatural value can be accomplished.

That message came through loud and clear. One reviewer discarded Connolly's thinking: "The title story… is not only sentimental; it is based on an unsound theology of prayer."[5] If Connolly were writing theology, this point would have to be considered. Do people go to Hell because there is no one to pray for them, as the seers of Fatima reported that Mary said?[6] Connolly, however, is using a theological proposition as an aesthetic device: what if people cannot be shown divine or supernatural mercy except through prayer, especially intercessory prayer? What kind of stories would such a teaching create? As the joyfully unexpected ending of "The Reason for Ann" illustrates, it makes for tales that affirm God's justice yet showcase his lavish mercy. And Connolly, who

---

5.   Review of *The Reason for Ann*, *The Catholic World* 177–178 (1953): pp. 394.

6.   A different rendition of Mary's words is that "many souls are lost from God because there is no one to pray and offer sacrifices for them." This translation leaves open the possibility that there are souls who can find God again in this world when prayers are finally offered for them; it also allows the possibility of eternal loss for those who freely reject God and never have anyone else to pray for them. See Donna-Marie Cooper O'Boyle, *Advent with Our Lady of Fatima* (Manchester, NH: Sophia Institute Press, 2018), pp. 39–41.

in *Mr. Blue* had written a modern St. Francis of Assisi tale, was likely very familiar with the Franciscan devotion of praying for those who have no one to pray for them. This devotion was popular, in fact, among Catholics in general at the time; one 1950 children's book encourages young ones to pray for the "many souls in purgatory who have no one to pray for them."[7] Of course, praying for those who are already on their way to Heaven (those in Purgatory) is distinct from praying for those apparently on their way to Hell. Connolly's title story in this volume finds that the latter proposition makes for the more adventurous tale in his time and circumstances.

"Love, Tomi"

The same reviewer critical of the theology in "The Reason for Ann" found "Love, Tomi" the best selection in the book. "Carefully wrought," the reviewer wrote, the story "shows, with restraint and artistry, a boy's admiration and love for his father."[8] That the story is epistolary or written as one long letter serves to heighten the drama of a son's summative communication with his Dad. From a literary point of view, the story is instructive in its nuanced portrayal of the son as typically masculine yet unusually perceptive—a clue to the reason for which may be found in the boy's burgeoning prayer life.

The story depends, too, on a Catholic understanding of redemptive suffering: that bearing such difficulties in

---

7.   Gerald T. Brennan, *Angel Food for Boys & Girls*, Volume I (Charlotte, NC: Neumann Press, 2013), chapter 14.

8.   Review, *The Catholic World*, p. 394.

union with Christ will not only bear fruit in the next life but also in the here and now—and one might actually glimpse some of those very fruits. One of Tomi's epiphanies in the story unites his father's redemptive suffering with divine providence: how God has already in his family's life arranged or governed things such that a much deeper suffering could be actively avoided. Tomi comes to terms with the beauty of these teachings through writing this very letter to his deceased father.

Thus, Connolly is up to something more with the epistolary form of the story. A priest known for being "strict and stern" invites Tomi to write the letter in the first place; his advice is something more than feel-good sentimentalism or pop psychology. His counsel is more in keeping with the aesthetic theory advanced by Tolkien: "In Fantasy [the Christian artist] may actually assist in the effoliation and multiple enrichment of creation."[9] Writing his letter with supernatural intention, Tomi may rightly and reasonably hope that its contents will help his biological father—and himself.

By ending the story on an association between Tomi's biological father and God the Father, Connolly opens up the entire narrative as a spiritual colloquy. The letter Tomi has written is as much to God the Father as it is to his birth father. In that sense, the story functions as a prayer, a pouring out of one's affective life in thanksgiving to the one who grants life. Connolly advanced this theme throughout his fiction, often asking his readers

---

9.   J. R. R. Tolkien, "On Fairy-Stories," in *The Tolkien Reader* (New York: Del Rey, 1966), p. 89.

to consider that spiritual fatherhood, rooted in God the Father, is what brings about the genuine friendship and intimacy that effects *metanoia* or conversion of life.

"The Pigeon from St. Bartholomew's"

By the 1950s Connolly had become involved with highly successful money-making films, but he did not compromise his literary taste or his aesthetic principles. "The Pigeon from St. Bartholomew's" is an excellent example of Connolly's art, stands as one of his best short works, and should take a place of prominence in his oeuvre alongside *Mr. Blue* if only because the story's protagonist, Mr. Somerset, is Mr. Blue in reverse—an anti-Blue, so to speak.

Blue lives on top of a towering apartment complex in a packing crate, offering up prayers on high; Mr. Somerset lives in The Towers, an exclusive building in one of the fanciest parts of town, and he looks down on all below him impersonally—a word Connolly emphasizes in the story. Blue walks through the sites of the American Revolution as he tells his narrator-friend his plan to revolutionize the soul through total self-offering; Mr. Somerset walks to his temple, the United Nations, judging those lower than himself and imagining a utopian revolution of pure utility. Blue dies a joyful martyr, having begun a Catholic apostolate among the poorest of the poor, his life sacrificed for an alcoholic for whom no one else seems to care; Mr. Somerset demeans the alcoholic who lives next door and dies by accident after fleeing a Catholic church, the victim of—quite literally—a pigeon drop. Examples of other similarities could be multiplied.

Mr. Somerset might as well be Blue flipped head over heels, which is what "somerset" means: to somersault. If Connolly did not consciously craft this tale as a "reverse Mr. Blue," the comparisons are staggeringly coincidental.

As usual, however, Connolly has a deeper meaning in store. Two of the most conspicuous words in the story work together: "adductive" and "ciborium." Like his use of the word "embolus" at the end of *Mr. Blue*,[10] Connolly here uses prominent words with clear literal meanings that also draw the reader deeply into the theological mystery of the story. Literally, adductive means the power to draw a part into its greater whole: Mr. Somerset, along with the crowd, is pulled into St. Patrick's, the famous Catholic cathedral. That moment is significant in and of itself, given the history of St. Patrick's, one of the most storied American churches. For instance, it played a role in the Catholic Worker movement founded by Dorothy Day and Peter Maurin, a living example of a program supporting the poorest of the poor. They reached an audience of hundreds of thousands with their one-cent *Catholic Worker* newspaper: "The bundles of papers were delivered by a volunteer named Dan Orr, who had a horse and wagon; whenever they clopped past St. Patrick's Cathedral, he claimed, the horse genuflected."[11] Such humor was right up Connolly's alley, and the author had indeed envisioned and fictionalized the beginnings of such Catholic outreach in *Mr. Blue*.

10. *Mr. Blue*, introduction and notes by Stephen Mirarchi (Tacoma, WA: Cluny Media, 2015), pp. 123, 196–97.

11. Paul Elie, *The Life You Save May Be Your Own: An American Pilgrimage* (New York: Farrar, Straus and Giroux, 2003), p. 88.

Further, the history of the word adductive is theological and necessarily controversial: an adductive power or motion is "characterized by the bringing of the body of Christ into the bread during the Eucharist (by substitution rather than annihilation)."[12] The word has been at the heart of Protestant debates over the Catholic doctrine of transubstantiation, namely in arguing against the substantial change of transubstantiation by proposing instead a change in location of Christ's body. The famous British priest Frederick William Faber, a convert to Catholicism with John Henry Newman during the Oxford Movement, argued that the idea of Eucharistic adduction is intellectually insufficient: "It does not seem then that a merely adductive act will satisfy the requisitions of the mystery."[13]

Connolly's use, therefore, points to the crux of the story: the question of Mr. Somerset's redemption. His being pulled into the Church without a free act of intellect and will on his part is insufficient; one does not experience conversion adductively. At the same time, Connolly asks his readers to consider that the drawing power of Christ must rest on his True Presence in the Eucharist. Christ indeed promises that "if only I am lifted up from the earth, I will attract all men to myself,"[14] and that word is fulfilled, according to the Catholic intellectual tradition, through Christ's True Presence in his Church, especially in the Eucharist. Thus, Connolly

---

12. "Adductive, adj.". *OED Online*. March 2019. Oxford University Press.
13. Frederick William Faber, *The Blessed Sacrament* (Baltimore: John Murphy & Co., 1855), p. 81.
14. John 12:32, Knox translation.

both affirms the Catholic Church's true drawing power through the Eucharist yet denies that an adductive form of that drawing can be salvific. Redemption must be transubstantial. Connolly was directly contributing to the Catholic renewal that flourished in 1950s America: "Most centrally, the renewal of liturgical concern was directed toward the Great Prayer of the Church[:] the Mass, the Holy Eucharist."[15]

Connolly drives this point home by using the word "ciborium" in the next paragraph to describe the canopy over the altar at St. Patrick's. The more common name for this canopy is a "baldacchino," though in a Catholic architectural context it is roughly synonymous with "ciborium." Once again, however, Connolly has chosen a keen wordplay. A ciborium also refers to the sacred dish in which hosts are reserved in the tabernacle or used to serve the faithful. Connolly's choice of "ciborium" thus builds on his use of "adductive": he is highlighting the doctrine of the True Presence in the Eucharist that Catholicism teaches, and that has the power to draw all humanity into Christ's Mystical Body. For Connolly, Mr. Somerset's redemption cannot happen through the utopian dreams of the United Nations or any other secular organization in which people invest salvific claims. Further, Mr. Somerset's ultimate incorporation in the Mystical Body of Christ cannot *de facto* happen through the Episcopal St. Bartholomew's, a church that does not believe in transubstantiation and thus cannot offer the faithful the

---

15.   Sydney E. Ahlstrom, *A Religious History of the American People* (New Haven: Yale University Press, 1972), pp. 1014–15.

actual *substance* of Christ's Body. Like Flannery O'Connor, Connolly says "to hell with it"[16] to adduction or any other teaching that reduces the fullness of the Eucharistic mystery. As O'Connor would write to one of her questioning correspondents, "For us the Church is the body of Christ, Christ continuing in time, and as such a divine institution... If the Church is not a divine institution it will turn into an Elks Club by and by & can be dispensed with."[17]

Where does that leave Mr. Somerset's redemption? After absconding from St. Patrick's, the protagonist makes his way as quickly as possible to his "church," the United Nations, only to have a flower pot come sailing down on his head, courtesy of a scared pigeon that knocked it off a ledge, killing him instantly. The narrator then tells us: "Mr. Somerset was buried from St. Bartholomew's." The title of the story now makes more sense. The wayward pigeon that inadvertently killed Mr. Somerset was not of the St. Bartholomew's Episcopal group; it was apparently from St. Patrick's. Thus, the title can refer to that bird only obliquely. The title more fully refers to Mr. Somerset himself: a "pigeon," in the common parlance of the times, is someone naïve or foolish, a scapegoat. Connolly thus turns the entire story on its head: the protagonist, who believes himself superior to others, is actually the most gullible character of all. Further, since that bird uncannily kills Mr. Somerset by

---

16. Flannery O'Connor, Letter "To A.," *Flannery O'Connor: Collected Works* (New York: Library of America, 1988), p. 977.

17. Ibid., p. 1099.

causing a flowerpot to fall on his head, the character has been the victim of a "pigeon drop," a common term for a type of confidence game.[18] Looking at the context, we can see Connolly's deeper meaning: those who exchange the True Presence in the Eucharist for any dilution of it are the chumps of the world.

For all his insistence on the fullness of the faith in Catholicism, Connolly was dedicated to ecumenism, as the last, surprising line of the story shows. The very bird that killed Mr. Somerset is compared to the righteous who batten on spoil from 1 Samuel 2. That section of Scripture—Hannah's prayer—contains numerous memorable lines about God's breaking down the mighty, lifting up the poor, shattering his foes, and leaving the wicked to "perish in the darkness."[19] We might conclude that Connolly was trying to emphasize the reality of Hell, the genuine possibility of eternal loss freely chosen. Other writers at the time were certainly not shy about the lessons of hellfire and brimstone—typically the sphere of forthright prophets—especially O'Connor: "No American author of the fifties was more closely identified with the biblical prophets than" she.[20] O'Connor published "A Good Man Is Hard to Find" in 1953, with its memorable villain The Misfit, who knows Christ is the answer but

---

18. See, for instance, Ralph Ellison's 1952 novel *Invisible Man*, in which the narrator in the space of two city blocks is labeled both a "field [nigger]… from the South" and a "young New York [Negro]" and is accused of perpetrating a "pigeon drop" confidence game. Ralph Ellison, *Invisible Man* (New York: Modern Library, 1994), pp. 321, 323.

19. 1 Samuel 2:9, NAB translation.

20. Jason W. Stevens, *God-Fearing and Free: A Spiritual History of America's Cold War* (Cambridge: Harvard University Press, 2010), p. 253.

rejects him anyway as he continues his cross-country kill-ing spree. Four years later O'Connor would publish one of her most disturbing stories, "A View of the Woods," in which the elderly protagonist strangles his granddaugh-ter to death and flees from a vision of God into eternal darkness. Though both of those stories contain O'Con-nor's trademark Southern humor, neither of them treats the final destination of its characters with anything less than metaphysical solemnity.

Neither does Connolly with Mr. Somerset, but the reader should note that the character dies *by acci-dent*—and by a rather comic accident, at that. The pun on "pigeon dropping" should be enough of a clue that Connolly intends some humor in Mr. Somerset's demise. Further, the other, Episcopal pigeons at the end of the story are eating just fine—but the Catholic one, as it were, makes off with the best piece. Adding together the other elements of the ending—Mr. Somerset's Christian burial, the fact that he has been saved from making it to the United Nations where presumably his rejection of God would have become irrevocably firm, and other details—we see how Connolly can have it both ways. There is redemption for Mr. Somerset, pigeon and anti-Blue that he is, for he was on his way to perdition, and he will still have a long way to go in the next life—a journey on which the real Blue may be able to help him.

"Natural Causes"

Of all the stories in this volume, only "Natural Causes" had never been published. Like "Love, Tomi," the story is epistolary, this time from a girl's point of view, and readers may not suspect until the end of the letter that they have been reading a suicide note—albeit a lengthy one.

Connolly's principal aim in the story is to dramatize the breakdown of the family in the face of the deadliest temptation for people of good will: acedia, or spiritual sloth—here, specifically, the pursuit of lesser goods at the expense of greater ones. Connolly took the threat of acedia so seriously that he dedicated an entire book to it, 1951's *Dan England and the Noonday Devil*, his most theologically rich novel. Continuing the theme of that work, Connolly has the protagonist in "Natural Causes" note how busy-ness has torn apart her parents' marriage: her mother is, ironically enough, "busy with the Children's Hospital Drive,"[21] disappointing her father. He compensates by becoming as occupied as his spouse; both have become "so busy."[22]

Left to her own devices, Betsy discovers the wonders of modern sociology, a course in which she learns "so many more ideas"[23] about families. Connolly indicts this kind of thinking as an accessory to the assault on the traditional family, even putting into the sociology professor's mouth a wholesale rejection of "Western Culture"[24]. At the same time, Betsy had been praying "more than I ever had in my life before,"[25] which eventually helps her to see through the sociologist's dogmatic relativism

21.   Myles Connolly, *The Reason for Ann & Other Stories*, introduction and notes by Stephen Mirarchi (Providence, RI: Cluny Media, 2019), p. 112.

22.   Ibid., p. 113.

23.   Ibid., p. 120.

24.   Ibid., p. 124.

25.   Ibid., p. 120.

and, Connolly implies, leads her to write the confessional-style note in the first place.

As Connolly denounces these early rumblings of doctrinaire multi-culturalism, he points to the holiness of small practices that stave off the imperiousness of modern technology. Betsy remembers nostalgically how her parents would insist on ignoring the telephone during dinner, and how that lay asceticism fostered their familial intimacy in "the jungle"[26] of the city, a description Connolly emphasizes. At the end of the story, when Betsy's estranged parents are dealing with her suicide attempt, they both agree to ignore a telephone call—a clear, if small, dedication to beginning their vocation afresh. For Connolly, the intrusion of technology is symptomatic of acedia, for it demands that we often pay attention to lesser goods rather than our vocational duties.

If Betsy's survival comes to us as a surprise—and it should, given how Connolly foreshadows the opposite—we might ponder the story's title further. As it turns out, the pills Betsy took had a manufacturing defect—lucky for her, perhaps, or Providence, and a side jab at quality control, too. One reviewer in Connolly's time saw Betsy as a kind of Cupid with a death wish, someone who "drastically reunites parents considering divorce."[27] Connolly rather portrays Betsy as genuinely heartbroken and refreshingly free of melodrama: "Loving too much is a natural cause, isn't it?"[28] Loving lesser goods too much is

---

26. Ibid., pp. 103, 115, 121, 127.

27. Review, *The Catholic World*, p. 393.

28. Connolly, *The Reason for Ann*, p. 126.

indeed all too natural; such is the lot of secular humanism and acedia alike. Responding rightfully to supernatural causes requires discernment, fidelity, a rejection of novelty, and perseverance in the ordinary, seemingly small things of everyday life, of one's vocation. Such humble holiness keeps the noonday devil at bay.

"Seminary Hill"

For many readers, this story will be the most controversial in the volume. As the first edition's dust jacket proudly proclaimed, "Seminary Hill" is a tale based on an actual attempt by Communists to infiltrate a Catholic seminary. Given that this story appeared in early 1953, readers might jump to the conclusion that Connolly had bought into McCarthyism. That judgment might be all but ratified when they learn that Connolly also co-wrote the screenplay for 1952's *My Son John*, a film about a Communist spy whose failed efforts lead him to publicly repent and become, unwittingly, a kind of Catholic martyr.

Some historical context, however, is in order. Even before 1950, Fulton Sheen—the most visible Catholic in mid-century America and one of the brightest apologists of the century—had "branded communism the Antichrist," and in mid-1949 the Vatican officially pronounced Catholics who became members of or even supported the Communist Party "under excommunication as apostates of the Catholic faith."[29] The stakes were obviously high

---

29. Frank J. Coppa, "Pope Pius XII and the Cold War: The Post-war Confrontation between Catholicism and Communism," in *Religion and the Cold War*, ed. Dianne Kirby (New York: Palgrave, 2003), pp. 60, 62.

for Catholics. Popular media bolstered their fears: "The mainstream Catholic press was among McCarthy's most fervid supporters. Hardly an issue…passed without a major article on communism, usually painting the threat in alarmist, if not apocalyptic, terms."[30]

Not everyone was convinced, however. "Lay Catholics were much less supportive of McCarthy than the Church leadership," and "in the final analysis…the anti-Communist consensus was far too broad to be dominated by Catholics."[31] For the first time in recent memory, "a prevailing national consensus [was] finally coinciding with long and strongly held Catholic views."[32]

In terms of McCarthy himself, "liberal bishops… repudiated McCarthy, and most Catholics, while remaining anti-Communist, rejected his outrageous tactics."[33] One historian admits that, despite McCarthy's often being wildly wrong, the Senator did not always miss the mark: "[McCarthy's] popularity reflected a widespread, and not wholly inaccurate view, that communism had in fact exerted a significant, if secretive, influence in parts of the American labor movement as well as the entertainment industry since the 1930s."[34] And though McCarthy was Catholic, "[McCarthy] was above all a political opportunist who showed little concern for the religious

---

30. Charles R. Morris, *American Catholic: The Saints and Sinners Who Built America's Most Powerful Church* (New York: Vintage, 1997), p. 248.

31. Ibid., pp. 248–49.

32. Ibid., p. 250.

33. Timothy Walch, *Catholicism in America: A Social History* (Malabar, FL: Robert E. Krieger, 1989), pp. 84–85.

34. James T. Fisher, *Communion of Immigrants: A History of Catholics in America* (Oxford: Oxford University Press, 2002), p. 121.

aspects of his crusade."[35] Many Protestants, actually, led
showy charges against their own. Methodist J. B. Matthews[36], for instance, publicly accused "'seven thousand
Protestant clergymen' as either party members" or col-
laborators.[37] Thus, write two historians, "the net effect
[of McCarthy] on American religion…and especially
upon liberal Protestantism, was to weaken its moral
leadership."[38]

As for *My Son John*, the film has, for better or worse,
been lumped in with what many critics simply term
anti-communist propaganda. One historian complains
that "the film is littered with crude religious symbolism"
and notes that one of the producing studio's executives
was "an example of those militant Catholics who understood communism as Christian heresy."[39] One scholar
calls the picture "a solemn film that lacks any of the
light touches and ingratiating comedy that characterize" Catholic director Leo McCarey's "best work."[40] A
contemporary reviewer in the *New York Times* exoner-
ates McCarey entirely and places the blame for the "flop"

35.   Ibid.

36.   For a detailed history of Matthews' political and religious journey, see Nelson
      L. Dawson, "From Fellow Traveler to Anticommunist: The Odyssey of J.
      B. Matthews," *The Register of the Kentucky Historical Society* 84:3 (Summer
      1986): pp. 280–306.

37.   Edwin Gaustad and Leigh Schmidt, *The Religious History of America: The
      Heart of the American Story from Colonial Times to Today*, rev. ed. (New York:
      HarperOne, 2002), p. 339.

38.   Ibid., p. 340.

39.   Tony Shaw, "'Martyrs, Miracles and Martians': Religion and Cold War
      Cinematic Propaganda in the 1950s," in *Religion and the Cold War*, p. 218.

40.   Richard A. Blake, S.J., "The Sins of Leo McCarey," *Journal of Religion and
      Film* 17:1 (April 2013), p. 7.

of a film entirely on Connolly's shoulders: "Connolly… had contributed many a bullying speech to Frank Capra's movies…McCarey's human touch came at last to serve a conservatism that choked compassion."[41]

One historian concludes that such "Goldwynesque family sagas" as *My Son John* "helped to endow the Cold War with the black-and-white moral clarity most people and official propagandists yearned for… The Catholic Church in the West had good reason to thank the cinema during this period."[42] We cannot overlook, for instance, that the once-Catholic communist spy who recants in *My Son John* "at the end…becomes more hero than traitor."[43] Similar to the economy of intercessory prayer in "The Reason for Ann," in this film the spy's reversion to his faith is "due at least in part to his parents' prayers for him."[44] For most critics, Catholic theology became a convenient, if not watered down, literary device in the film.[45]

Given this history, it would not be right to characterize the story "Seminary Hill" in this volume as Connolly's literary attempt to capitalize on the Communist scare. It would be more correct, though still superficial, to observe that the story is the author's ideological rebuke of Communism, an unveiling of its true face for those still not

---

41. Stuart Klawans, "A Kind Man Who Became A Hard Man," *The New York Times* (15 December 2002), p. 15.

42. Shaw, "'Martyrs, Miracles and Martians'," p. 226.

43. Blake, "The Sins," p. 27.

44. Ibid.

45. Readers wishing an introduction to the intersection of Catholicism and film may consult Richard A. Blake, S.J., *Afterimage: The Indelible Catholic Imagination in the Works of Six American Film Makers* (Chicago: Loyola Press, 2000).

persuaded of its genuine threat to the spiritual fabric of the country.

On a much deeper level, Connolly is doing very much the opposite: Catholics who genuinely live their faith have nothing to fear from Communism, nor from any enemy, ideological or otherwise. Though Felix starts his spying mission with all the fervor of a "Red," he is gradually and surely converted away from betrayal by one simple fact: Fr. Andrews loves him as a father loves his sons—as the Father loves His Son. Connolly paraphrases one of the most beautiful yet difficult Gospel teachings by having the story proclaim that a lived-out, persevering love of enemies will eventually dispel hate. To put it another way, an enemy who understands that he is unconditionally loved also understands that betrayal is out of the question. Connolly wisely has Felix *ipso facto* trust the seal of the Sacrament of Confession, for such a wild promise could only be held by one who wills the good of the other *in persona Christi*. Connolly thus makes a startling statement with the story: if we are genuinely looking for a rebuke of Communism, we will find it in the sacramental love Catholicism teaches—the kind of love the senator from Wisconsin increasingly left behind. What *My Son John* could only do elliptically or blatantly Connolly accomplished literarily in "Seminary Hill" through the gradual art of deep characterization and the aesthetic manipulation of time: he showed that Catholicism lived out in all its mystery had the real substance of answers to the prodigious problems of his times.

"The Big Red House on Hope Street"

The venerable Catholic magazine *The Liguorian* reviewed *The Reason for Ann* when it came out, admiring the book as a whole: "With a master's touch [Connolly] portrays his characters in situations that are unusual."[46] In their short review, they highlighted "Big Red House" as "a well told sketch" and one of the reasons "Catholic authors would do well to imitate this talented writer."[47]

At sixty pages in the first edition, the story is indeed a novella; it reads like a fictionalized screenplay, with each scene thought out in how it builds on the last, and with Connolly's mastery of cinematographic narrative. The story is also one of his most straightforward: the telling is of a piece with the simplicity of its message, the gradual conversion from a life of dissipation to a path of holiness. That the tale happens almost exclusively in a monastery of religious sisters and dramatizes their differences not only for comic effect but for contemplation of their vocations marks it as a forerunner or predecessor of books like Rumer Godden's *In This House of Brede* (1969).

Like the rest of the stories in this collection, "Big Red House" exhibits Connolly's deft balancing act of inspiring cinematic storytelling—and its necessarily sentimental, though not sentimentalist, element—and his intellectual engagement with timely religious issues. Connolly's art thus runs counter to the prevailing national spirituality of the times, what one historian classifies as "the *political*

---

46. Review of *The Reason for Ann and Other Stories*, *The Liguorian* 41 (1953), p. 381.

47. Ibid.

usefulness of God and prayer for the United States."[48] By emphasizing the complexity and intellectual power of theology proper; Divine Providence as a surprising and welcome help to humanity's free will; and a place for sentiment that allows its authentically human expression without succumbing to emotivism, Connolly wrote stories that restored the role of reason to its proper place in aesthetic expression. *The Reason for Ann* stood as a bulwark against the nationalistic fideism of the 1950s, just as it asked its readers to go along on spiritual journeys sometimes harrowing, sometimes uplifting, always adventurous—telling "in concrete terms man's relation to his God and to his soul."[49]

~Stephen Mirarchi
Atchison, Kansas
Tuesday in the Octave of Easter, 2019

---

48. T. Jeremy Gunn, *Spiritual Weapons: The Cold War and the Forging of an American National Religion* (Westport, CT: Praeger, 2009), p. 61.

49. Carty, "Myles Connolly," p. 9.

*

The Reason for Ann

There was a mist around them, so at first you could not make out much, about the two young men except that they were both tall, and one was dark and somewhat delicate and the other was fair and sturdy. They stood side by side before two ledgers, and now and then they peered into the mist, watching something far off, and now and then, after peering into the mist, they made an entry in the ledgers. Their manner of making the entry was careful, slow. Some entries were made in red, some in black, and they were painted on rather than written, as if it were the purpose of the two men to make the entries endure a long, long time.

The dark young man saw something beyond the mist that held his gaze. The other joined him in his looking. They leaned forward, head to head.

"Drinking," the dark young man sighed.

"As usual," the fair youth added coldly.

The two worked at their books for a while.

"No good, never was," the fair youth grunted. "Look, Gerald." He waved to the other's book. "Look at the record. Red almost all the way. Drink. Women. Brawling."

He gestured down into the mist. "Now, look. A woman—a new one."

Gerald joined him, nodded sadly. "Yes, Basil. She's the third this week."

"And very common. Cheap. Very." Basil was exasperated. "Listen…listen to him, will you?"

Gerald cocked an ear, listened. A man's voice could be heard coming up through the mist. It was a rich masculine voice, vibrant with a forced earnestness, obviously assumed for the occasion. It grew louder, nearer, as they listened.

"Beautiful," pleaded the voice, "can't you understand? I'm lost. I've lost myself—I've lost myself in you. I'm not me anymore. Come into my arms and give myself back to me. Come. Will you? Will you, darling?"

The voice stopped. Basil shook his head in disgust. "Such a cheap attempt at impassioned speech! It's a mockery—a mockery."

"Yes, I know." Gerald smiled a wisp of a smile. "Still, it's—it's amazing how he can put so much feeling into it, time after time. He has a store of genuine fervor."

"Harpstrings! The same old flapdoodle, word for word!" Basil was annoyed. "He's an unmitigated fraud."

Gerald's face was gently eager. "Look," he whispered, "he's ordering champagne. Two quarts. He hasn't more than four dollars in the world."

"He'd better order it quickly," Basil commented coolly. "The husband is on his way."

"A husband?" Gerald seemed surprised. "O'Sullivan doesn't know. The woman—she didn't mention it."

"O'Sullivan makes women like her forget," Basil remarked.

Gerald shook his head slowly, not taking his eyes from the mist. "Poor O'Sullivan," he lamented softly. "And with that smile too."

"Smile or no smile, he's doomed," Basil said. "Doomed."

But Gerald continued to look down on O'Sullivan with mild and faintly smiling affection. And as he looked, O'Sullivan became slowly visible through the mist.

O'Sullivan was a full-sized man, with big hands and big shoulders. He humped awkwardly over the table and held the woman with his eyes, held her as fast as if he had her pinioned. His smile was good, as the gentle Gerald suggested. It broke like light over his face and stayed there, wrinkling from his full, avid mouth into the corners of his hungering eyes.

The woman was warm and soft, all body.

"Darling," whispered O'Sullivan, forcing as before, "are you going to stop the march of the sun and the stars? Are you going to crush the flowers in their growing? Come. Love me. Love me bravely, madly."

"Sh-h-h," the woman interrupted, looking anxiously about her. "Don't talk like that. I don't want people to think I'm—I'm common."

O'Sullivan laughed again. He glanced around at the people at the tables. "But these aren't people, my precious. They're mechanical devices for the transmission of money. They're weighing machines, slot machines, mechanical banks, food-grinding machines, washing machines. They're all headed for economic security—and insensibility."

"Gee, you're funny. You talk funny. You're sort of—of abnormal. Did anyone ever tell you that?"

O'Sullivan grinned. "I'm the only normal person I ever met. I'm as normal as a horse or a barracuda or a chimpanzee. Everybody else is abnormal."

"Oh," The woman stared at him, a slight shadow of fright in her shining eyes.

Up beyond the golden mist, Basil scowled.

"It's dreadful," he moaned, "dreadful. The way he uses good poetic words for his sordid ends. It's nothing short of sacrilegious. And the worst part of it is he thinks he's God's darling."

"It's true, Basil. It's true." Then, Gerald added mildly, "But he has imagination, you must admit that."

Basil snorted. "Imagination! Humph! Imagination is the source of sin and discontent."

"And joy," Gerald put in meekly. He gazed into the mist. "Look, I suppose that's the husband now."

Basil nodded. "And those two burly men with him are detectives. Private detectives."

"Yes, I know," Gerald said. "No one can have kept the record of O'Sullivan for twenty-six years without knowing what a detective looks like."

Basil shrugged. "Well, here comes the brawl."

"It should be lively," Gerald said. "O'Sullivan is quite good in a brawl."

The brawl was lively. It started with O'Sullivan accusing the husband of being an imposter. A detective told O'Sullivan to shut his trap. But O'Sullivan couldn't stand rudeness—or so he said—and he let the detective have a quick hook that floored him. The woman screamed. The husband, pale, ran to her side. The second detective took a swing at O'Sullivan, and O'Sullivan let him have it too.

Now the first detective was up off the floor and the bouncer had arrived. O'Sullivan levelled out the first detective again, this time for keeps, and went for the bouncer. The bouncer took longer than the others—fifteen or twenty seconds longer—and O'Sullivan had barely finished him off when the second detective was up from the floor. By now, O'Sullivan was in his glory. He had his back to the wall and was lashing out with power and precision. His smile was large and handsome. He sent the second detective back to the floor beside his sleeping brother and slapped down a waiter who had come up to attack, waving a chair.

Meanwhile, the manager had telephoned the police and at a moment when O'Sullivan was polishing off the bartender and a pair of chivalrous customers, there came the siren of a police car racing down the street. O'Sullivan stopped at the sound, then turned, started full speed for the kitchen, crashing over tables as he went. Suddenly he stopped, reversed and rushed back to the table, where the woman sat rigid with terror.

He shoved the husband aside. "Pardon, please," he said. He bowed to the woman. "I'm sorry, beautiful," he said, "but I have to go now."

The police were at the door. O'Sullivan bowed to the husband. "I still can't believe there's a husband," he said. "It's too unfair." Then he was off again.

O'Sullivan slammed into the kitchen as two policemen swung open the front door.

The policemen looked across the shambles that had been a cocktail room and saw O'Sullivan disappear. Immediately they were after him, swiftly, but with the grim economy of movement that all good policemen have.

Gerald, enchanted, looked down through the golden mist. "It's going to be a chase," he murmured. He turned to Basil, his eyes glowing with admiration. "I know he's a scoundrel, out and out, but I must confess he's diverting."

Basil was completely disgusted. "He's a walking degradation. Do you call that diverting?" He shook his head unhappily. "Gerald, if you weren't an angel, I'd begin to worry about you."

Gerald sighed. "It's O'Sullivan. Nothing seems quite in order after he passes."

Basil looked out beyond the ledgers, out into the vast and swirling distance. "Sometimes I wish I had another job, a cleaner, more orderly job. Like keeping the planets in their places. Or winding up Time." He scowled. "I'm fidgety, Gerald. We have no business getting fidgety. I'm not my angelic self; I'm not myself at all."

"Neither am I," Gerald agreed.

"You're aware, I suppose," Basil said coolly, indicating the ledger with a rigid finger, "you haven't yet made an entry of the affair with that married woman."

"No, not yet," Gerald murmured. "I'll do it now."

He dipped his brush in red and began carefully to make an entry. His ledger looked more like an ancient illuminated missal than a modern account book. The open page was decorated rather than inscribed, and the words, graceful and delicate, were like so many flowers. Basil's ledger, on the other hand, had a stern and almost scientific appearance. His entries were mostly numerals, dates and computations, and they lined the page in precise, well-behaved columns.

Gerald could not keep his mind on his work. "I wonder how he's coming out with those two policemen," he said. He peered down into the mist. "Look," he whispered excitedly. "Look at that O'Sullivan go."

O'Sullivan was going, there was no question about that. The night was dark, and O'Sullivan's speeding car, with the lights off for concealment, was a dark streak in darkness. O'Sullivan leaned over the wheel, his eyes searching the blackness of the country road as the car roared down it. Behind him, a thousand yards, the police car skimmed the road, its siren whining, its searchlight fingering the darkness ahead.

O'Sullivan gave his car all it had. But it was not enough. The police car gained, gradually but relentlessly cutting down the distance between them.

Gerald was tense. Basil, in spite of himself, was watching the wild chase with interest.

Suddenly, Gerald shouted, "That curve in the road. He doesn't see it! Look!"

"How could he expect to see it with his lights off," Basil grimly commented.

No. O'Sullivan did not see the sharp turn in the road. It swerved up at him out of the blackness, slapped up at him so abruptly that even O'Sullivan, whose coordination was flawless, jumped in his seat. He was headed off the road at eighty miles an hour and dead into a cement protection wall. He stamped down the brakes, swung the wheel. The car skidded wildly, clutching the edge of the road.

"He'll make it!" Gerald shouted.

But Basil coldly shook his head. "See that patch of oil on the road ahead? See it?"

Gerald saw the patch of oil, but O'Sullivan did not. The wheels hit the oil, lost the little grip they still had on the road. The car swerved, spun, and then, completely out of control, skidded crazily off the road as if it were greased and on glass. O'Sullivan was helpless. The car grazed the far end of the protection wall and went crashing down into a gully. It slid forty feet, then rolled over completely, landing flatly back on its wheels at the bottom. It came to rest abruptly and stood in the blackness as if it had been parked there.

The police car, unaware of the whole event, roared by overhead, its siren still whining, its searchlight still exploring the darkness. The roar and the whine and the light whirred and blurred by in an instant. The darkness was deeper than before.

After a moment, O'Sullivan opened the door of the car and stepped out. He rubbed his head and felt the back of his neck as if to make sure he was still alive. Then, he looked up at the ridge of the road, just discernible against the muddy sky, and grinned. His grin lit up the murk around him.

Gerald smiled his little smile. "That grin of his. I can't get over it."

"Well, he's going to get over it. That's about his last allotment of luck." Basil glanced at his ledger. "He's had far more than he deserved, far more than I'd ever have given him if I were running things."

Gerald sighed. "Yes, I suppose he has." He looked

over his book, ran a finger down a column. "That's the last of his mother's prayers, the one that saved him just now. He's used them all up."

"Poor woman," Basil said. "She left him such a great wealth of prayers too. Only an extraordinary scoundrel like himself could have run through so many prayers at twenty-six." He pointed sternly to the ledger. "You haven't yet, you know, entered that affair with a married woman."

"So I haven't," Gerald sighed. He picked up a brush and began to shape it between his thumb and forefinger. "More red ink," he said limply. "Just more red ink."

Gerald and Basil had a difficult time of it trying to find a reason for Ann. O'Sullivan's mother's prayers had been all used up. O'Sullivan's own prayers when he was a boy were routine things, few and indifferent, and the little value they possessed, Basil pointed out, had been expended years before. What was the reason for Ann? That was a sticker even for a pair of angels.

"It's sacrilegious," Basil had scowled when first he had seen Ann and O'Sullivan together.

They both looked down and watched a girl in a pale blue dress walking in a garden. The leveling afternoon sun shone in her eyes and on her hair. Even Basil found it difficult to conceal his admiration.

"No perfume, no jewelry. I like that," Basil said.

"Ann," Gerald whispered. "Ann. Such a beautiful name. I didn't think anyone called her daughter Ann any more."

"Very few. Ann is a little simple and unaffected for nowadays. I imagine her mother had no social-inferiority complexes," Basil said.

"Probably never read the society columns at all," Gerald smiled. "Look, Basil. Look how easily she walks, how weightlessly, as if she were one of us."

The two watched the girl in the blue dress, Gerald with enchantment, Basil with cool but evident appreciation.

Gerald sighed. "She has the poise of an archangel."

"Her smile is reserved," Basil added. "She does not waste it. She gives it as a gift. I like that in her."

Gerald nodded. "She has never wasted herself. She is as new as the day she was born."

"No rust or rot."

"Like a seraph."

The two angels, their heads together, continued to look down at the girl who walked in the garden. There was a long silence. Finally Gerald turned away.

"I know it's an almost irreverent thing to say," Gerald murmured, and his face was troubled, "but do you know for the first time in all my eternity I have misgivings about my good fortune—in being an angel, I mean."

"Hush," Basil reproved him, and his voice was gentle for him. "Do you want sorrow and heartbreak?"

"No," Gerald hesitated, "but when I look at her I do not think of sorrow and heartbreak."

"But that is her lot, Gerald." His voice was kind. "She is beautiful, but she is imperfect. She must suffer and grow old and die."

"Death will be afraid of her. He will go to her timidly, on tiptoe," Gerald said softly. He watched a while. "Look," he whispered. "The flowers seem to turn to watch her as she passes."

Basil smiled his customary cool smile. "I cannot believe

that you, Gerald, an angel, a pure spirit, blessed with the beatific vision, have been diverted by the world's oldest illusion."

"What illusion?" Gerald faced him.

"Woman. Her physical beauty is largely the creation of man's desire," Basil was matter-of-fact. "Really, I suggest you brush up on your philosophy. You are beginning to sound a little like O'Sullivan."

Gerald pointed toward the garden. "Look. Isn't he coming now? She's smiling. She hears his footsteps."

"Yes, poor creature," Basil said. "He's still home on leave, and still in his pilot's uniform."

Gerald nodded. "I was sure he'd be back in the ranks by now."

Basil shook his head sadly. "She is lost. Never will she be able to see his infamy through the uniform."

"But he—" Gerald stumbled mildly. "I sort of think he looks handsome in it, don't you? See the pair of wings on his chest."

"He has a new coating of conceit, that's all! It's shameful to let a scoundrel like that have wings."

"But such impractical and unangelic wings, Basil. Don't grudge him those."

"I do. Look at how importantly he struts. He is sure the war was sent so he might have an airplane. It is a noble justice that his wings will carry him to his doom."

"Look how they walk toward each other in the sunset; look how her eyes shine," Gerald whispered. "They are in love. Just now they seem immortal."

Gerald and Basil were bright and knowing, as angels are, but neither of them had ever been able to understand the reason for Ann. For Ann in O'Sullivan's life, that is. And yet, O'Sullivan's first meeting with Ann was such an accident, or rather such a series of accidents, as Gerald insisted, it could only have been according to plan.

That year when the Chinese communists entered the Korean conflict, O'Sullivan decided his country had a war on its hands, and he went to Boston to enlist. He was crossing the Common toward Tremont Street at ten minutes past eleven on December fifteenth. Had his train from New London not been a half hour late he would have crossed the Common at ten forty instead of eleven ten. And had he continued on with the train to the South Station instead of getting off at the Back Bay Station, he would not have crossed the Common at all. And he would not have met Ann.

For Ann was crossing the Common at ten minutes past eleven on December fifteenth on her way to a shop on Boylston Street. She carried a good armful of packages, the last of her Christmas shopping. Had she not met her Aunt Abby in the book store and chatted fifteen minutes, she would have crossed the Common at ten fifty-five instead of eleven ten. And had her Aunt Abby not told her that Cousin Philip was coming home from Washington for Christmas, she never would have remembered Cousin Philip and she would not have crossed the Common to the leather-goods shop to buy him a billfold for Christmas. And she would not have bumped into O'Sullivan.

Neither saw the other till they bumped. O'Sullivan was craning his neck, looking for a flag or a poster that would locate an Army recruiting office. Ann was looking off the other way to see if the ice was frozen in the Public Garden. Besides, there was a brisk wind blowing and she had the collar of her fur coat high up around her face and couldn't see much anyway.

So they bumped. Ann held tightly to her packages. She begged his pardon. He begged hers. He moved to one side to let her pass. But she moved to the same side to let him pass, and they bumped again.

O'Sullivan grinned. But Ann did not notice him. Deftly, this time, she stepped to one side and passed him, continuing on her way toward Boylston Street. As she passed, her fur collar flapped open and he saw her face, looked into her eyes. That one look stopped him, stopped his heart, stopped his breathing. There was a gaping hiatus in his existence as he stood and watched the girl glide away from him, watched her melt into the Christmas crowds of Boylston Street.

When he recovered, it was too late. She was gone. Nonetheless he raced along to the street, searched the crowds, searched the endless procession of faces. But she was nowhere.

He walked up to a policeman. "Punch me in the face, will you? Hard!"

The policeman stared. "Wh-what's that? What do you want?"

The policeman's voice brought O'Sullivan back to the pavement. "Forget it," he said. "It wouldn't help. I'm just a chump, that's all."

He strode away. The policeman looked suspiciously after him a moment, shrugged and continued on about his business. O'Sullivan was wild with himself. Indeed, he could not recognize himself. Never had he been knocked off balance before. Never by a girl, certainly.

Mechanically, he found the recruiting office. His mind was still a little punch-drunk. He could not remember his age. He could not recall whether or not he had a middle name. He was sure he was an American citizen and that was about all. The recruiting officer was busy and became impatient.

"Speak up," he said sharply. "You mumble like you were in a muddle."

"Well, I am in a muddle!" O'Sullivan came to life.

"You want to get into the Army to get out of the muddle?" the officer asked quickly, suspiciously.

O'Sullivan was annoyed. "It just happened to me ten minutes ago."

"What happened to you?" The officer studied him.

O'Sullivan looked off into space. "She did," he said.

The officer indicated the enlistment blank on the desk before him. "I think maybe you better give this a few days' thought," he said.

The truth broke on O'Sullivan. "Oh, I know what I'm doing, captain. I had my mind on something else for the moment." He indicated the enlistment blank. "Let me have it. I want to join the Army."

"Come back in a few days," the officer said. "Come back when your mind is a little clearer. Good day. Next."

O'Sullivan got to his feet. For a moment, he considered lifting the captain to his feet and knocking him down. But he remembered the girl. "Okay, then. Maybe it's a break. Maybe I'm going to get married."

He turned and strode out to the street. There he began

again to search the endless parade of bobbing faces. After an hour, he gave up. He went into a saloon and had two straight bourbons.

"I guess I should have enlisted," he told the bartender. "I'll never see her again."

"The Army's no protection against women," the bartender said. "Poverty and prison, they're the only protection. And poverty isn't too sure."

O'Sullivan finished his drink. He went out to the street and began to search the faces again. He went back to the Common and paced the path on which they had bumped. He went to Boylston Street and paced the sidewalk. Finally, faces became little more than a blur to him. He gave up.

He looked around for another saloon. He found one and went in and had two more straight bourbons. When he came out, he saw the blue flag of a navy recruiting office down the street. He went to the office. Despair had cleared his head now and he had no trouble enlisting.

"What's the most dangerous branch of the service?" he asked the lieutenant in charge. "I mean the one with the highest mortality rate."

"Battle duty is dangerous enough for any branch," the lieutenant remarked, smiling.

"I've just had a blow, a kind of shock," O'Sullivan explained, "and I'd like to get over it as fast as possible. How would an attack bomber be?"

"Take it easy," the lieutenant advised with a twinkle. "Time and the Navy cure all things."

"I've come to the right place, then," O'Sullivan grinned. "Thanks, lieutenant."

They shook hands and O'Sullivan turned and left the office. Outside in the corridor, he took the wrong door, went down the wrong corridor and opened another wrong door. He found himself looking into a small office lined with filing cases.

A girl stood before one of the filing cases. She turned slowly, a moment after O'Sullivan had opened the door. It was Ann.

Now, Gerald and Basil, watching Ann and O'Sullivan in the garden, pondered the record.

"Why did she have to be in that office at that moment?" Basil questioned, and there was something almost disagreeable in his voice. "Why?"

"One of those little miracles, one of those infinitesimal miracles that really run the world," Gerald replied.

"But why should a scoundrel like O'Sullivan have a miracle of any sort? Why?" Basil was getting impatient with the sympathetic Gerald.

"The Master is an artist, Basil, as you know. He rarely does anything obvious. While the poor humans search the skies for great wonders," Gerald sighed, "He works in secret, disguising His hand; and they never know."

Basil looked over his ledger. "That Ann should have been the lieutenant's daughter is understandable enough. She might have telephoned him as she always did. But to go there that day, which she had never done before, and to go into that office—"

"She wanted to help out. She volunteered because of the rush of enlistments."

"Yes, I know all that." Basil retorted. "But why did she

happen to be there in that office at that very minute?" He groaned. "Oh, I wish I had never seen that O'Sullivan."

Gerald suddenly looked up. "I have an idea, a little idea," he said. Hurriedly he began to turn back pages of his ledger. He stopped many pages back. "Here," he whispered excitedly. "Here. Perhaps this is it."

Basil looked over his shoulder at the page. "Are you sure this is O'Sullivan's account? There are several black entries on the page."

Gerald smiled. "This is an exceptional page." He moved a finger slowly down the page. "Remember Penelope?"

Basil thought a moment. "The fat girl the men called Nellie?"

Gerald nodded. "Yes, Nellie. Black Nellie. But her real name is Penelope—" He hunted for the real name, found it. "Penelope Purly. She came from Pasadena, California."

"No end of entries, at any rate," Gerald agreed, still moving his finger down the page. "Ah, here we are." He read a moment, then turned to Basil. "She died, remember? After her shack burned down."

Basil nodded. "A man by the name of Sniver set fire to it. A very moral man. A leader in the community."

"Yes. He was the censor of the films in that area." Gerald looked off into the golden distance. "One autumn night he did it, a rather sharp night. All Nellie saved was a robe and a pair of slippers."

"A very flimsy robe and a very fancy pair of slippers, as I remember them," Basil commented coolly.

Gerald nodded, "But not very warm. Not very warm,

especially for a chill autumn night. Nobody would take her in, remember? After the crowd had gone, she kept herself warm by the smoldering embers of her shack. When their warmth died out, she became cold and ill. A fireman had saved an old rocking chair from the flames. She sat on it and wept, wept. Alone there in the dark she wept."

"Yes, I remember," Basil said. "I remember the whole business. O'Sullivan, on his way home from a carousal in New York, heard of the fire and went out and picked her up and took her to his home. Is that what you mean? Is it because of that noble deed"—Basil was ironic—"you believe O'Sullivan met Ann?"

"Oh, no," Gerald returned. He looked at his ledger. "No, I don't think I even gave him a merit for the deed. No, no, I didn't."

"He was a friend of hers. It was the least he could have done."

"Yes, I know," Gerald said mildly. "But there were other friends of hers in the town, hundreds of them, and they hid from her. Indeed, as I remember it, they—as well as the rest of the town—were scandalized by what O'Sullivan had done." Gerald returned to his ledger. "No. It wasn't that I was looking for."

Basil was indifferent. "After she died, he took her to church and buried her. Is that it? Is that the deed?"

Gerald smiled. "No, but it was—sort of magnificent, wasn't it? Remember how he filled the little church with flowers."

"His theatricalism, I'm afraid," Basil said.

"He sold his beloved piano to pay for it." Gerald's eyes were soft as he remembered. "It really was magnificent.

He was the only one in the town who went to the church. He went right up to a front pew and sat there. Alone. But he wasn't defiant. He wasn't thinking of the gesture the way he usually does. He was really grieved. He was—he was almost reverent."

"Now, Gerald!" Basil objected.

"Well, I mean—he was reverent for him," Gerald replied meekly.

"And is that the reason for Ann? Is that what you think?" Basil was annoyed now.

Gerald shook his head. "No, Basil," he said softly. "No. Though I did give him a merit for it." He turned back to the ledger. "Remember Pimkin, the undertaker?" he smiled, as he searched the entries. "Remember how he stood outside the church and hid behind that huge oak tree, afraid someone would see him?"

"I didn't care for Pimkin at all," Basil said.

"Not a bad man, just a coward," Gerald commented. Then, his face lighted up as only an angel's face can light up. "Ah, here it is. Here is what I was looking for."

Basil leaned over and looked. "Nellie's death?"

"Yes," Gerald whispered. "Nellie's death. From the pneumonia she caught that night. O'Sullivan had put her in his mother's bed in his mother's room. She had come up here the year before. Remember? It was a sweet room, quaint and a little cluttered, but cluttered with loved and treasured things. A homey room. A good mother's room."

"Yes," Basil admitted, "it was a warm and human room. There aren't many of them down there nowadays."

But Gerald was intent on the ledger. "Nellie's death was one of the pleasantest we've ever had. O'Sullivan held her hand and told her amusing stories and made light of everything."

"Some of those stories were a trifle ribald, weren't they?"

Gerald smiled. "Not 'a trifle,'" he said. "O'Sullivan was never 'a trifle' anything. They were outrageously ribald, several of them. But they didn't seem so to Nellie. They were plain healthy stories to her. She had the gift of laughter, as O'Sullivan said."

"Perhaps. But she wept when she died," Basil commented coolly.

"Yes, but I think you missed the point there, Basil," Gerald returned, "They were not tears of anguish or despair. They were tears of gratitude. Remember her last words? 'I feel good, O'Sullivan, thanks to you. I always wanted to die in a decent home and in a decent bed. I feel good.' Remember how she leaned over and kissed his hand? 'God bless you, O'Sullivan,' she whispered. 'God bless you.' Then she sobbed a little and smiled a little and that was the end."

There was a pause. Basil looked afar off at the spinning constellations. "I'm afraid I did miss the point, Gerald," he said.

Gerald turned away from the ledger, faced Basil. "I'm sure that is the reason for Ann meeting O'Sullivan—that last prayer of Nellie's. I'm sure it's the reason Ann bumped into him on Boston Common. I'm sure it's the reason she was in that little office in the recruiting center the moment O'Sullivan blundered in."

Basil thought a moment before he answered. "It could be," he said. "But how much better it would have been if

Ann had met someone else—some good, sensible, thrifty and sober man. But O'Sullivan! Perhaps we should be looking for the reason for O'Sullivan and not for Ann."

"I doubt if we could find it," Gerald said. "We're only angels."

"Yes," Basil nodded grimly. "God only knows the reason for him."

Gerald looked down through the golden mist. "Well, there he is," he said, "smiling, talking, very much O'Sullivan. There he is, and no question about it."

Basil looked. "But he's not talking the way he usually does. He's not so lush or highfalutin. Notice that?"

"It's the Ann influence."

O'Sullivan, walking in the garden with Ann, had something on his mind. There was no doubt about that. At the moment, he was walking in silence, and the smile was gone from his face. Ann, content, walked by his side, at gracious ease in the silence. Now and then she looked up at him with quietly adoring eyes. Her adoration was grave, self-possessed. It seemed the more she gave, the more she was herself.

They paced the garden once, twice, three times. Finally, at the magnolia tree near the far wall, Ann stopped. O'Sullivan stopped with her. A full minute passed and no word was spoken.

Then Ann smiled. "Tell me," she said.

O'Sullivan did not smile. "It is a hard thing to do."

"Will it hurt you?"

"A great deal." He hesitated a moment, then spoke. "Ann, I'm a mug and a mushhead. I'm forty kinds of a skunk. I'm a first-class all-around mistake of a man. I'm a loud tin horn on heels. I'm an imitation hoodlum who's no good for anyone else on earth except himself."

"You're good for me," Ann said quietly.

O'Sullivan shook his head. "Don't make it any harder, honey. I know what I am. I'm about one thin shave above a bum. I'm a walking load of trash. But that—" His voice caught a moment. "But that isn't why I'm not going to ask you to marry me. I'd ask you to marry me in a minute. I'm selfish. I want you. I need you. You're a straight-through ticket to paradise. I've never stopped at anything before. I'd certainly never stop at anything now."

Ann looked up at him, and her look, which was the gift of herself to him, stopped his speech. "So far as I'm concerned," she said in a soft, level voice, "you asked me to marry you that first day you saw me in that office, and I said, 'Yes.'"

"Oh, darling, darling," O'Sullivan pleaded, "don't talk, will you? Don't say another word till I finish. I'll never get said what I want to say, what I've got to say."

Ann looked away, as if making a resolution, then looked back at him, and he went on. "Tonight I shove off. Korea, I think. Which is all right with me. I didn't want to tell you before because I wanted to remember you up to the last the way you'd be if I were here to stay. I wanted it to be all everlasting, these final few days. I didn't want fear of the end to ruin the meanwhile. I'm a weak slob, as you know, and I almost told you a dozen times. I didn't think I could carry off the deceit. But somehow I did. So I'm telling you now." He took her shoulders in his two huge hands. "I leave at six. In an hour. I want to ask you to marry me. But I'm not going to do it. I'm going to hate myself for it I'm going to hate myself and all the world, and hate it all with passion, when I leave here and you're not mine. I'll never forgive myself, but that's the way it's got to be."

The sun was now behind the magnolia tree, and the brandies and leaves of the tree broke its glory into shadows. Ann stood without moving, patient, gentle before the man she loved. The girl's face had become a woman's in the minute that had just passed—had become a woman's, richer and even more beautiful. She kept the silence he had requested. O'Sullivan took his hands from her shoulders. "Ann," he went on, quietly now, "I've got a kind of a hunch I'm not coming back. I've never been very practical. I've never put much stock in sense, and I'm going to take a beating for it. I've always relied on my instincts. I've followed my impulses. I wanted it that way; I liked it that way. Such was me, I felt, the best of me as I was made. It would have been as foolish for me to have been sensible as for a hawk to try to be a hen. Maybe I wasn't right. I don't know, and it's too late for me to try to figure it out now. But I do know this: Up in the air where I'm going, my impulses aren't going to be much help. Up in those brawls of machines my instincts are probably going to be in the way. I'm not a good risk, as I see it. Outside of you, I don't care. I never cared. But that's why I'm not asking you to marry me. It's why, standing here and looking down into the abyss of your eyes and knowing that in you I begin and end, I'm still not asking you. It's probably just another instinct, but I'm holding to it. I've known many women—and I've loved one. The one I've loved I want to leave as I found her."

There was a mist in Ann's eyes. The sun had slipped below the wall and now the shadow was heavy and unbroken around them. There was a trembling silence for a moment. Then Ann spoke. Her voice was a whisper. "You can never leave me as you found me."

Abruptly, O 'Sullivan grabbed her in his great, awkward arms and kissed her. "Goodbye, everybody, everything. If I did not have to go now, I would never go. I'm glad I left the telling to the last." He kissed her again. Then he turned quickly and walked out of the garden, never looking back.

Ann kept a grip on herself for a moment. "Good-by!" she called to the empty garden, "good-by!"

Then she broke. She broke as Ann would break, with her weeping inside of her. There were tears, but the muffled sobs, the choked heart cries convulsing her body were more eloquent of her pain than all the wailing in the world. She sat down on a garden bench, sat there a long time while the shadows deepened until the one, single vast shadow of night was around her. Her body shook in the darkness, but there was no sound.

Gerald, up above the golden mist, turned limply away. "Poor soul," he murmured. He seemed as unhappy as an angel could be.

"It is a pity," Basil said quietly, and there was something like sympathy in his voice. "But tears are part of her lot, Gerald. She is a woman. Out of her pain comes life."

"Out of her pain comes wisdom," Gerald murmured. "It is pain that makes women wiser than men, makes them more aware of eternal significances."

Basil glanced at Gerald, smiled his cool smile. "You

are a sort of poet, Gerald. Sometimes, if I didn't know you better, I'd suspect you were a dreamer."

Gerald gave a little start, as if caught in some guilt. He looked carefully around him to make sure they were alone. Then he whispered to his friend, "Sometimes, Basil, I'm afraid I am a dreamer. Sometimes I think I see more to truth than can be measured and ordered. Just as there is more to reality than can be touched and seen. Sometimes I have a sort of sympathy for the discord, for the distortion. Just as I'm inclined to prefer O'Sullivan in all his villainy to the thrifty, well-ordered, careful man."

"Gerald!" Basil was aghast. "This is subversive!"

Gerald was humble. "Yes, I know, I know," he sighed. "I'm—I'm afraid I am a dreamer."

"But you can't be a dreamer!" Basil exploded. "Heaven is the end of all dreams! You know that as well as I do."

Gerald was defeated. "Yes, I know that," he said meekly, almost sadly. "Heaven is the end of all dreams."

There was a great silence—such a silence as there can be only where time and space do not exist. Basil checked the rows of dates and figures in his ledger. There was no need for it. He did it only to try to keep from further discussion. Gerald turned his attention back to the girl in the garden.

She sat in the dark, her body shaking with her grief as before. She was alone in the dark; she seemed alone in the vastness of the world.

Gerald looked down on her, his face softened by her grief, his eyes warm and kind. "Poor soul," he whispered again.

Now Basil was irritated. "Please, Gerald," he said, "be sensible. There's nothing we can do. Nothing." He brushed a hand across the page of his ledger. "O'Sullivan is doomed. It is written."

"Yes, I know," Gerald said. He thought a moment. "I suppose I should give O'Sullivan a merit for that speech in the garden."

"Give it to him. But it isn't going to help him in the judgment. He's too far behind. He isn't going to live long enough to catch up."

Gerald began to prepare a brush, drawing it between his thumb and forefinger. "I'll give it to him," he murmured. "I want to use a little black ink."

After a moment Gerald went on, "It's so seldom I have a chance to work with black ink, I feel a little bit strange about it." He turned to Basil. "Sometimes I wish I had your job, Basil. Dates, facts, figures. Vital statistics. This moral end of it that I have, these merits and demerits, can become so confusing."

Basil nodded. "I wouldn't have your job for an archangel-ship." He waved to his ledger. "Mine is clean, orderly, exact. No blurs, no guesses. There is O'Sullivan, factually and scientifically, from the day he was born—the second, the minute, the hour—till the day he dies. There can be no casuistry about that."

Gerald peered timidly over at the page. "It is neat and clean," he admitted. He let his eye move slowly down the page. "Um-hm'm. It's all there." He turned away before his eyes reached the bottom of the page. "I don't want to read the end. I don't want to know till it happens."

Basil smiled. "Sometimes I think if you weren't an angel you'd be a weakling. Go ahead and read it."

Gerald shook his head. "No. I don't like finality."

"I'll read it to you." Basil ran his finger along the last entry on the page. " 'Parachute fails to open.' That's it. That's the end."

"'Parachute fails to open,'" Gerald repeated mechanically. "And that's the end."

"The end," Basil said flatly. "And a good thing too."

The sky was a vast, pale, hazy blue vault, empty except for a flight of light Navy bombers and one great floating island of solid white cloud high above the bombers. Below, the Pacific was a shimmering spread of dark, wrinkled blue satin.

The bombers, carrier-bound after an attack on a communist ammunition dump, soared serenely, levelly through the blue haze. One plane—the one in the tail-end slot—flipped its wings, flipped them suddenly and then stopped, like a dancer doing a hip shake. It looked for the moment as if the plane were in trouble. But the performance was repeated, and repeated again and again, rhythmically, at intervals, with a certain human expression of joy about it. It could not have been a plane in trouble. Nor was it. It was O'Sullivan.

O'Sullivan, in the pilot's seat, was singing, giving play to his high animal spirits. It was raucous, crass, a fighting song. At each pause in the song, he flipped the plane. This was O'Sullivan's way of telling sky and sea of his good health and good spirits.

Luke, his gunner, was on the interphone. "How

in—how do you think I'm going to count these bullet holes if you're gonna keep on shimmying? The old gal's about to fall apart now. So'm I."

O'Sullivan grinned. "How many you counted so far?"

"Hundred and fourteen," Luke replied. "But I ain't got to the tail yet."

Suddenly O'Sullivan looked up. He whistled. "Don't look now," he called to Luke, "but do you see what I see?"

Luke looked up and saw what O'Sullivan saw. Against the bottom of the great white cloud about six thousand feet above them was an ancient arid battered bomber, limping along,

"You mean that old Russian DB-Three?" Luke asked.

"It's insulting," O'Sullivan said. "Downright insulting."

He slowed down, let the flight get on ahead. Then, slowly, he started to climb.

Luke's eyes popped. "Hey! Yuh're not—"

"Sure," O'Sullivan grinned. "Get a hold of the flyswatter."

"But—but," Luke sputtered, "I don't want to get out of line, but he's bait. You know that, don't you?"

"Of course he's bait," O'Sullivan answered. "And inviting us up instead of down. That's what makes it so insulting."

Luke shrugged. "Okay," he said. "I figure I'm on over-time anyway."

"That's the spirit," O'Sullivan said. "Radio's busted and the boys are out of sight. We've got the world to ourselves."

"We should have been knocked off weeks ago, the way we operate," Luke said. He turned to man the mounted machine gun in the rear cockpit. He gave a glance up at the bomber limping under the cloud.

Suddenly out of the white belly of the cloud dropped two far-away specks.

Luke swung back to the interphone. "See 'em!"

"Yup, only Yaks. That makes it more insulting."

"Two of 'em!" Luke shouted, "an' don't count out the bait!"

O'Sullivan grinned. "Great," he said. "We outnumber them one to three."

Another speck fell out of the white fleece. "See that one, do yuh?" Luke called. "Do yuh?"

"Makes it more even," O'Sullivan said.

Luke jumped to the gun. The Yaks streaked down— the three of them. O'Sullivan turned sharply and headed for them, passing up the bait. He headed straight into them as they came down.

The Yaks, startled by the sight of a single bomber driving straight into them, began to fire frantically. Their aim was erratic and they did no serious damage. O'Sullivan held his fire till they were close to him. Then he let go. Excited, the Yaks flashed past him. He hit one as they passed. It belched flame, then dropped like a steaming smoke pot to the shimmering blue water far below.

O'Sullivan cut back at the bait. The DB-Three had slipped a thousand feet away to watch the slaughter. Abruptly, O'Sullivan dived down on it, his guns blazing. The plane, bewildered, pulled up, and O'Sullivan cut it across the belly. It fell apart.

"Wunnerful," O'Sullivan grinned, "wunnerful."

Gerald, up beyond the golden mist, was excited. "It is sort of wonderful," he whispered to Basil, not taking his eyes off the flight. "Isn't it?"

"Killing is never wonderful," Basil said coldly.

"Yes, I know, I know," Gerald admitted. "But he—he has a certain audacity about him. That's what enchants me."

Basil frowned. "Foolhardiness is what it is. The only truth he ever spoke was when he told the girl he had no sense." He nodded down through the mist. "Look. The others are coming back up for him. It'll be all over in a few seconds now."

The two Yaks were streaking back for him. There was a whirling brawl. Luke got one of them. Then, suddenly, O'Sullivan's guns stopped firing.

Basil nodded grimly. "That's it now."

"But look," Gerald whispered excitedly; "look. The last of the attackers is fleeing. O'Sullivan's own planes are coming to his assistance. See them?"

"It's too late," Basil said. "It's all over. See O'Sullivan—"

Gerald saw O'Sullivan. He was wounded in the shoulder, the chest, the arm. His face was grey, his big awkward body lopsided. He was trying to signal Luke, who was blazing away—happily, but futilely—at the fleeing Yak, already out of range.

"He won't jump until he signals his gunner," Gerald whispered, and there was pride in his whisper. "If he passes out at the controls, he knows it's the end for both of them."

"I don't think he knows much of anything at the moment," Basil said matter-of-factly.

"I'm not so sure," Gerald said. "He's thinking. He's using his logical faculty. His mind is fogging up, but he knows if he doesn't jump now, he'll never be able to jump. Still, he won't leave his gunner." Gerald was very proud. "It's what the humans call courage."

Basil shrugged. "It isn't going to help O'Sullivan," he said coolly.

"Look!" Gerald cried. "There, he has his gunner's attention! They're going to jump!"

Luke jumped first, a clean clear jump. His parachute billowed open, swinging Luke back and forth like a pendulum. O'Sullivan, a convulsed hulk of a man, weak, fumbling, groping, slid back the canopy. Feebly, like a young child crawling over the fence of its play pen, he lifted one leg out to jump. But there at the edge of the pit he slumped and hung, his consciousness ebbing. He could not see now. The plane, its controls bullet-riddled, began to circle crazily. Blindly, O'Sullivan held on.

"Poor soul," Gerald said softly.

"If he'd had less Scotch during his life," Basil said sharply, "he'd have more stamina now." Basil turned away. "He'll be up here in a few seconds. I think I'll go up and listen to the judgment. It won't take long," he added coldly.

Basil went away from the ledger, went off and up toward the vague, distant source of the golden light. Gerald kept his eyes on the plane below.

O'Sullivan, limp, sagging, groped for the cord of his parachute. The plane lurched abruptly downward.

The sharp movement threw O'Sullivan off into space. He tried to pull at his parachute cord. But his strength was gone. Unconsciousness surged over him, drowned him. A dead weight of flesh and blood and bone, he fell, spun downward toward the wrinkled dark blue satin spread below.

Gerald turned away. He bowed his head in his hands over his book. A pot of red ink turned over, spilled its redness over the desk. But Gerald did not bother to turn it back up. His head stayed bowed in his hands. He looked, at the moment, like a human being, a brother, a father, a friend who has lost a loved one.

Presently Basil came back to his ledger. His face was dark with annoyance. "It's odd," he said.

Gerald did not hear him.

"I don't understand it." Basil shrugged. "He didn't show up."

Gerald, incredulous, stared at Basil. "He—didn't—show up?"

"No," Basil said; "I don't understand it at all." He went to his ledger, examined it carefully.

Gerald, tense, watched him. "He didn't show up," he repeated mechanically.

"No!" Basil was almost angry. "He didn't show up." Basil glanced down through the mist. Abruptly, he stiffened. "Look!" he cried. "It can't be! No!"

Gerald, hardly daring to look, went slowly, cautiously to his side. He gaped at what he saw. "Yes," he whispered, "it is."

"I can't believe it," Basil mumbled.

It was easy to understand why Basil found it hard to believe. O'Sullivan, his unopened parachute tangled in the strands of Luke's parachute, was riding with him, swinging in a rhythmic arc, sinking toward the sea. The parachute was carrying the two of them, heavily but surely, to safety. An American plane circled them as they fell.

Gerald's face was aglow with delight. "He must have tumbled into Luke's parachute as it swung widely beneath him," he said.

"Yes, he must," Basil said coldly. "I don't think it came back up and invited him in."

"It might have," Gerald said meekly, "you never can tell."

Basil gave him a sharp glance to see if he was rubbing it in. But Gerald, innocent as the angel he was, continued to look down at O'Sullivan, settling in space toward the sea.

"I usually can tell," Basil said acidly. "It is all written." He waved to his ledger. "Facts, dates—" Suddenly he remembered. He rushed to the ledger. "It can't be wrong," he said excitedly.

Gerald smiled. "You never can tell," he murmured again.

Basil turned a page of his ledger. "What's this?" he cried out. "What in eternity is this?"

Gerald came and looked. The page was covered with entries. Gerald smiled. "Most of them black," he said.

Basil darkly shook his head. "This wasn't here before," he said grimly. "This page was blank." He turned back to the page before it. "The chronology ended back here. I'm absolutely certain of it."

"He must have been given a reprieve," Gerald said gently.

"The scoundrel!" Basil was exasperated. "I don't understand it."

Gerald turned back to peer down through the mist. "I—I—I have an idea, a little idea," he murmured. "Let's see." He looked here and there through the mist. Something caught his eye. "Of course, of course," he said. "Look, Basil. Look in that chapel—Ann."

They looked down at Ann. She was in a little chapel, on her knees, praying. She was like a flower, the stem bent gracefully with the weight of the blossom. Her eyes were closed, her face was grave. But she was calm, serene as ever.

"Of course," Gerald said again. He turned to Basil. His eyes were alight, but he spoke very gently, "I understand it now, Basil—the reason for Ann."

"That is something I'd like to know," Basil said.

"O'Sullivan," Gerald went on gently as before, "he's the reason for Ann. One day she will be a mother and she will have O'Sullivans of her own. Then, there will be other Anns to pray for the new O'Sullivans. And so it goes. If there were no girls like Ann to worry about men like O'Sullivan, there'd soon be no men like O'Sullivan."

"What in eternity is the reason for an O'Sullivan?" Basil asked sharply. "That is something no one can answer."

Gerald nodded slowly. "We can only guess." He looked up and off toward the source of the golden light. "He must like the O'Sullivans," he whispered. "He gives them the Anns." He smiled, turned to Basil. "Did you ever notice the women He gives to the good men?"

Basil threw up his hands in despair. "It's too much for me," he groaned. "It's all so erratic and disorderly and unscientific." He turned, looked up toward the golden light. Then he turned back to Gerald. "Why should He like the O'Sullivans? There is no place for whim and fantasy in the supreme economy."

"I'm not so sure," Gerald replied. He was gentle, very gentle. "Perhaps He has imagination, Basil. Perhaps heaven is not the end of all dreams."

But Basil had turned away. He was filling an ink-pot with red ink.

✳

Love, Tomi

It's funny, Pop, but it didn't occur to me till a few months ago that I ought to open up and tell you how I felt, and then the weeks went by, and the first thing I knew it was too late. Each day, as the time got shorter, I'd tell myself I was going to get together with you but somehow I never did. I couldn't, I guess. I didn't have any trouble telling Mr. Sturgis, the football coach at school, that I thought he was pretty good. And I didn't have any trouble at all telling Father Bonaventure, when he left the Mission, it wasn't going to be the same without him. But I couldn't get myself to open up to you. And when you left, I not only couldn't tell you how I felt, I couldn't even say goodbye.

Well, Pop, I'm going to try to tell you now. I hope it isn't too late, that's all.

I guess I just took you for granted, Pop, like the house and the Mission and the ocean. I suppose plenty of kids are like that. We're interested mostly in ourselves and our own plans and what happens to us. With me, it's always been as if I were sort of standing on your shoulders and looking far away down the road, like I was standing on a rock, or like the way you used to stand in the bow of the *Northwind*, searching the sea to the horizon. I'm writing from my room on the second floor, at the old table near the window, and I can see the *Northwind* riding easily in the bay. I've got her moored fast, and I've got the skiff stowed away up in the sand under the pier and everything's shipshape the way you'd want it. The water is grey-green and cool-looking and out a way there are some white caps showing. The breeze is southwesterly and a bit sharp. It's a pretty morning for a sail. I guess maybe I shouldn't mention all this, knowing how much you love the *Northwind*, and the sea.

As I was saying, I always took you for granted, Pop, like, I guess, other kids take their fathers. But then, when a few months ago I found out about you, I didn't take you for granted any more. You didn't know I knew about you, and you never suspected how hard it was for me to keep from saying something, as I watched you. Only you kept smiling all the time, I guess I would have gone to pieces. You were great, Pop, and I should have told you.

Once, one evening, I almost did tell you. I went up to the Mission to get some lemons. The monks always let me pick all the lemons I wanted, though I never told anyone at home where I got them. I used to charge Mom ten cents a dozen and she used to be surprised and used to ask where on earth I got them so cheap. That evening, before supper, I had picked the lemons and was walking through the cloister with Brother Lawrence when we stopped at the church door. Then, I saw you sitting inside in the shadows. It was dark in the old chapel and I could just make you out. I stood and watched you, and I guess I choked up some, because Brother Lawrence kept watching my face. I was wearing sneakers and Brother was wearing sandals so you did not hear us. In fact, you never knew I saw you.

Brother Lawrence told me you always came up to the Mission about that time every evening and had been coming for years, on your way home from the store. I never knew you went there, Pop. You never said anything. And you had been going up there night after night, praying for us, I suppose. It did something to me, Pop, and that night, after supper, I tried to tell you how I felt about you.

You were sitting out on the porch in the dark, sort of dreaming. I came out and sat on the rail and tried to talk. But the silence was too much for me to break. "What a silence it was. It seemed as if the only sound in the whole town was the tinkle of Mom and Consuelo in the kitchen doing the dishes. Consuelo was staying home pretty much those nights. I wonder if you ever noticed that. John was staying home a lot, too, when he wasn't down at the store. If you noticed the change in us, you never said anything.

Well, anyway, that night I tried to talk, but as I say, the silence between us was too much. It was like a weight that was too heavy for me to lift. And then, you began to talk. You told me you were going to take a vacation, and that you and I were going to go for a long sail in the *Northwind,* just the two of us. You'd let me be the skipper and you'd be the crew. We'd go out to San Clemente Island and then, maybe, put into San Diego. We'd try to make San Diego on Saturday night, you said, because on Saturday night sailors take over and it's a real seagoing town. We'd sail in through the great Navy ships anchored in the bay—cruisers, carriers, destroyers, submarines, even a battleship, maybe. They're a great sight, you said, and would make me feel pretty proud of my country. Though, you added, they never would affect you in the same way that sailing ships would affect you—ships crowded with canvas, like great white birds, that's the way you put it, ships like those your grandfather and granduncles sailed out of Boston and out of Salem.

It was a wonderful cruise you planned, Pop. But I knew you would never make it. I knew then you would never sail the *Northwind* again. Not very far, anyway. And I filled up and I couldn't speak. I couldn't tell you what I wanted to tell you. I never even tried again.

I don't think I'll ever forget that June morning I went down to the drugstore to tell you about Consuelo. I'm calling her Consuelo here and not Connie, because that's what you always called her, and that's what you liked everybody to call her. And maybe, too, in what I'm writing from now on, I'll call the drugstore a shop the way you always called it.

I didn't want to tell on Consuelo, I didn't want to look like a squealer. And besides, I knew how much you loved her. I knew that for you she could do no wrong. I didn't want to hurt you.

The night before that morning I went down to the shop, I hardly slept at all. Just about sunrise I got up and went down to the water and walked along the beach. Walking there, with the sandpipers scooting before me, and the gulls and pelicans taking off as I neared them, wheeling in the sky till I had passed, then settling down again, I felt natural and more peaceful and I was able to think more clearly. I always feel more at home by the water, Pop, than I do in the house. The way you did. I can't imagine you anywhere more than a few hundred yards from the ocean. Nor me, either.

I'd been worrying about Consuelo for some time. She's so pretty, and so sophisticated, and sometimes she looks more like she's twenty-two than eighteen. Uncle Luis says that girls with Spanish blood in them are like that, and she gets it from Mom. Mom and Consuelo are a lot alike, there's no question about that. Their eyes seem to be always on fire, and they move about so quickly. I'll never forget the first time I saw Mom asleep, I couldn't believe it. I thought she was dead. I touched her cheek as softly as I could to see. And right off, she was sitting up and smiling at me, her eyes flashing as if she had never been asleep at all. Consuelo likes clothes and excitement the way Mom does. So does John. The three of them have that Spanish blood all right.

I guess, as Uncle Luis says, I take after you, Pop. I know my hair grows straight and kind of close to the head the way yours does. You and me never seem to need a haircut while John always does. His hair grows especially on his neck, where ours never does. Uncle Luis says John should have been named Tomi after Mom's father, and I should have been named John after you. However, I kind of like the name, Tomi. But I guess Uncle Luis is right. I can talk about boats and things, like you. But I can't talk about people and money and clothes the way Mom and John and Consuelo can.

How I used to envy Consuelo those times when you brought her home a present and she would throw her arms around you and almost scream, "I think you're just the most wonderful daddy in the whole wide world!" Mom could do that, too. And John could do it in his own way, slapping you on the back or putting his arm through yours. But I never could. I guess maybe that's why I never could tell you how I felt, Pop. Maybe you were never able to tell your father, either. I wish now I had asked you about that.

Well, that morning, I waited till you had gone to the shop and then I walked down after you. I walked slowly so you'd be well settled by the time I got there. I had finally decided to tell you about Consuelo. She was going to run off to Mexico with Bert Mellowes that night and get married.

I had no idea then, that what I was going to learn at the shop that morning was far more serious than what I was on my way down to tell you. The elopement seemed like nothing after I learned the terrible news about you. But I've wanted for a long time to tell you about Bert Mellowes and Consuelo and the elopement, so I might as well tell you about them right now, and after that I'll come to what is most on my chest, and that's about you, Pop.

Mom knew about the elopement and John knew about it. So did Uncle Luis. But they never told you. They never told me, either. I guess they figured us being sailors together, I might tell you. Mom thought it wonderful for Consuelo to get a husband who was smart and had money and a big cafe like Bert Mellowes. She was pretty sure when they came back you'd forgive them all. She knew how much you loved Consuelo.

I didn't like Bert Mellowes right from the start. He was always laughing too much for one thing. And his teeth were too shiny, and his clothes were too fancy, and I didn't like that flashy red convertible he used to drive, either. Mom and Consuelo and John said I was just small town. Maybe I am, and, if so, it's all right with me. And I guess people with Spanish blood have a tendency to like red, and shiny teeth, and people who laugh most of the time, but I don't. That laughing business, for example, never sounded on the level to me. There isn't that much to laugh about, I figure.

Also, when you have a paper route, you pick up odds and ends of inside information that other people don't get. Early in the morning I used to see a lot of strange people leaving Bert Mellowes' place over the cafe, people I never saw before or afterwards, and they didn't look regular to me. And besides, Jim Grady, the postman, and I are pals, and nobody knows more of what goes on in town than the postman, Pop, not even a druggist like you. Jim told me about Bert Mellowes having a telephone bill of sometimes two hundred dollars a month from telephoning all over the United States, and especially to New York and Detroit and Chicago. He said he figured Mellowes was probably in some sort of racket. But nobody would listen to Jim.

Everybody loved Bert Mellowes like Mom did, from the Mayor and the Chief of Police down, and they thought he was just a good-hearted rich restaurant man, as I guess they should have, seeing all the presents he gave them, including television sets. Bertie, they all called him. They thought Jim Grady was sort of cracked, like Mom and Consuelo thought I was.

When I told Mom I had an idea Bert Mellowes was no good, she told me I was too young to judge people, and that Bert Mellowes was kind and generous and good-natured, and Consuelo was lucky to know a man like that. There weren't men like him in Seaview, she said, and very few like him in all California, if any. He was going to give John a good job after he graduated from High School, Mom told me, and that made me look even more foolish.

I guess you never were wise to Bert Mellowes. But I must say, Pop, I was pretty proud of you that day he offered to build you a new shop, a shop much fancier than the one the chain store has. Mom's heart was all set on it, and John and Consuelo thought it wonderful. In one way, I suppose, they were right, Pop. You worked awful hard and awful long hours in that dusty little shop without making much out of it.

But, anyway, I was pretty proud of you that day you turned down Bert Mellowes' offer.

I can still see his face when you thanked him and told him you were not in the store business, you were a chemist. But in a minute he was laughing and saying he thought that chemist sign you had over your shop couldn't be very good business in this day and age, and those big glass bottles of colored water in the window were away out of date.

I can remember how nice you were with him, even though I had an idea you didn't like his laughing very much. You told him all of the physicians in town, all the top ones, anyway, sent their important prescriptions to you to fill, and you felt that was the sort of good business you wanted. It was a responsibility and it gave you a feeling you were doing something worthwhile. And so far as the big bottles in the window being out of date, you said that being out of date was sometimes being up to date.

He really listened when you told him how you used to get kelp on the beach and dry it and sell it to people who needed iodine in their systems, and how the chain store people laughed at you, but how now they've come around to seeing the need for iodine so they put up the dried kelp in pills in fancy bottles and sell it at fancy prices, and call it an "iodine ration," as if it were something new. And you told him the same about a lot of other old remedies, like iron and calcium and sulphur, that the chain store sells now as if they were recent discoveries. I could see he was pretty surprised. He had never met anybody who was poor and still stuck up for his work, I guess. And, as I say, Pop, I was pretty proud of you.

I always liked your little dark shop with all those shelves with nothing but those shiny bottles with the big labels on them. It always looked mysterious and important. I never told you but that's what I want to do when I grow up, be a chemist like you. Unless I can go to Annapolis, the way we used to talk.

Of course, I was to blame for Bert Mellowes meeting Consuelo, in the first place. I don't know if you know about that. Remember when he first came to town and bought the Bayside Cafe, and turned it into a night club, he ran an ad in the Monitor saying, "Now the nights at Seaview will be as bright as the days"? Well, it made me mad, and I wrote him a letter telling him we liked the nights at Seaview the way they were, quiet and dark and starry, and it'd be a good idea if he kept on going to some other town, some bigger town, like San Diego.

He laughed a great deal at my letter, I guess, and when he found out I was the paper boy he thought it was a great joke. Later, he gave me a ship's clock for a present but I gave it back. I liked it but I wasn't going to take it from him. I told him so, and he started laughing. If I had been big enough, I'd have punched him right on the nose.

It was the next day that I was walking down Main Street with Consuelo and he drove up in that red convertible. I could see he was all eyes for Consuelo and was slowing down to a stop, and I tried to pull Consuelo into the Five-and-Ten to get her away. But she had seen the big red car and was all eyes for that, the way he was for her, and she wouldn't move. He gave me a big hello, and the next thing I knew he was talking and laughing with Consuelo. He drove her home, and that's how it all began.

I could have kicked myself many times after that, especially since Consuelo had begun to go out pretty regularly with young Dr. English, Dr. Evans' assistant, who came to the house when Mom had the flu and Dr. Evans was out of town. It was when he came to the house to see Mom that he met Consuelo, and it looked like a sure thing to me. It looked like a good thing, too. The Doc is kind of serious, but, from listening to him, I got an idea he takes his job the way you always said a Doc should take his job, like the father up at the Mission takes his job. He had lots of offers to practice in Los Angeles as a heart specialist but he came down to our little town so he could work general with people. I guess you know all this better than I do, seeing he is around the shop so much, but I don't think you knew about Consuelo and him. He's pretty much on the quiet side.

It was only the night before I went down to the shop to see you, that I found out about Consuelo's going to run off with Bert Mellowes to Mexico. I'll tell you how I found out. It won't bother you now.

You never knew it but for a long time, on many nights when you were working late at the shop, Uncle Luis would come to the house with a bottle of wine, sometimes two, and he would drink the wine and get very tipsy. He was Mom's favorite brother, and I guess that's why she never seemed to mind. He was a bachelor, she said, and he got lonely sometimes for a home. But what he really came for was to have me read to him. Yes, Uncle Luis, Pop. It's hard to believe but that's why he came, for me to read to him. He'd bring all sorts of books, good books, too, like Shakespeare and Dickens and Edgar Allan Poe—he liked Poe especially—and he would give me fifty cents to read those books aloud to him. He liked sad stories best, and he would sit and drink wine while I read, and sometimes he would get big tears in his eyes and sometimes the tears would fall in the wine in the glass. He couldn't read very well himself but I think he knew almost every word of those books by heart. He certainly would correct me quick if I missed a line or made a mistake.

I never told you about Uncle Luis because I was afraid you'd be mad at him for getting tipsy there with me around. But I didn't mind. I liked to read to him, except sometimes when I read late and then went to bed, I saw all sorts of creeping things in the shadows, especially after reading Poe, and sometimes I would have dreams that frightened me.

Everybody in school used to wonder why I was so well-read and how I knew so much about books, and why I used to write so well and win all the honors in English. Well, Pop, that was all from reading to Uncle Luis.

Sometimes, when I was reading and Uncle Luis had drunk a whole lot of wine, he would begin to talk to the bottle, just as if it were a human being. He'd make comments on what I was reading, and sometimes he'd get very confidential with the bottle and tell it what was on his mind or unload his troubles to it. He called the bottle, "Lugo," though why I never knew, and the more he drank the more confidential and affectionate he became with the bottle. "Lugo," he'd say, "you're all I have. They're only two of us left, Lugo, you and me. We're going to have to stick together."

Sometimes he would tell Lugo about all the wealth his forefathers had, and about land stretching inland from the sea through the foothills to the desert, miles and miles of land given to his forefathers in the early days by the King of Spain. But the forefathers sold all the land and spent all the money.

"They were no good, Lugo," he'd say to the bottle. "They were selfish. They did not think of us. Now, I have to come to a stranger's home to drink my wine. Let us never be selfish, Lugo." Then, he would cry into the wine. I know you don't like me to talk this way, Pop, but I think it could have been that Luis' forefathers were very much like Luis.

Sometimes, he would talk to Lugo about you, Pop, talk just as if I weren't even around. You are a stranger to him, and he doesn't understand you very well. He likes you but he talks as if California is his country and you are a sort of visitor here, I think he sometimes wishes you had stayed back in Boston and not come to California and met Mom.

"Mr. Butler gets up early in the morning, Lugo, which no true son of California should ever do," he would tell the bottle. "And he walks through the orange groves, and along the roads lined with date palms, and through the apricot trees in bloom, and he does not see them or smell them. He still blinks at our sunlight, and refuses our wine. Mr. Butler is a stranger, Lugo. We must be kind to him." He always calls you Mr. Butler, Pop.

"Well, that night before I went down to the shop, Uncle Luis, came over with two bottles of wine. I was reading *Bleak House* at the time and was well into it, but he was in a happy mood and made me put *Bleak House* away and read *The Pickwick Papers* and especially the chapter where Sam Weller testifies at Mr. Pickwick's trial, a chapter which Uncle Luis knew almost by heart. I figured something good had happened to him because when he started to talk to the bottle he didn't feel sorry for himself, and didn't talk about the past and his forefathers and all those other stories he kept telling over and over.

This night, he began to talk about the future and what great plans he had. "We shall be wealthy and happy at last, Lugo," he told the bottle. "We have long been brave and we are going to be rewarded."

After he had finished the first bottle of wine and
had started the second, he began to talk of Bert Mellowes, singing his praises, and saying what a fine husband
Bert Mellowes would make and what a lucky girl Consuelo was, and I knew something was up. And then he
said, "Soon, Lugo, after the boy and girl are one, he the
wealthy and jovial and generous, she the lovely and kind,
after heaven has looked down on their union, then will
our hour come. We are to go to work for Mr. Mellowes,
Lugo—or, as he, the generous one, says, we are to work
with him—and we will have gold jingling in our pock-
ets, and we can hang gold pieces on our ears, if we wish,
Lugo." And then he made a toast with a great glass of
wine, saying "To tomorrow night, Lugo!", and I was
pretty sure of what was happening.

He made more and more speeches, and his words got
all jumbled up and crazy, but I could make out enough to
be certain of what was going on. I guess he had forgotten I was there or else he thought I knew what he knew.
It was the next night that Consuelo and Bert Mellowes
were going to elope to Mexico and get married.

The print blurred on the page, and I couldn't read any
more. I said my eyes were tired. Uncle Luis was too full
of wine to listen any more, anyway, and he babbled away
to the bottle until it was almost empty. Then, he took the
bottle with what was left and went out, singing, with the
bottle swinging from one hand.

I couldn't sleep that night, and I got up and walked
along the beach, as I told you, and then, finally, I decided
to go down to the shop and tell you. I knew Mom thought
she was doing the right thing, and was sure you would

agree with her after it was done. But I think I know you, Pop, in some ways better than Mom, we being so much alike.

Well, I never did get to tell you, and I guess you know why now.

I went into the shop and you were busy in back with a prescription. Dr. Evans and Dr. Hall, the X-ray man, were standing by the counter waiting for you, and talking in low voices. I went in behind the side counter, as I always do when I'm going in back to see you, and the counter was piled high with bottles the way it always is so they didn't see me. I figured from the way they were talking in low voices they were talking about you, so I guess I had my ears cocked. Then, when I heard what they were talking about I stopped and stood still. I couldn't have moved if I'd wanted to.

Dr. Hall nodded back toward where you were, Pop, and asked Dr. Evans, "How long do you figure?" And Dr. Evans said, "About four months, top." Then, Dr. Hall shook his head very slowly and said, "I knew that from the pictures. Those stomach C.A.'s can get along pretty far before they give any notice."

I've listened to doctors in the shop talk long enough to know my praying has always been for things like a new bike, or when I wanted to put on thirty pounds so I could play football, or the time when you were thinking of buying the *Northwind* and I prayed that you would get it. But now, when I wanted to pray to keep you from dying, I couldn't find the words. I just knelt sort of numb, and kind of hoped, I guess, that my being in church on a sunny afternoon might help somehow.

Time passed without my knowing it, and then suddenly the church was dark and the shadows of the palm trees were very long beyond the open side door, and on the other-side of the church the stained glass windows were on fire from the sunset, and I jumped up and ran for my bike and raced home. Why I raced home I don't know. All I knew was I had to get there. When I went in through the kitchen door I heard Mom and Consuelo in the front room laughing together, the way they always do so you can't tell which is which. I stood still in the kitchen for a moment and listened to them, and then for the first time I remembered about Bert Mellowes and the elopement and why I had gone down to the shop to see you that morning. It all seemed years away, like something I remembered seeing when I was a baby. Then, I heard John upstairs whistling. I listened a little while longer and then I went on through into the front room.

When I walked into the front room, and Mom saw me, she quickly shut the suitcase which was open with clothes in it on the sofa, and put the suitcase in the closet under the stairs where we keep the rain coats and umbrellas. She and Consuelo stopped laughing. My face must have looked strange to them for they both watched me sort of worried, as if they were afraid maybe I knew about the elopement. Nobody said anything, and then John, all dressed up to go out for the evening, came down the stairs, still whistling.

The moment John was in the room, I said, "Pop has cancer and is going to die." I hadn't planned to say it, but I knew you would be home in a few minutes, and somehow

I felt it would be good for them to know about it right there and then, and I just blurted it out.

Well, regardless of what Uncle Luis is, I guess, Pop, what he says about Spanish blood must have some truth in it, or else Mom's Spanish blood must be pretty good. Not one of the three said a word and I, thinking I knew them very well, had expected screaming and a whole lot of panic.

Mom sat slowly down on the sofa and slowly blessed herself. "No, Tomi. It can't be true. It can't be." Her voice broke a little, and I knew she was working hard to keep a grip on herself. Then, I told them what I'd heard at the shop that morning, "No, Tomi. No. It can't be true," Mom said again, but without hope now.

"Poor Pop," John whispered.

Consuelo began to sob, then she stopped herself. "He's known for a week, and he's never said a word," she whispered.

John now sat down and stared at the floor. "He seemed in better spirits the last few days than for a long time," he said. "I guess he's putting on an act so we won't suspect anything."

Now, Mom began to cry, but very softly and mostly to herself. Then, Consuelo began to cry, and in the same way.

"It's a tough break," John mumbled, "a tough break." And then he was sobbing, but trying hard to keep it to himself.

I guess I should have cried, too. But I couldn't. It wasn't till John had commented on it, that I realized what a great thing you had been doing, Pop, keeping your terrible secret to yourself just to save us all trouble, and even pretending to be in fine spirits. I filled up with pride and admiration, but I couldn't cry. I had an idea you wouldn't have liked it. I figured you were doing what you were doing to save us from crying.

The telephone rang. It continued to ring. Nobody cared, but after a while I went into the hall and answered it. It was Bert Mellowes.

Mom and Consuelo and John all looked in a kind of bewilderment at one another when I told them he was on the phone. Then Mom said to Consuelo, "Go tell him we'll have to forget about it. For some time, anyway."

Consuelo went out to the telephone and was back in less than a minute. Then, I said to Mom, "We shouldn't let Pop know we know, Mom. What do you think?"

"Oh, no. Never," she answered quickly.

Just as she said that you pulled up in the sedan and stopped in the driveway. You got out and came around the front door. Mom and Consuelo quickly dried their eyes, and John blew his nose.

You came in that night as you'd always come in, smiling, with a little pat on Mom's cheek and a little squeeze for Consuelo, and saying, "And how are my two little girls tonight?" Then, you looked John and me full in the face, still smiling, and said as you always said, "And how are the two men?"

You were tops, Pop. You had come home many times from your little shop, I knew, with disappointment in your heart, and sometimes maybe, with despair in your heart, and you'd never changed, and now, tonight, you came home with death in your heart, as you'd been coming home for about a week, and you hadn't changed, either. Yup, you were tops.

We put on a pretty bad performance that night, and I guess if you hadn't had the worry of the shop on your mind at that time;—you were hiring Mr. Higgins to help out (business had picked up, you said, but we knew it hadn't), and had to hurry back to show him the ropes— you'd have seen through us. John all of a sudden began to pretend he had a great interest in pharmacy and I saw you look at him sharply. You had always wanted him to study pharmacy and be with you in the shop but he'd never listen to you. He wanted to be a salesman, he always said, and travel around from one big city to another. So, that night you were surprised, and you said, "I might take you up on that, John." Then, you added with your little smile, "If the feeling you have doesn't blow over." I guess you remember all this.

Mom waited on you hand and foot till I was sure you would suspect something, and Consuelo kept talking about you taking a long vacation, maybe even driving back to Boston, and I was more of a clam than usual, hardly being able to speak even when you asked me a question, and we all were so nervous and unnatural, it was a good thing, as I say, you had the shop and Mr. Higgins on your mind or you'd have suspected something.

Later, as day after day, and night after night, we watched you dying, usually smiling and with never a moan or a complaint, we got to be much better at playing the game. The sight of you, carrying on the way you did, Pop, built us up, gave us a courage I'm sure we never would have had otherwise. We all seemed to grow bigger and finer, watching you, admiring you. I think now, we actually did grow bigger and finer right under your eyes. Maybe it's because you had the idea your family was pretty good to begin with, that you didn't suspect us. And maybe we just sort of began to live up to your idea of us. I shouldn't wonder but that's it.

That first night, when I was in bed, Mom came in and sat on the edge of the bed, and asked me if I was sure I was right about what I'd heard in the drug store because she couldn't believe you were any different from what you'd ever been. I told her what I saw in your face after the doctors had left the shop and you leaned on the counter and looked out into the sunlight on the street. Then, she began to cry but very softly, and I put my arm around her and we began to talk about how wonderful you were, not only then but all the years before, how hard you always worked, day in, day out, without any complaint, and how almost everything you did was for us, like how you almost never bought any clothes for yourself but always made your two girls, Mom and Consuelo, have the best clothes you could afford to buy, and the great plans you had for John and me, and how there had been times when you had to go without lunch to pay the premium on the life insurance policy you carried for Mom and us— things like that, we talked about, and it was the first time since I'd grown up that Mom and me were so close.

Then, Mom told me about the elopement of Consuelo and Bert Mellowes that had been planned for that night, and how now her conscience bothered her for not telling you, and how grateful she was for knowing about you being so ill and what the shock would have done to you if the plan had gone through. I didn't say I knew any-thing. I just let Mom talk. I could see all she had done and planned to do, she had done only because she thought it was going to be wonderful for Consuelo.

Mom sure liked Bert Mellowes. He was so happy and generous, she said, and he didn't smoke or drink. Some day, she said, maybe Bert Mellowes and Consuelo would have a nice church wedding and everything would be fine. I didn't say anything then, either.

We must have talked for an hour, and I guess I got to know Mom better than I'd ever known her. I got to see she's like a child, Pop, just a little girl, like Consuelo, and I can see more and more now what you mean when you call them your two little girls. When Mom left, I kissed her good night, something I hadn't done in as long as I could remember.

I lay awake a long time, doing some thinking. I decided I'd have to do something about Bert Mellowes but just what I didn't know. And I decided I'd open up pretty soon and tell you how I felt. But, as you know, the days and the weeks and the months went by, and I never did, and then, somehow, it was too late.

Well, that night before I went to sleep I went to the window and looked out at the *Northwind* riding at its mooring on the water. There was moonlight all around her and the bay was very calm and quiet. And I remem-bered all your plans, your dreams for your old age as you called them, and how you were going to do nothing but sail up and down the coast from Mexico to Canada with your family, and how you used to say that was the only happiness you ever wanted and it was well worth working for and waiting for. And then, I remembered what Dr. Evans had said that morning about you having only four months left, top. It was a pretty hard fact to accept, Pop. The *Northwind* would be here four months from now and we'd be here, but you wouldn't, Pop. Then, suddenly, for the first time I began to go to pieces. I got angry, got mad at God and the world, and I wanted to run out into the street and scream my anger everywhere and at everybody. Then, I remembered how quietly and bravely you had accepted the fact, had taken the death sentence, and I felt ashamed of myself, and in a minute I was calm again. I drew down the window shade against the moonlight, and went back to bed.

Just as I turned away from the window, I heard someone drawing down the window shade in your room across the hall, and right away I knew it was you. You had been looking out at the *Northwind*, too.

Those months went fast, Pop. Your courage couldn't keep you from growing thinner and greyer, nor your shoulders from getting bent, nor your walk from slowing down to little more than a shuffle. The hardest thing for me to watch was the twinkle fading out of your eyes. The little smile around your mouth never went, not for good, anyway, but the twinkle disappeared, and after a while there were mostly shadows in your eyes.

Still, you made no comment or complaint. Once, I remember, when we were standing outside of the shop, a Mexican funeral procession went slowly by on its way up to the Mission. They had come in from the hills, and the casket was on a farm wagon drawn by two horses, and the friends and relatives, men, women and children, followed the wagon on foot. The wagon was filled with flowers, mostly dark red hibiscus blossoms and white oleander blossoms and there were so many of them you could hardly see the casket, and the people following the casket also carried flowers, but they carried mostly red roses. It was a sunny bright morning, but the breeze that comes off the sea sometimes in late summer was blowing across the town, and, as you remember, it would blow some of the flowers off of the wagon on to the street, and the flowers lay in the street and the people walking behind the wagon tramped over the flowers. You watched the procession, leaving its little broken trail of flowers in the bright sunlight, until it was out of sight and then, after a moment you spoke, and your voice had a little sadness in it. "Death seems like a stranger," you said, "like an intruder in this bright and colorful country. I wonder if it is harder to die here than it is elsewhere, like in Boston, for instance." That was the only time I ever heard you give any hint that maybe you were doing a lot more thinking than you ever let us know.

I used to watch you all of the time, Pop, and I figured one day you'd break, but you never did. At first, when you couldn't eat very well, you used to say you were giving up certain foods because they were too rich for you. Then, later, you used to say it looked like you had an acid condition, and food was bad for it. Finally, you said you guessed you had ulcers but not to worry for the doctors were getting so they could get rid of ulcers pretty quick nowadays. When someone, who hadn't seen you for a long time, would remark about your thinness, you would joke and say it was a good thing because thin people usually lived longer.

I can still see you getting up in the morning and going to work just as if life were the same as it always had been, and there wasn't anything wrong at all. And sometimes in the beginning you almost had us believing it, but the time came when you could spend only an hour or two at the shop, and then the time came when you couldn't go to the shop at all. You never said anything, and we couldn't either.

Bert Mellowes came around to the house a lot at first, especially at night when you were in bed, but Consuelo thought his laughing was sort of out of place, though she could not explain why to him, so she told him not to come. After that, when she saw him she saw him down town, I guess, or at the cafe. Dr. English used to come around the house to see you during those days on times when Dr. Evans would be in San Diego, and he would loiter around in the front room, and for a time I thought Consuelo and he would take up again. But those gifts that Bert Mellowes sent, flowers and candy almost every day, and special gifts about every week, like perfumes and fancy soaps, and things like that, kept Bert Mellowes right around the house almost more than if he had been there.

You seemed to grow gentler with Mom and Consuelo as the weeks went by, and you kept telling John and me little things, like how you kept your accounts at the shop, and how the car needed a new fuel pump, things like that. And you used to give us little items of advice, but mostly you kept telling us we were good boys, as if you wanted to be sure we'd always remember what you thought of us. I remember, Pop. I remember every word you said, and everything you did. It's just as if I were listening to you and watching you right now. If that's what you wanted to do, Pop, you certainly did it.

Then, came the day you went to the hospital, and time was running out fast.

I can still see you at home that last day, sitting in the front room where you had called us, waiting for us all to sit down.

It looked, you said, as if your sickness was more serious than you thought, and you guessed you'd have to be going to the hospital for a spell. A hospital's a much better place for treating the sick anyway, you said, with its nurses and equipment, and you'd have a much better chance to get well quicker there.

Then, you saw that none of us was surprised, and none of us said anything, and you knew all of a sudden that we knew, and I remember the wonderful look on your thin, tired face.

You didn't speak for a long time. No one spoke. Then, at last, you said, "Well, well. That's pretty good, pretty good," and you spoke very softly, and I think then, Pop, I saw what looked like your twinkle back in your eyes.

You hadn't told us how ill you were, you explained, because you hadn't wanted to spoil the summer for us, and then your little smile came on your grey face, and you said, slowly, very slowly, "I always knew my family was all right, all of you. I can go now, happy and in peace."

Then, you got up, and making your way by yourself the way you always insisted, you left the room and went to the front door to go to the car, and we followed, and no one cried, not even Mom.

You remember all this, I guess, but I don't think you had any idea how I felt, and how great I thought you were, and especially how great you were when you told us that you didn't say anything about your illness because you didn't want to spoil the summer for us. I can still see you saying that, Pop, with your little smile on your face, and you were great. It'll be a long time before I forget it.

I knew that ride to the hospital was going to be our last ride together, and I had been dreading it. But it wasn't so bad after all. We felt so proud of you, and, I guess, we kind of felt proud of ourselves because of the compliments you'd given us. You made little ordinary remarks as we went along, like about the new paving job, and how Mrs. Sullivan's house needed painting, and I can't tell you how normal, and just like it used to be, it made us all feel.

I remember, too, how, when you were in the hospital and all comfortable in bed, Mom started suddenly to say some prayers in Spanish, and she was trembling, and you patted her head and quieted her and said, "I haven't waited till now to say my prayers, Mrs. Butler." I guess I'm not going to forget that, either.

Well, Pop, driving home from the hospital we all felt fairly good, considering. It was you who had done it, of course. It was you who had made us all feel that way. And then, the strangest thing happened. It was almost, Pop, as if you had arranged it.

We were driving across town all very quiet, thinking and not saying anything, when we noticed the newsboys running around, hawking their papers in great excitement.

We came to a stop sign and John stopped the car, and I leaned out and bought a paper. Mom and Consuelo, who were in the back seat, leaned forward and we all read the headlines together.

None of us said anything. We all looked at one another and we all had the same thought but still none of us said anything. That was the paper that told of Bert Mellowes being arrested by Federal officers that day on a narcotics charge. You read all about it yourself, the next day, about his using his place in our little town as a headquarters for a ring that ran dope up out of Mexico, and how his name was not Mellowes but Mello, and how he had a criminal record and had been mixed up in a lot of killings in Detroit and Chicago, and had had three or four wives, and the rest of it. You read about it yourself, as I say, but you never knew how we were involved, and how he was going to run off with Consuelo that day I went down to see you at the shop. If I hadn't gone down to see you, and hadn't heard about your illness, and hadn't gone home that evening and told the family, Consuelo would have married Bert Mellowes, and maybe John and Uncle Luis would have been mixed up with him, and there'd have been nothing now for all of us but heartbreak and all kinds of unhappiness.

All I could think in the car that day was that somehow you had saved us from all this. You didn't know you had, and you didn't plan it, of course, but still that was the way it worked out. I know that's what we were all thinking in the car that day when we looked at one another, Pop. And I still have that feeling, the feeling that even your dying took care of us, Pop, just as your living did. And I wanted to tell you that, too, and especially.

Well, I guess that's about it, Pop. Everything at home is going pretty well, considering. That Spanish blood of Mom's is all right, and she's been tops, brave and smiling, and always wanting to help us, like she's trying to take your place, and Consuelo and Dr. English are going together again, and it looks like it's going to take this time, and John is spending all his spare time at the shop with Mr. Higgins and liking it, and in two weeks he goes north to study pharmacy the way you always wanted him to, and I got hold of a Blue Jacket's Manual, and am studying it, just in case, when I get through high school, I get a shot at Annapolis, and that's about the way things are right now, which is pretty good, don't you think?

Now, I'll tell you how I came to write this, and then I'll be finished.

The other day when I was going goofy, thinking about how I'd never opened up to you when you were around, I was up at the Mission getting some lemons and I saw Father Anthony walking in the cloister, so I decided to go to him and tell him how I felt. He understood it right off. You know how strict and stern he is, well, when I told him about us, I think I saw something like a tear in his eye. He was like me with his father when he was a kid, he said. And when I told him I'd been thinking lately of writing down how I felt in a sort of letter but I knew that was foolish, because it would be a letter I never could mail, he said he wasn't so sure it was foolish, and he told me to go ahead and write it. Since no one had any idea how great God's kindness was, he said, no one could definitely say you wouldn't learn somehow what I'd put down on paper. That's the way he talked. It didn't help me too much till he told me to remember that God is a father, too, and that started me to thinking.

So, here it is, Pop. Love, Tomi.

✳

The Pigeon from
St. Bartholomew's

Mr. Somerset stood at a window of his suite high in The Towers and looked out on the wide world. What he saw pleased him, and Mr. Somerset was not easy to please.

Spring had come to Manhattan. Mr. Somerset's window faced north and beyond to the west he could see the Park, a woodland valleyed among massive cliffs of brick and stone, budding gray green in its annual adolescence. He noted the warm blueness of the sky, the warm brightness of the sunlight, the gleaming slender silver of the Hudson in the distance, the darker, wider silver of the East River just below him. It was a beautiful world, he mused, a vast, clean, glowing impersonal world.

At Fiftieth Street and Park Avenue, directly below, the pigeons from St. Bartholomew's steps suddenly swirled up into the air, fluttered indignantly over the church dome and, after a moment, reluctantly settled on nearby roofs and ledges. There, Mr. Somerset knew, they would wait impatiently until the vulgarian who had disturbed their dignity went his inconsiderate way.

Mr. Somerset liked watching the pigeons, liked their fat, lazy grace. Once, in a time long past, he was wont to disdain as daft those poets who pined lyrically to be a bird, a flower, a cloud; but no longer. Now, in his graying years, he believed the poets saner than they knew or, perhaps, saner than he knew. So Mr. Somerset, being Mr. Somerset, mused as he looked out from his lofty window on the wide world.

Charles, Mr. Somerset's valet, a solemn, shadowy little man, noiselessly entered the room carrying Mr. Somerset's homburg, his ebony, silver-handled stick and his gray gloves. He stopped at a discreet distance, watched the slender, tall silhouette of Mr. Somerset against the sunny window. After a moment, he coughed a small polite cough. Mr. Somerset turned.

"I imagined the homburg, sir," Charles said, presenting the hat and gloves.

"Yes. Yes, Charles. Thank you." Mr. Somerset carefully put on the homburg. "I shall go to the office as usual."

"You will not forget, sir, to stop at Mr. Legant's on your way out."

"What do you suppose Mr. Legant is doing up so early? He must not yet have gone to bed." Mr. Somerset began the slow ritual of putting on his gloves. "Did he seem sober when he called, Charles?"

"He seemed cheerful as he always does, sir."

"Well, cheerfulness is hardly heroic on his part, Charles. Mr. Legant is very rich."

Charles waited in deferential silence until the ritual of the gloves was finished. Then, he said, "Would you mind, sir, if I left a little early today? It is Easter Sunday."

"So I saw in the papers, Charles." There was the least curl of irony in the corners of Mr. Somerset's thin-moustached mouth. "You are not thinking of going to church, are you?"

"Yes, sir." Charles was respectful.

"You, Charles?" Mr. Somerset moved his head from side to side slowly in mock despair. "On such a beautiful day, too?"

"I always go on Easter Sunday, sir." Charles passed him his stick.

"Yes, I seem to remember now. There're more candles lit today, isn't that it?" He moved toward the door. "More words from the pulpit. New hats. More tall hats, too. More flowers, particularly lilies. You have no idea, Charles, how I detest Easter lilies. They are so blandly artificial, so hypocritically pure. Well, go, Charles, as you wish. The show will be a good one I'm sure."

Charles opened the door for him. "Thank you very much, sir.

Mr. Somerset passed Mr. Legant's suite on the way to the elevators. He had gone some steps beyond the door when he remembered. He returned, pressed the door button.

Mr. Legant, tall, fleshy, an oldish forty, formal in a well-cut gray morning coat and finely striped trousers, opened the door. "Good morning, Professor," he buoyantly greeted Mr. Somerset. "Come in and have a drink."

Mr. Legant waved a long, pale hand to a small table at the window. The window looked toward the east and the morning sunlight lavished its good spirits on the table, flowing over white linen, glistening in the glass, of two slender-stemmed wine glasses, glowing on a silver bucket and its bottle of champagne.

Mr. Somerset gave a slight shrug of annoyance. Neither the idea of the wine nor the other's ebullience pleased him. "Thank you but it's a little early, don't you think, Freddy?"

Freddy laughed. "That's the idea. It's rash. It's imprudent, drinking in the morning. A gesture of reckless defiance. It's revolutionary, sir. You have no idea the good it will do you."

Mr. Somerset coolly studied the alcoholic brightness in Freddy's eyes. "You are a toss-pot, Freddy."

"A drunkard," Freddy, smiling, corrected him. "An impetuous seeker of the Absolute, sir, a passionate lover of the Beautiful Now. You'd never understand, Professor."

Mr. Somerset's annoyance became more apparent. He lifted his stick toward the wine bucket. "Is that why you asked me in?"

"No. No, it isn't, sir." Freddy now spoke with a lofty solemnity. "I wanted to invite you to go to church with me."

"You, too? Is everybody drunk?"

"It's Easter, Professor." Freddy moved toward the wine bucket. "Beautiful Easter. I thought it'd be nice for us two sinners to go to church together."

"It's the alcohol, Freddy. *You* don't believe in Easter."

Freddy, about to pour himself a glass of wine, stopped, pondered gravely. "No, I guess I don't, Professor. I don't know much about Easter. I just had a feeling I—I ought to be grateful—make a gesture—you know—"

"Be grateful for what? Your preposterous wealth?"

"For the wine, sir." Freddy filled a glass. "For the beautiful wine." He sipped from the glass. "It is beautiful wine, Professor. And for all the rest of it—" He waved his glass vaguely toward the window—"for the beautiful view—the beautiful view including you, Professor—"

"I can see, Freddy, I won't have to worry about you going to church." Mr. Somerset watched him in cynical amusement. "One lovely bottle will lead to another, as one always does."

Freddy stuck out his jaw in a defiance that was solemn and comic. "I'm going to church. You'll see." He indicated the gray coat and striped trousers with an almost childish gesture of hurt. "What do you suppose I put these clothes on for? I'm going to church, Professor. You'll see."

Mr. Somerset shrugged. "Yes. I'm sure. Well, I must be on my way." He pointed his stick out the window at the United Nations Building, rising against the East River at the foot of Forty-Second Street. "*That'll* be my church today."

Freddy looked down at the huge glass-and-steel prism of the Secretariat glittering in the sunlight.

"A big committee meeting today, I'll bet. Special for Easter." His soft amiability returned to him. "Do something for me, will you, Professor? Tell your friends down there to turn off the lights when they go home at night. They leave them burning to all hours, all of them. It messes up my night view of the river."

"It could be my friends are working nights down there, Freddy, working for the good of the world—for you, Freddy."

Freddy drank from his glass, grinned. "You really think you're going to save the world by committees, don't you, Professor?"

Mr. Somerset smiled. "Well, somebody's got to save it, Freddy. Alcohol hasn't done it, not even in champagne bottles in silver buckets." He turned easily toward the door. "Nor have your churches done much to save it, Freddy. Not much that I've observed in any event."

Freddy chuckled, sipped his wine. "The churches have quite a problem, Professor, with people like me."

Mr. Somerset lightly tossed his stick, waving goodbye. "Don't go to bed in those lovely clothes, Freddy," he said at the door. "It would be very unbecoming to a passionate lover of the Beautiful Now."

The door closed behind Mr. Somerset. Freddy, still chuckling, poured himself a second glass of wine.

Mr. Somerset stepped out into the sunlight of Fiftieth Street. Ordinarily he turned right and strolled east to the river and the Secretariat. But today the Easter promenade on Park Avenue, particularly the bobbing parade of women's gay hats, gave promise of game for his satiric eye. He strolled leisurely west, crossed to St. Bartholomew's.

The pigeons, down from their roofs and ledges, fluttered thick on the church's steps, swarmed around a tall, soft-faced woman in a new pink hat and new pink suit, feeding them cake from a cardboard cake box. Mr. Somerset stopped, looked on, meditatively tapping his stick on the sidewalk. A sickening pink.

On her way to church, Mr. Somerset mused, but must feed the poor birds. Bird lover. Kind soul. Yes, of course. Also such an easy way of attracting the eye. Attract the pigeons and you attract the eye. People were stopping on the sidewalk, especially women. They were stopping on the steps on their way into church. Especially women....

Yes. The bird lover. How much better the pigeons, Mr. Somerset mused. How completely themselves. Fat, all of them. And getting fatter. It had been a mild winter. No worry about diets, no worry about their figures. No worry about Easter or showing off pink hats and pink suits. No concern about church, either. Church was cornices, ledges, wide eaves, casements, belfries, comfortable for roosting. Church was steps, wide steps and bread crumbs and cake. What folly the woman in the pink hat and suit, what wisdom the pigeons eating the cake.

Mr. Somerset shrugged ever so slightly, turned away. Superstition, exhibitionism. And vulgarity. Worst of all, vulgarity. How were order and elegance ever to be brought to the world? Mr. Somerset waited for the traffic light to change to green and crossed the Avenue.

People. Men and women, with women more manifest. People going to church. People coming from church. People parading to be seen, with women more manifest. Fatuous, foolish. He thanked his genes, and the genes of his ancestors, for his sapience, his fastidiousness, for his self-sufficiency.

Now, this girl coming up the Avenue, this girl with the waxen face, the Easter-lily face, and the round, moist eyes. The blue hat was cheap and new, the blue coat was cheap and old, old and gawkily short and out of fashion. He knew that face, its ingratiating mouth, its waxen innocence. Of course. The cashier at his barber shop. So, she too was in the parade.

She came near. She would speak to him with her ingratiating mouth.

He would tip his hat, manage a small smile and move on without pause, without breaking stride.

But no. She passed him. She did not speak. She did not see him. She continued up the Avenue.

He stopped at the corner, tapped his stick, watched her. He watched and he saw why she did not see him. A man. A chubby young man in a new gray felt hat and a new light gray worsted suit. A good suit, though the cut of the shoulders, the narrow round cut seemed an affectation on him. It was spring, and an ardent air was over the Avenue. The young man followed the girl, his eyes never leaving the back of her neck. As if he were trying telepathy. As if he would drive his desire right into the back of her neck. It was a radiant spring day.

Mr. Somerset watched. The young man had no need of thought transference. Mr. Somerset could read the girl's mind in the movement of her body. She slowed down, stopped by a religious goods store. It was deftly done. He could see the girl show a sudden pious interest in a statue of the Madonna and Child and a display of the book: *Happiness Through The Conquest Of Desire.* The book hadn't sold very well. There must have been ten copies still in the window. Strange. Those blue sky books always sell, however inane. Especially religious blue sky books. Nothing like religion, Mr. Somerset mused. How to be everything through religion. How to be brave, how to be healthy, how to have peace, how to live longer. Through religion. Had anyone written a book on how to get thin through religion? It was an idea. Asceticism made stylish. Pray and grow thin. Yes, strange how *Happiness Through The Conquest Of Desire* had not sold. At Easter Time, too.

Still the shop was doing all right. Here it was deep in the elegance of Park Avenue, near the Waldorf, near the Ambassador, near Sherry's. Nothing like religion.

Mr. Somerset tapped his stick, watched the girl's moist eyes grow more moist, as she studied the Madonna and Child and read the jacket of *Happiness Through The Conquest Of Desire*. The Easter-lily face went well with the religious goods store window, he thought. So did the faded blue of the cheap coat. The young man joined her at the window. He looked into the window. Quite a book, he said after a moment, quite a book. She gave him a cold stare. An instant's cold stare. Then she smiled…

Mr. Somerset shrugged. Woman: the dove who swallowed the serpent. He liked his definition. They would probably go to church together, the young man and the girl. They could very well sit by the woman in pink who fed the pigeons. Or by poor frightened Charles, shadow of a shadow. Or by drunken Freddy. It was all tawdry, vulgar. Vulgar as the cardboard cake box, or alcohol in the morning sunlight, or the gawky, cheap blue coat.

The genii of the city streets were to be thanked for the pigeons.

Mr. Somerset continued his stroll east. He crossed Madison and moved along by St. Patrick's to Fifth Avenue. He stopped again. But this time he tapped his stick in considerable uneasiness. It was much more disconcerting here on Fifth. More people. More exhibitionism. More hats. More women more manifest. More people going into St. Patrick's.

There were pigeons here, too, a fluttering multitude of them. But there was no woman in pink here with a cake box. And people were thicker here. The Avenue before the church was amazed with them. The church steps dribbled black with them. There were more children here, too. The sidewalk, the steps were pimpled with them.

How much better the poor pigeons, the poor dispossessed pigeons. The good, simple, natural, nonsectarian pigeons. The liberal, tolerant, secular pigeons. Loving all churches, favoring none. The noble, cosmopolitan pigeons, citizens of a world society. Yes, St. Patrick's Easter was a bad day for them. Much worse even than St. Bartholomew's Easter.

Mr. Somerset's stick tapped the street in staccatoed vexation. For him, the vulgus was glutting the Avenue, a heavily moving, turgid sludge of superstition and exhibitionism. Park Avenue was the Academe beside Fifth. But the coolness of his agnosticism, the intellectual discipline of years, stood nicely by him. He managed a dispassionate, almost casual mien. His stick slowed gradually to rest.

Now, Mr. Somerset's seeking eyes came brightly to attention. Across the Avenue, before the facade of the International Building in Rockefeller Center, rose the bronze giant, Atlas, holding the firmament on his shoulders, holding a bronze skeleton firmament on his shoulders, a ribbed universe, airy, geometric, like a great gyroscope. Mr. Somerset's vexed spirit delicately found peace. His poise settled fastidiously over him again.

He moved with tranquil dignity across the Avenue, his eyes not leaving the huge statue. How delicately, how massively, it seemed to Mr. Somerset to rise above the ragtag, the bedizened parade. He came to a stop before it, reverently raised his head. Not to the pagan god holding the heavens two thousand years too late did he reverently raise his head, but to the cold, bronze grace of the giant and the rhythmic impersonality of his firmament.

A span of infinitude away from the sludge of humanity, this bronze god. A span of infinitude away from poor, fearful Charles and champagne-tearful Freddy, from the pink hat and pink suit and the cake box, from the girl and the young man looking at the Madonna and Child in the store window. The Madonna and Child, that was it, the Historic Exaggeration, the Apotheosis of the Personal. Yes, that was it, Mother and Child, from Crèche to Pieta, from cradle to grave, the smug magnification of the individual, the gross glorification of the home, of all the ancient sentimentalities.

Mr. Somerset, leisurely, relaxed, moved along the Avenue. A display of Maori weapons of war in the window of the British Empire Building drew him to it. Darts, spears, javelins. Beautifully drawn, beautifully made. A superior people, the Maoris. The family existed among the Maoris but was never recognized as a unit, never permitted to function as a separate household. A wise people, the Maoris....

A tall, thin young woman in a long black coat came to the window, stood beside him, stood very close beside him. Her black hair was pulled tight around her head by a black veil knotted at her chin. Her face, he could see in the window, was thin, was eccentrically thin with protruding, wide cheekbones and finely lean jaws. A sometimes patrician face. But the coat was wrong, a black, heavy winter coat.

Slowly the girl opened the coat, opened it wide, held it open. Mr. Somerset did not need to look. In the shiny window, he could see the whitish reflection of her body. Darts, spears, javelins and the whitish reflection of her body. Slowly the girl closed her coat.

Mr. Somerset's poise was shaken for an instant, but only for an instant. How crude, he said to himself, how shockingly crude.

"My baby's hungry." The young, trembling voice finally protested the silence.

"How inept," Mr. Somerset spoke with metallic grace, "how inexcusably inept to have a child one cannot feed."

"She's a beautiful child." The voice was low, pleading. "It's Easter. I want her to be happy on Easter."

He turned to her, saw her eyes were gray, fine, her mouth large, obvious. "*You* believe in Easter?" The smile was chill, sardonic.

She looked sharply away. "I—I know I'm wicked—but it isn't because I want to be." Her voice broke. "Yes. I believe in Easter. God help me."

"The Magdalen of Fifth Avenue?" The sardonic smile grew ever so slightly. "Well, I suppose this is one way to express your faith."

Her lips trembled. "You don't think I like what I'm doing, do you?"

"And you believe in Easter?" He shook his head slowly in mock solemnity. "The Magdalen of Fifth Avenue seeking her Christ."

Abruptly, she slapped his face, and just as abruptly she turned and fled. His stick fell from his hands. When he had retrieved it the girl was gone.

Mr. Somerset sought to see her but his vision blurred. The delicate wire of his being quivered. His cheek continued to sting from the slap. This was vulgarity, indeed, this harlot....

It was Easter, she said. And the beautiful baby, the beautiful hungry baby. A sales talk for Easter. The plea tender, the plea pathetic. A deceit, an insulting deceit. The beautiful baby, the beautiful hungry baby on Easter. Sobs from a harlot, tears from stone. The Easter story....

The Fifth Avenue Magdalen seeking her Christ. His answer had been good, he thought. Pictorially worded, shrewd, restrained. With the touch of malice that makes the artist. A silver rapier. A ruby-jewelled silver rapier. And her rebuttal, a slap. The dialectic of woman. The primitive logic of the harlot.

Mr. Somerset's vision cleared. The Easter parade went on as before. The gay hats bobbed, the canes gesticulated. A young policeman, face pink, shoes a-shine, buttons glowing, came up the Avenue. For a moment, Mr. Somerset was tempted. He had faith in policemen. The instruments of authority, the agents of truth. What is truth? "The majority vote of the nation that can lick all the other nations." That was the answer that Holmes, the American jurist, had given Pilate. Mr. Somerset liked that answer.

Now, here came the agent of truth, pink-faced, shoes a-shine, buttons glowing. It was a temptation to tell him of the harlot.

But Mr. Somerset withstood the temptation. When you play with mud, you get covered with mud. He turned into the channel, into the fountained, flowered stone

courtway sloping down from Fifth Avenue to the Lower
Plaza. Mr. Somerset stopped as he entered the courtway.
The harlot's slap vanished into the sudden beauty of the
courtway garden, into the sudden beauty of white birches
and cherry blossoms, of yellow forsythias, of rhododen-
drons rose-purple, of azaleas pink and white. The fountains
purled, the flower reflections splashed in the oblong pools.
The sunlight shafting down the great stone ravine was a
shining trellis for leaf and branch, bud and blossom. It was
sanctuary for Mr. Somerset, and release, and balm.

He took a deep breath of gratitude and moved on
toward the Lower Plaza. Yes, those poets who pined to
be bird and cloud and flower were wise indeed. He had
not felt so completely pleased since earlier that morning
when he looked far out over the wide inanimate world
from his window in The Towers and found it good.

Waiters were setting out tables under red and white
parasols on the floor of the Lower Plaza. The United
Nations flags tossed happily from a score and more of
slender staffs on the ramparts above. Parasols, flags, flowers. Color, and more color, gleams of color, daubs of color,
squares, rounds, slivers, ribbons of color, and high over all,
the great canopy of color, the blue arch of sky. And into
the blue of the sky, cleaving it, piercing it seventy stories
above, the towering building, the dominating building of
the Plaza.

Mr. Somerset's gaze swept up the soaring lines of the
mighty building, up to the top reaches of the many-win-
dowed monolith, up to its summit piercing the blue satin
of the sky. Mr. Somerset's being was swept up with his
gaze. Utilitarian, he mused, functional, but majestic, more

inspiring than minaret or obelisk or Gothic spire. None of the vapidities of superstition here. No tortured arches. No curlicued aspirations. No praying stone. No symbolism. Size, power, mass. Man's own mighty monument, not to the gods or to the Muses, but to himself. A magnificent marker on his long road to self-sufficiency.... Self-sufficiency, the fulfillment of mankind's being, the perfection of mankind on earth.

Mr. Somerset happily swung his stick. It was an exhilarating idea. Total self-sufficiency, the perfection of mankind on earth. Exactly the inspiration for his paper before his Committee. He would go to work on it at the office that very day. Mr. Somerset turned back to Fifth Avenue. He was as jaunty as he, being Mr. Somerset, could be.

People still blotched the Avenue. The parade, it seemed to Mr. Somerset, was thicker now, more viscid, more garish. He crossed at Fiftieth Street and was suddenly caught up in a human stream that swept toward the great open doors of St. Patrick's. Mr. Somerset, more tolerant now in the warmth of his new inspiration, coursed along with the crowd. The great entrances to the Cathedral fascinated him. The tall, arched apertures, flanked by their open bronze doors, were like sluice gates draining the human flood from the Avenue, drawing in the crowd with some deep, adductive power, some vast suction of their own. Mr. Somerset found himself on the steps. He found himself in the Cathedral. He found himself in a press of bodies against the last pew.

Far down the lofty, vaulted Gothic cavern of the Cathedral, down through the shadowy gray dusk, a dusk

dimly glass-stained red, blue, green, Mr. Somerset could
see beyond and above the massed kneeling thousands
the gleaming, candle-starred altar, canopied by its golden
ciborium, filigreed and slender-pillared, a jewel glowing
in a distant dark. He could see the celebrant in his white
vestments, another Abraham, another Ambrose, at the
altar of sacrifice. It was quite good, Mr. Somerset mused,
an imaginative New York reproduction of an antique, a
recaptured moment of a distant and discarded past.

He became aware of the Easter lilies that banked the
sanctuary. The flower of bland artificiality, of hypocritical
purity. Immediately, the charm of the scene dissolved for
him.

A priest, in black cassock and white surplice, came
forward from the sacristy, crossed the sanctuary, mounted
the steps to the pulpit. The congregation cleared its
throat for the priest. He wished everyone a happy Easter, a very happy Easter. He read routine announcements.
He named the newly dead of the parish and led prayers
for them. Mr. Somerset's cynicism glinted in his bluish
eyes. Death on Resurrection Day. Never let up. Death was
their business. Death on Resurrection Day. Very good,
indeed....

The priest began to read the gospel for the day, "At
that time, Mary Magdalen and Mary the Mother of
James, and Salome brought sweet spices that coming they
might anoint Jesus...."

An undistinguishable woman in a rear pew began to
sob.

"And very early in the morning, the first day of the
week, they came to the sepulcher...."

The woman's sobbing grew. It was painful, piteous sobbing. An usher, cutaway-coated, stripe-trousered, glided to the pew. He stood at the pew, looked down in concern.

Mr. Somerset saw the woman now. He recognized the black hair, the eccentrically thin, wide cheekboned face, the black winter coat. The Magdalen of Fifth Avenue.

Mr. Somerset shuddered. The Magdalen of Fifth Avenue. The sobbing ebbed.

"...go, tell His disciples, and Peter, that He goeth before you into Galilee. There you shall see Him as He told you."

The priest finished the gospel. The sobbing ceased.

Mr. Somerset was chilled. This was tawdry drama. Even for a church. Raw, immature. The usher should get an Easter lily for her, put it tenderly in her hand. Perhaps she would open her coat for him.... He backed away, made for the vestibule, for the door, for the glittering Avenue.

Outside, quickly now, with purposeful step, he strode east toward the river and the Secretariat.

He crossed Madison. He crossed Park. As he crossed Park, services at St. Bartholomew were letting out and the first scattered members of the congregation were emerging into the sunny spaciousness of the church steps. But Mr. Somerset, still deep in purpose, was unaware of the world around him. Thus, he did not see Freddy in his bowler ease out of the church. He did not see him stop on the steps, slip a cigarette from a silver case that flashed in the sun, light the cigarette, inhale it deeply, and start leisurely back to The Towers. And he was well beyond the church and out of view when

Freddy was suddenly swarmed over by a great swoop of pigeons, an innocent enough happening but a happening that led to what many world statesmen considered a very great disaster.

Freddy had not seen the tourist with a camera toss the handful of popcorn onto the sidewalk at his feet. His eyes, unused to morning, were squinted against the streaming sunlight. His nerves were taut, tensely impatient for a return to the sedative champagne. It is easy thus to understand why he was so thoroughly shocked by the swirling onslaught of the pigeons. Add to this that Freddy had no use for pigeons, that he considered them gross and dirty, and there is no reason to seek further cause for his immediate panic, for his rushing about like a madman, flailing his arms at the pigeons, kicking, shouting at them.

Never had the pigeons at St. Bartholomew's seen anything so vulgar, never had they been so affronted. They stampeded into the air in frenzied, noisy flight, wildly seeking sanctuary far from their usual retreats. Gone was their lazy presumption, gone their fat, easy grace. They were, for the moment, every bit as inelegant as the panic-stricken Freddy.

One pigeon, a grayish blue pigeon of lighter hue than the others, seemed particularly shocked. This pigeon was longer-necked and not so fat as the rest, and not nearly so well-favored, and might well have been a newcomer, might well have come over from St. Patrick's. He took off like a frightened swallow and sped down the chasm of Fiftieth Street.

Louisa had just come home from church. Her mistress had just gone out to church. Louisa thought it an expedient time to tidy up the living room before going to the kitchen to begin the Sunday dinner. She dusted a little here, vacuumed a little there. Then she noticed the Easter lily on the piano.

"You look a little peaked, poor thing," she said to the lily. "I'll just put you out in the Lord's good sunshine for a while and you'll be yourself in no time."

Louisa opened the window and put the lily out on the ledge in the clear sunlight ten stories above the sidewalk. It was a large lily in a large pot. The ledge was narrow and slightly sloped. The lily's place was precarious.

"You just hold tight there a minute," Louisa told the lily, "and I'll get a piece of string and tie you in safe and snug."

Louisa left the window to get the string.

In the sky above the window, the bluish gray pigeon, the long-necked, thin pigeon, circled, seeking a place to light.

On the sidewalk ten stories below the window, Mr. Somerset, walking to the music of his bright, new faith in self-sufficiency, strode almost vibrantly toward the river and the Secretariat.

The white-flowered lily attracted the pigeon's eye to the ledge. He fluttered to the ledge, alighted beside the lily. A wing feather brushed a lily leaf.

The lily pot tipped, tumbled.

Louisa, returning with the string, saw the lily tumble, saw the pigeon flee. She ran to the window, looked out, looked down the ten stories to the street.

Louisa screamed, jumped back into the room, her hands pressed violently to her eyes.

Mr. Somerset was buried from St. Bartholomew's on Easter Wednesday morning.

Mr. Somerset's widow made the funeral arrangements by transatlantic telephone from Paris. She was attending a world conference on The Future of Marriage and was unable to be present. None the less, it was a solemn and imposing occasion. The front pews of the middle aisle were well filled with representatives of the nations of the world. Many members of the diplomatic corps had come down from Washington to attend. The President had sent a member of the Cabinet as his own special representative. It was a solemn and memorable occasion.

Freddy, in formal morning attire, sat alone in an empty pew half way down the church. His eyes were misty with wine and tears.

Charles, Mr. Somerset's valet, sat in a shadowy pew in the last row with three old ladies. The little man sat in distress rather than in sorrow for he could not take his gaze from the white Easter lilies that adorned the chancel.

Outside, on the sunlit steps on Park Avenue, a soft-faced woman in a pink hat fed the pigeons from a cardboard cake box. One pigeon, blue-gray, long-necked, thinner than the others, made off with the largest piece of cake.

✳

Natural Causes

The young girl slowly entered the apartment, quietly closed the door and stood with her back against it, her eyes moving about the living room with a curious slow intensity. It was a gray-green room, a misty room with the June noonday light filtered through pale green Dutch curtains. The carpet and walls were gray, the upholstery dark green, the lamps dark red, and dark red the tole boxes of deep green philodendron on the mantle over the gray-brick fireplace. A gray-green room, a misty gray-green room stained with dark red, the way it had always been.

It had been her Manhattan home all of her life, this mid-town East Side apartment, as much her home as any cottage or mansion, and this room had been the heart of it. It was her room. She had never permitted her mother to change the decor. It was a focal place in her growing up. A family place. An important place in her dream of love and courtship. She had been drawn back to the room. It was her room. It was one of the first rooms she had ever known. It was now to be the last.

Her slow gaze came to rest on the piano. Her intensity sharpened for an instant then grew dull again. A framed

photograph was easeled there on the piano, a new photograph tilted back facing the room as once her father's
photograph had done. Mr. Brownlee's photograph, a living likeness, handsome, sensual, possessive. Too living,
too possessive. It had not been there when last she was in
the room during the Christmas holidays.

She moved away from the door to the piano, her
tawny hair and the tawny light-wool jacket that all but
matched her hair making a wan yellow blur through the
misted light. She turned the photograph softly down on
the piano, softly because she must not hate.

She went to the desk by the window. The wide, wal-
nut desk she loved with its glowing satinwood inlay and
its little brass handles shining in the soft light. With
its ancient silver ink stand with the little white candle
that was never used. The desk where she had written
her thank-you notes, bread-and-butter notes, Christmas
cards, birthday cards, valentines, especially valentines to
Bill. She took a small package from her jacket pocket, put
it carefully on the desk by the inkstand.

She looked at the clock on the wall above the fireplace,
the round gilt-and-rust tole clock that had measured the
happiness of years of hours. The delicately ornamental
black hands marked eleven minutes past noon. She continued on across the room to the hall and went down the
hall toward the rear of the apartment. She walked with a
quiet deliberateness.

She stopped at the door of the large bedroom, looked
in, her eyes moving about with the same slow intensity
they had had in the living room. They rested on the great
four-poster bed with its white, frilled canopy. There she

had been conceived, there she had been born. Her father had insisted the delivery be at home. No cold, metallic hospital for his wife. No even single night's separation for him and his love.

Now, again, her intensity suddenly sharpened, then dulled. On the table beside the bed were two champagne glasses, side by side, touching, with violet lipstick on one of them. The girl moved slowly several steps into the room. On the old highboy against the wall was a faded white orchid corsage. Two or three days old, a week even. Father must still have a key to the apartment. Mother could never endure white orchids. How careless of him. Even with mother living at the beach. Not that she would have cared, not much anyway. Weren't they all modern, intelligent people? Still, he must have had more than one bottle of wine.

She drew back to the door, looked again at the room, at the bed. How her father had changed in seventeen years. She turned and quietly, deliberately as before, went back to the hall. Quietly, deliberately. She must not hate.

She went into the single room that had been her bedroom. She stopped just inside the door. The room had no magic for her, no nostalgia. It had been redecorated each autumn after they returned from the beach, year after year, according to her mother's whim. Yellow and white. Blue and yellow. Rose and gray. Papered walls. Painted walls. According to whim. Victorian. French provincial. Colonial. Playful. Placid. Ardent. According to whim.

The room was her mother's story, not hers. The living room was she. She had fought for that. Only the pictures on the walls were hers. Boats, sailing boats, all with white canvas showing. Real boats she had known during her Connecticut summers. Some she had sailed in the Sound. One in particular. The little catboat she had sailed to win the junior regatta. The little gold tiller awarded her was still on the dresser.

She remembered how proud her father had been of her. His pride had been her greatest pleasure in her victory. He had taught her to sail for he had been a sailor in his day. The best damned navigator from Bar Harbor to the Bahamas he used to say of himself when he was in his cups. She had not failed him. She had been aglow from head to foot in his pride of her. That day he invited everybody in sight to the house at Noroton to celebrate. By dark he was tight. He kept singing off key, "Who's my daughter? *She's* my daughter," to the music of a popular tune. He would give her a squeeze and sing the words off key for he had no ear. "Who's my daughter? *She's* my daughter." He would pour himself another Scotch and water and sing the words off key again. And again. But she did not care. She was proud of his pride in her. She was happy.

She went to the dresser and picked up the little gold tiller. It seemed very small and very far away. She had been only fourteen when she had won it. Only three years away and a little more, three years and three centuries.

Delicately she put the little gold tiller back on the dresser. It had had its day, its beautiful day, and the day was over. That day and many days were over. She went to the closet, took out a white organdie evening dress and measured it against her body. It was last year's dress and a little worn at the bottom from much dancing but it would do. It had been her favorite formal. It would do better than any dress she had ever known.

She put the dress on and she put on the white linen slippers she had worn with it. She stood before the full-length mirror and studied herself. Quietly, deliberately, she studied herself standing in her white organdie evening dress, standing in the noon light in her white organdie evening dress.

In the mirror, she studied Elizabeth. Miss Elizabeth Williams. Betsy Williams. Also known as Skip, from Skipper. Seventeen years, nine months and some days old. Why bother to figure out the number of days? Or the number of years, for that matter. Five feet, five inches and one hundred nineteen pounds. Blue eyes. Brown golden hair. A college student. Freshman. A B-plus student. A in English. But that was yesterday. Not today. Not tomorrow, either. Hobbies: golf and sailing. Health excellent. American for a long way, with a leaven of French from her mother's mother. From Grandma Lemoyne. Dear Grandma Lemoyne. What would she think of her granddaughter Elizabeth, almost eighteen, standing there in an evening dress in the noon light, standing there with that strange look in her eyes.

She smoothed out her dress, quietly, deliberately. She turned from the mirror and went out into the hall. She walked back to the living room. She sat down at the wide desk at the window. Quietly, deliberately.

Dear Mother and Dad: You will, I feel sure, find this letter before anyone else does, and though it won't ease the shock of the moment very much it will in time, I hope, help you to understand and, perhaps, forget. Perhaps you should put the letter away for some quieter hour when you can read it at leisure for there's so much, so much I'm going to have to write. For I know I am going to have to write my whole heart out before I do what I'm going to do.

It has taken me a long time, Mother and Dad, to realize that you have a right to your own happiness. It is selfish for me to ask that you live any more for me. You did that for years. So I am going, rather than stay and mar or, perhaps, destroy your new happiness. And please don't think this is a sudden decision for it isn't. I've been moving slowly toward it ever since you first got your divorce. I feel for the first time in my life I'm being as unselfish as it is possible for me to be.

When first you separated and began to talk of divorce, I couldn't believe it. It just isn't possible, I kept saying to myself. Not you two, not my mother and father. It's not even imaginable, I said. Why, no man and wife were ever so completely meant for each other as you two. Never. I was so sure of that.

I remember in the old days when we'd go to church together and we'd go down the middle aisle to our pew in front and I'd drop back a little and watch the two of you—you, Dad, lanky and a little awkward with those wonderful suits just a little loose on you, just a perfectly little loose on you, and that easy little, smile on your long, lean face, and you, Mother, tall and slender and graceful, with your

hat, like some lovely small creature whose homeland only you knew, perched atop your pertly poised
head—I'd watch you, Mother, gliding, not walking,
your hand lightly on Dad's arm as if the two of you
had been born joined that way—I'd watch you both
and how proud I was of you! And how I knew all
the boys and girls in church envied me for having
the perfect father and mother! And how grateful I
was, and how when we got to the pew I'd pray and
pray, thanking God for you both.

I had many other special pictures of you, of you
two meaning so much to each other. One I remember of you both sitting side by side here before the
fire in the winter dusk having cocktails and hardly
ever speaking, and the dusk getting darker and no
thought even of turning on the lights—deep still-
ness and no thought of anything except each other.
It was nothing and yet to me it seemed almost
everything.

Another special picture I had of you was
Christmas Eve, that one night when visitors were
all shunted off and the telephone was not answered
and the only lights would be the lights on the
Christmas tree here near the desk, and you, Dad,
would bring out a bottle of your best wine and then
you would open the big window wide and in the
cold air we would look down on the city, down into
the great darkness shot through with millions of
lights, and you would raise your glass to Mother's
and say, "To our little home in the jungle," and
you both would sip your wine and give me a sip

and then you'd close the windows and shut out the world, and we three would be so by ourselves in the room here, and it was so exciting—so defiant—to let the telephone ring without anyone answering it. (I once wrote the scene for a composition at school and the teacher marked it, "Maudlin." But when the bitter hours came and I wrote bitter pieces they were always marked, "True to life. Excellent.")

Then there was that night when Mother had the members of her bridge set and their husbands over for a buffet and you got bored, Dad, and you drank a little more than usual and you went around making bad jokes and being, in the worst sense of the words, the life of the party, and Mother joined you and went around with you, among all those quiet conservative people, bravely laughing at your jokes and holding affectionately to your arm, with that lovely chin of hers loyally tilted up and her brown eyes glowing with challenge as if to say, "I don't care what you nice people think—I think my husband is wonderful." It wasn't an important picture of your life together but somehow I thought it fine, Dad. I find it hard now as I recall it to realize it was only a moment that passed, another moment that passed without having anything lasting to say after all.

There was another picture of you two I liked and that was when you'd be ill, Mother, and Dad would sit in by the bed reading to you hour after hour—you liked poetry and how he hated it— how he hated reading of almost any sort for that matter—and how he hated sitting still—and when his friends would call on the telephone, he didn't want them to know what he was doing and he'd be sheepish and lie that he couldn't play golf that day or go to the club that night because he had "a touch of a sore throat" or "a touch of sinus" and he was a very bad liar and he'd get mixed up and he'd finally say a quick, weak goodbye and hang up and go back into the bedroom, and he'd be even more sheepish there, and he'd lie about the phone call and say something like "The hell with the dentist," or "It's always money, money. I think I'll resign from the club," and you, Mother, you'd always see through him but you wouldn't let on. You'd smile and all your love would be in that smile, and he'd pick up the book and resume reading but more loudly, more defiantly, as if to prove to all the world that there was nothing under the sun he'd rather be doing than sitting there reading to you.

Oh, Mother and Dad, I had so many beautiful pictures of you through all those years—pictures of what I considered the perfection of you almost from my cradle-days—that when you first separated and began to make plans for a divorce, it was impossible for me to believe it. I would have died for the belief that you two were born to be husband and wife, and my father and mother forever and ever. But as time went on, I found out the pictures deceived me, that they were moments that passed, passed and left no trace. It is only now, now that I, too, am going to pass—only now that the picture of me is going to pass and leave no trace—that I can let myself retrieve the memory of those beautiful moments— those moments that lied to me so.

Now, sitting here with my decision made, I can tell you how fierce was my faith in you, Mother and Dad, my faith that you were meant to be, and therefore how heartbreaking was my disillusionment when I saw I had been duped—duped by life and my own wishful thinking—and by you.

I felt I had been made the victim of a great fraud. I felt as if God, through you, had lied to me. It was then that my childhood faith left me. I had prayed so hard and my prayers were never answered. I used even to walk around here imagining my prayers had come true just to prove the completeness of my faith. I would shut my eyes and declare to myself with all my being that you two were sitting here by the fireplace again, close to each other, in a deep quiet, with the dusk getting darker. Then I would open my eyes and, of course, you would not be here, no sound or sign of you. So, day by day, my faith was whittled away until it was no more.

I suppose I sound tragic. I hope not for I really am not. Not now. All my real sense of tragedy has long been blurred. I am rather pleased with myself that I am able to write this letter without any pain or difficulty. It could be that farewell letters, real, final farewell letters, pretty much write themselves. Or, perhaps, to be less dramatic about it, those A's I worked so hard for in English have now come to help me out.

But, Dear Mother and Dad, I was not always so calm, as you can see from what I have already written. Those first weeks and months were cruel. I still don't understand how I lived until today. You were selfish, coldly selfish, both of you, though I know you didn't mean to be. When I was divided up between you, so many days to be spent with one, so many days with the other, this week-end here, this week-end there, I felt as if I'd been divided up with the stocks and bonds and the real estate. I felt like another piece of furniture and not like a daughter who had been led to think she was the apple of your eye. And when you'd keep telling me not to be unhappy, I'd always have a home, I knew I'd never have a home again and I never had. I was old enough even a year ago to know that money and food and beds and television sets do not make a home. I knew that fathers and mothers, and love and loved ones made a home. In those days I wanted to face you and tell you you weren't being fair. I hadn't asked to be born. But I never did face you. Perhaps it was best that way.

Yes, I was bitter then. I had learned to love you both so much. Or perhaps it's truer if I say you both had taught me to love you so much. You made such a great fuss over me when I was little, and when I was big, too. I suppose I got to thinking we were all deeply in love with one another. Then when you two began to be strangers to each other, I felt as if you had broken some solemn promise to me. Later, I began to see that I—and your love for me—was

an experience you both had gone through, like a
honeymoon or a trip abroad, an experience which
in time you put behind you. Mother, when you
dressed me up so beautifully and showed me off at
tea, and, Dad, when you were so proud of my sailing
and bragged about me, you were not loving me so
much as you were loving yourselves. I was part of
your marriage career. I was a parental achievement.
Sometimes I was, I'm afraid, simply the thing to do,
the fashionable thing to do. You were no less selfish
when you made a great fuss over me than you were
when you divided me up with the stocks and bonds.
No wonder I was heartbroken. But it was all natural
and modern and I've forgiven you long ago.

This afternoon I, in turn, want you to forgive
me, too. I want you to forgive me any unhappiness
I may cause you. Be patient about it, and it will pass
in a little while, as my bitterness passed. In a very,
little while, I feel sure.

The girl, seated at the desk, rested the pen on the
ancient silver inkstand and sat back, exercising the
cramped fingers of her writing hand. Her cheeks had
small spots of color on them but they were the only
signs of emotion. She parted the pale green Dutch curtains with her other hand and looked out the window
as if she were checking the weather. At a little distance,
framed in a sunlit brick gorge, was a vista of the East
River with an arrogantly ugly black tug lazing it down the
shining stream. Beautiful as always, the river through the
gorge. In rain, in snow, in mist as in sunshine. Beautiful

for all the years, ever since her chin hardly reached the windowsill. And today, too beautiful, much too beautiful. The girl withdrew her hand, letting the curtains fall back into place. Her eyes were cloudy with the beauty she had seen, with all the remembered beauty she had seen. Her hand moved to the small package she had left on the desk. Slowly, she began to unwrap the package. Then her eyes fell on the last sentences she had written on the paper before her. She put down the package and picked up the pen again.

I'm afraid, now that I see what I've written, I do sound bitter. But I'm not, truly. Not now. It is only when I remember and tell of those other days, those heartbreak days—there were so many of them—that the old bitterness shows through. I don't think you should blame me too much.

Those first months when I was shuttled back and forth from the apartment here to that apartment Dad took for a while down near Washington Square were enough to make anyone bitter. You both tried so hard to be kind—tried so hard to prove to me you were more than doing your duty and that you each loved me more if anything than before. It was real suffering for me because each one of you alone was so incomplete to me. It was a situation I couldn't accept no matter how I tried. I was nervous and unhappy. I couldn't help it. You were kind, Dad, with the dinners and theatres but I knew you knew it wasn't working. At first you'd ask if I'd care to have a girl friend along. But at the end, before you gave up the apartment and moved to the Club, you'd insist I have someone along and if I didn't, you'd be ill at ease all evening. It wasn't a natural situation, not for me anyway, and you felt it as much as I did.

It was about the same with you, Mother. You were so sweet with your gifts and the shopping sprees and the teas, and in the daylight sometimes I'd forget, but when we'd come back here to the apartment, and dusk would come and outside the million lights of the city would go on—that wonderful hour I used to love—then I'd realize it was no longer home and we would never be three together again. You'd be your cheerful best and we'd even play the old game we played when I was little—"adventures" we used to call the game—sitting in the dark and looking out on the lights and making up stories about certain lighted windows and what went on behind them—romances and weddings, and burglaries and counterfeiters and spies plotting and murders, even—I think we both preferred the crimes to the romances—but the make-believe wouldn't work any more. It wouldn't work because I couldn't keep from listening for the key in the lock and waiting for you, Dad, to come into the dusky room, silhouetted tall and thin against the vestibule light and turn on the lights and say with your little grin something like, "How about us—can't we have our adventures, too?" Then you'd kiss us both— always you first, Mother—and from then on there'd be much light and noise and talk and laughter. Yes, I guess I was stupid—and selfish—to have expected the three of us to go on like that. It was too perfect.

Those evenings were bad enough, but those nights when Mr. Brownlee came—sometimes at the hour you used to come, Dad—those were unbearable. First of all, he didn't belong with you, Mother—not in my mind, I mean. Nobody belonged with you, Mother, except Dad. Nobody ever could. I know you can call me narrow-minded and old-fashioned but that's the way I felt and feel, and I can no more help it now than I could then.

Mr. Brownlee usually brought me little gifts—books and candy, mostly—and he always made a great fuss over me. But the more he brought me and the more fuss he made over me the more I couldn't stand him. I felt like I was being pawed. And when he told me he had a daughter my age—and how much like me she was and how nice it would be if we got together, I used to see red. I hated Phyllis long before I ever met her. I suppose because of that I wasn't fair to her when I finally did meet her in college.

One night he really made me ill—that was the night when he put his arm around me and was very fatherly and said we had much the same temperament, he and I, and so much in common and we were going to be such friends. I got cold all over and suddenly I wanted to strike him but then my stomach turned upside down and I left the room. I remember wanting to run but I didn't want him to know he could affect me that much so I excused myself, saying I had a whole lot of homework to do and I walked from the room. You, Mother, and he went out to the opera that night and I stayed home with Eliza and I was sick almost all night.

Do you understand now why when I remember these things I am a little bitter?

Worst of all during those times was the foolish hope I had you'd come together again. It was Grandma Lemoyne who encouraged the hope in me. Dear, old-fashioned Grandma Lemoyne, we are very much alike, I think—I want to think so anyway. Perhaps I was born too late and out of time and should have grown up in her day.

When I went up to Winchester to see her during the Easter vacation a year ago I was beginning to be discouraged. You see, at first I had an idea it was only a quarrel between you two and that after a while you would see the silliness of it and come together again. All I knew of the beginning of the differences was that once when you came home from the office in the evening, Dad, mother wasn't here to greet you and you were disappointed. You always wanted her here when you came home and she had always rushed home to be here when you came. Then a second time you came home and mother wasn't here, either, and then a third time. Mother was busy with the Children's Hospital Drive at the time and I'm sure she had no idea how deeply you felt. But you were hurt so you took to telephoning you wouldn't be home for dinner because you were busy and then you'd come home very late, and mother would think all sorts of things.

Then, charities or no charities, she wouldn't come home till late dinner time just to show you. Then, you both began to be so busy....

Anyway, that's how simpler—and silly—it seemed to me at the start. I couldn't believe you were tired of each other or in love with anyone else. And I used to sit around waiting for our lives again to be what they used to be. But you grew further and further apart and I began to be discouraged, for the first time.

It was then I went up to visit with Grandma Lemoyne. One afternoon during the holidays it was very rainy and windy cold and we sat in the great parlor before the small, perfect marble fireplace and had sherry and pound cake instead of tea and cookies and I began to choke up—I guess it was the sherry—and I told her all about you.

I expected her to be surprised but she seemed to know about the separation and wasn't too greatly concerned about it. You two had come to that time in life—"the difficult time" she called it—when change seemed desirable, especially a change of mate, because you yourselves were changing—but the time would pass and you would "return to your-selves"—that's the phrase she used—and later you, being the kind of people you were, would look back on it all as very foolish. She sounded so wise and so convincing.

"The later years are always happiest for well married couples," the dear little gray lady said, "for the last is always the best."

And then she quoted a poem I had not heard. I wrote it down.

> "In youth I sought the golden flower
> Hidden in wood or wold
> But I am come to autumn
> When all the leaves are gold."

It is by Chesterton and I thought it truth itself at the time Grandma recited it, gently, rhythmically smoothing her black faille dress, sitting before the coal fire in the brazier in the small marble fireplace.

Then, she gave me one of her rare smiles and said, "Remember what the steward said toward the end of the wedding feast at Cana in the Gospels, when the Lord changed the water into wine? 'You have kept the good wine until now.'"

Grandma seemed to believe the Lord was keeping the best wine for you, Mother and Dad, for your later years and she made me believe it, too. For a time. I so wanted to believe it. It was so beautiful a thought even for one as young as I was. And it seemed so perfectly applicable to you.

Poor, dear Grandma with her poetry and her Scripture, believing that all the leaves would eventually be gold for you and the Lord was keeping the best wine for you till the last.

You probably remember what happened when I came back from Winchester. After listening to Grandma Lemoyne I felt very young and foolish. I was sure I had been jumping at conclusions.

Of course, it was only a matter of time till you two would come together again. I was full of hope, and I decided I would hasten the time. I thought up a plan.

Now, I can see that my plan wasn't a plan at all—just a childish impulse born of my new hopes. I called you each to meet me in the lobby of the Waldorf, not saying I had called the other. It was important, I said, as I'm sure you remember. I knew with the Waldorf only two blocks from our apartment and only around the corner from your club, Dad, you two would arrive about the same time. I stayed out of sight over in the passage-way by the telephone booths and watched for you both. I wanted you to run into each other before I appeared. And sure enough you did, over near the entrance on the Lexington Avenue side. I walked over triumphantly to greet you. I was going to invite you into Peacock Alley for a cocktail. I was even going to have a cocktail myself. My first. I was going to talk to you both like a Dutch uncle and quote Grandma Lemoyne's poetry and be very sophisticated and grown-up and bring you back together that very evening. We'd all go back up to the apartment together. It would be dusk by then. I had canapes and wine on ice. We'd open the window and look down on my beautiful lights—on your jungle, Dad—and it'd be like old times again as if we'd never missed a beat in between.

Well, you know what happened. I guess nothing much else could have happened. You both pretended to be amused, but I could see right off how deeply uncomfortable you were. You saw through my poor, silly plot immediately and I suppose you felt as if you'd been tricked. I really don't know how you felt but I knew you wanted to end the farce as soon as it began. When I heard you, Mother, say you had an appointment at the hairdresser and you, Dad, say you had to drop back at the office to meet a man from South America—they were such bad lies, I couldn't keep from smiling, little as I wanted to. Then, you both laughed uncomfortably and said goodbye, you, Dad, going toward Park and mother going to the long stairway that led to Lexington.

I went back to the apartment. I didn't open the window and I didn't look at the lights. I threw myself on the sofa here and cried my heart out. It was the first time in my life I had cried like that. And, for the first time, the idea of suicide occurred to me. If Eliza hadn't been home that night I don't know what I'd have done.

But I came out of it, slowly but easily enough that first time. I had not lost my faith in prayer yet. Summer came, and the Sound, and the swimming and the sailing and the wonderful rainy days, and Bill, especially Bill. And again, for a while, I began to believe in Grandma Lemoyne.

Please, Mother, and Dad, always be nice to Bill. He may look like just another tall, dark boy to you but he isn't. He's got a lot to him, Bill has. Of course, as he says, he's been lucky in his way. He's one of six children and the house is a happy turmoil with brothers and sisters and friends and aunts and uncles and cousins, and his father and mother don't have much money, so the truth is, Bill says, they have so many problems, they don't seem to have any problems at all.

It was almost a wonderful summer. You won't mind now, Mother, if I say Mr. Brownlee's being in Europe helped. And Bill had suddenly grown older. He had become more of a person and more interesting. He was no longer that skinny boy from up the beach. He was going into his sophomore year at college. He began to be quite possessive and more than a little jealous, and I liked it. He didn't make any special point of it—he just acted as if I belonged to him and I liked it. I suppose I wanted someone to take me over. Perhaps I loved him then. I don't know. When you've grown up with someone, he has to go away from you—really go away—or you have to go away—to know whether you love him or not. Now that I'm going away, really going away, I know at last how much I love Bill.

The summer was wonderful until Labor Day. I know, Dad, you meant to do the right thing. But I resented your bringing Miss Ellender to the house more than I resented anything in my life before. I could see that you, Mother, didn't mind very much. You knew she was coming and you had the house shining and full of flowers as never before. I suppose you were curious to see her. It is the only explanation I can think of.

It was the modern, intelligent thing to do, as you explained to me before she arrived. We're all grown-ups, you said, and we must act like sensible people. Well, I couldn't act sensible. My dislike of Miss Ellender was deep—chemical, as my psychology prof in college would say.

It was mostly selfish, I suppose, bitterness over the loss of my last hope. Mother, you had Mr. Brownlee. But Dad, you hadn't yet to begun to build your own new world—not that I knew of, anyway, until that day. Then I saw you were becoming a stranger, too.

Miss Ellender is beautiful, Dad. I have to admit that. I also have to tell you I don't like her type of beauty. Her face, perfect as it is with its delicate features and dark eyes, is too small for her body, perfect though that is, too. I'm prejudiced, of course, after having admired you, Mother, for all these years, with the wonderful proportion between your face and figure.

And I didn't like her voice, Dad. You don't mind my saying so, do you? You'd want me to be honest, wouldn't you? She's much too—too physical when she speaks. I guess that's the nicest way to put it. It seemed a little bit artificial, or, perhaps, more than a little bit. With that beautiful figure, she doesn't have to put on a voice like that. And that lipstick-—that violet lipstick! She doesn't have to put that on, either.

Then she, like Mr. Brownlee, made such a fuss over me, especially when Mother wasn't around. She's at least ten years older than I am but she insisted on acting my age—or what she considered my age. She tried to be cute and insisted I call her Pen which I suppose is short for Penny. But I couldn't. The word simply stuck in my throat. Yes, I know I'm bitter about her and am prejudiced but I couldn't go without telling you how I felt.

Well, as you used to say, it's all water under the bridge. All I can do now is wish you all the happiness in the world. I won't be around to cast any shadows. Neither you nor Mother nor Miss Ellender nor Mr. Brownlee are going to have to worry, so far as I'm concerned, about us all being very modern and good fellows together. I can tell you, though, that that very night I thought of swimming out from the shore, swimming out in the dark as far as I could toward Long Island, and finally when I was exhausted and could swim no more, just give up. I'd be a good mile out by then and I couldn't swim back if I wanted to and if I got chicken and screamed no one would have heard me. I even put on my bathing suit and walked down through the darkness to the water's edge. But I suddenly realized all the dreadful publicity there would be and, Mother and Dad, in spite of Mr. Brownlee and Miss Ellender, I loved you too much to do that to you. I decided then and there if I ever did decide to go, I'd go in such a way that no one would ever know. Selfish I could be, but I was determined I wasn't going to be mean.

Later that night, Bill came along with his uke and—well, anyway, none of it makes any difference now.

When college began a few days later, I got caught up in the novelty of my new life and the excitement of making new friends and I almost forgot that I'd ever had such terrifying thoughts at all. Almost. For Phyllis Brownlee, as you know, was in my class and she came always as a shadow of remembrance into any bright moment of forgetfulness I might happen on. She was forever coming up to me and saying things like, "Isn't it going to be wonderful when you and I have the same home?" Or she'd run up with an open letter and say, "Daddy says next summer maybe the four of us will go to Europe together! Won't that be wonderful?" Please don't ever say anything to her. That's kind of silly, Isn't it? I know you won't. It could be that her attitude to her home and parents was much wiser than mine. It's certainly more modern and sophisticated, as you would say, Mother.

Still, even with Phyllis in the background, I came home for the Christmas holidays full of a new hope. I had been praying more than I ever had in my life before. And I had been doing quite a bit of thinking. I had been taking a sort of preliminary course in sociology under Dr. Cassell and I was beginning to see there were so many more ideas of home and marriage than those Grandma Lemoyne and I believed in. I promised myself I was going to be intelligent. It was childish of me and out of date, I kept telling myself, to try to keep you two for myself. You had your own lives to live. Why should I try to make your lives conform to mine?

Especially, why should I go on wanting you to be unhappy for my sake? I prayed and prayed that I wouldn't be selfish any longer.

Christmas was in the air, beautifully and vividly and ever present in the air as it always is for me in mid-Manhattan. I was determined to live up to the Christmas spirit. I stopped being moody and moping about. I even tried to be gay. Till Christmas Eve.

I'm sure neither of you ever suspected how deeply unhappy I was underneath, at Christmas time or in the months before. I was never much for talk, and on the subject of your divorce I was mute. If I had ever been able to unburden myself, even a little, perhaps I would not have to be writing this long letter of confession now.

Christmas Eve began perfectly, almost like old times. Only the Christmas tree was lighted in the apartment and outside with the coming of dusk there were flurries of snow. It was the first snowfall of the year in New York. Remember, Mother, how you stood by the window and looked down on the lights shining through the dusk and the snow, and how you repeated Dad's words, or rather used them in your own way, saying, "We should be grateful for having such a lovely little home in the jungle."

For one whole minute I felt all the perfect happiness of all the Christmases when we were three alone together. In fact, when the doorbell rang, I was sure it was you, Dad. It had to be to make the picture complete. It wasn't, of course. It

was Mr. Brownlee and Phyllis, loaded with packages. I didn't even get up from my chair. I was rude,
I know, Mother, and you were a little annoyed. I
don't blame you. But I can't blame me, either. How
that Phyllis slobbered all over me and how I didn't
want her or her father's gifts! Then, they weren't
here three minutes with all their noisy cheerfulness and chatter when you arrived, Dad, with your
armful of presents, letting yourself in by your key.

It was the first time you had met Mr. Brownlee
and you both put on such an act of being good
fellows together it directly made me ill. Remember
you followed me back to my room, Dad. You put
your arm around me the way you used to and I
think for a moment you had an inkling of how deep
was my hurt. But I lied to you and said I was woozy
from the rich food I had been eating, the sort of
food I was not used to in college. You believed me
and you kissed me. I nearly went to pieces.

I wonder now—suppose I had gone to pieces
and told you how I felt about you and Mom—about
the tragedy of the Christmas Eves that would never
be again—about my heartbreak—I wonder what
would have happened?

Nothing, I'm sure. Nothing but more unhappiness.

Well, that was about the end. I knew then it
was the end for me. The next day, Christmas Day, I
refused to go to church as you remember, Mother.
Instead, I drove down to see Bill. I told him everything. I had to tell somebody. Good old Bill. He
immediately proposed we run off and get married.

We'd get in his jalopy and drive down to North Carolina or some place and lie about our ages, if we had to, and set up our own home somewhere. It was wonderful of Bill. But I couldn't do it to him. I couldn't spoil his college career for one thing. And I couldn't wish a dismal person like myself on him for another. I wasn't going to ruin his life. Bill deserves far greater happiness than a mixed-up person like me could ever give him. But I didn't tell him it could never be. Instead, I suggested we both go back to school and in the spring we'd make our plans. I tried to be very bright and eager.

But Bill didn't want to wait. I could see then that his wanting to marry me wasn't pity. He loved me. I cried and cried and when he got worried about my crying, I told him it was because he had made me so happy. That wasn't the reason, of course. But he had made me happy.

I went back to college. But I wasn't interested. I continued to do all right in my studies but that was only because I had to study to keep myself from going off the deep end. I knew then that no matter how I tried I couldn't be modern and sophisticated. Not about you, Mother and Dad. I had so much wanted to believe with Grandma Lemoyne that the best was yet to be for you and one day we would come to the autumn when all the leaves were gold. But the day finally came when I couldn't believe any longer.

Well, there isn't much more to tell. My confession, as I want to think of it, is almost finished. Yesterday, at school, Mother, I received your letter telling me you and Mr. Brownlee planned to be married in September. Phyllis received a letter from her father in the same mail telling her the same news. She was very excited. I suppose you and Mr. Brownlee planned it that way. I had expected the news sooner or later, yet when it came it was a shock to me and I couldn't realize it, and I kept mumbling over and over to myself, "No, no. It can't be. No, no."

Phyllis met me in the yard and I hardly saw her. The memory of it is hazy and unreal. I know she was puzzled why I wasn't jubilant. I remember her saying, "I hope it'll be a big wedding. We'll have such fun! Do you like champagne?" But I couldn't say anything. I stared at her for a moment and then moved on. I was conscious of her looking after me with a puzzled and uncertain light in her eyes. I think finally she began to have doubts about the fun of having me for a sister.

I went to class that afternoon. I went only because I was suddenly very lonely—and I thought in class with the girls around me I'd find some kind of companionship. But I was lonelier there with my classmates than I was alone in my room.

It was Dr. Cassell's class and it seemed after a while as if he were talking to me and for me. He wasn't, of course. It was merely the way I felt. I remember him saying that we are all inclined to exaggerate the importance of ourselves. He said it was Western Culture that had encouraged this wrong idea, teaching as it did this exaggerated importance of the individual. He talked of the billions of people who had lived and died—of the hundreds of millions in the world today—of the millions in China and India—of the thousands that were born every day and the thousands that died every day. Wasn't it conceited, he said, for us to prize our own little lives so highly?

As Dr. Cassell talked, I grew lonelier and lonelier. I had always followed my heart, and my heart had always told me I was important, and our home was important, and our loving one another was important, and all sorts of little things were important—like not answering the telephone on Christmas Eve or like your hand, Mother, on Father's arm as you walked down the middle aisle at church. Now, as I listened to Dr. Cassell, I began to feel that my heart had lied to me, too.

Have you ever been lonely, Mother and Dad, really lonely? It isn't just a sort of blue mood the way the songs have it—and it isn't just an empty feeling such as I used to have when I was small and both of you would be gone away over night. It's not being just friendless and alone. It's not having no one to love you. Not for me, it isn't. It's wanting to love someone so terribly much and not being able to. It's a real hurt and the pain is real, more real than any pain I can imagine. I pray you'll never be really lonely, ever.

I've tried to arrange everything so there will be no publicity or scandal, and I won't, I hope, be of any trouble to you. I left college and came down to see Dr. Bowen this morning. I told him I couldn't sleep and my heart hurt. I told him I had shortness of breath but I was lying, and I was also lying when I said I had shooting pains up and down my left arm. I heard once that pains in the arm like that sometimes went with a bad heart. But the hurt in my heart wasn't any lie. The doctor was a dear as he always is. He listened to my heart and said it did sound as if I had a little murmur but it was nothing to worry about. He gave me a prescription for some pills and the address of a place to go for a cardiogram and all the while he was talking the way he always does about how pretty I'm getting to be and about the blizzard the night I was born and things like that just like a country doctor.

I didn't go for the cardiogram but I did get the pills and I've thrown four of them away so it'll look like I took them. I went over to Seventh Avenue to a soda fountain that some crazy boys once pointed out and bought a bottle of sleeping pills. If you're young enough they'll sell them to you without asking any questions. Nobody there has any idea of my name or anything about me so you have nothing to worry about. I'll get rid of the sleeping pill bottle and no one will ever know about it, and I'll put Dr. Bowen's bottle on the table here by the sofa. Dr. Bowen will say it was my heart and it all happened from natural causes and there'll be nothing unusual in the papers and after a while, Mother and Dad, you can go on living your own lives as you were meant to do.

Dr. Bowen won't be wrong. Loving too much is a natural cause, isn't it?

It is getting dark now. The late June dusk is coming in with the mist from the River. It has been a long day and I'm tired. Pray for me—pray that sometime we three will come together again—if only for an hour or two like those old hours at dusk here when we were in our own little home in the jungle. With all my love. Betsy.

The room was deeply dark, and the green and red were melted into the darkness, and only the gray of the ceiling showed in a delicate pattern of light reflected from the glittering dark beyond the window. Then the door opened, framing the light in the vestibule.

The young woman coming through the door could see the long white blur on the sofa. She stopped, pulled back into the vestibule. "What is that—there on the sofa," she whispered.

The tall, thin man behind her switched on the lights.

He saw the girl as if asleep on the sofa, her head on a pillow, her face turned toward the window. He went to her and stood looking down at her a moment. Then he discovered the bottle on the table beside the sofa. He picked up the bottle, read the label.

"What is she—asleep?" The young woman whispered from the vestibule where she still stood, fearful of coming farther into the room.

The man leaned over the sofa, put his hand on the girl's head. He dropped to his knee, put his ear against her chest.

"Betsy," he called, "Betsy." Then, louder, he called, "Betsy! Betsy!"

Abruptly, he leaped to his feet, rushed to the telephone near the hall. Fiercely, he dialled a number.

The young woman drew back into the vestibule. Her lips were like a violet scar on her blanched face. "I'd better not be found here, do you think?" she whispered, her voice now trembling with fear.

The man, fiercely dialling at the telephone, was no longer aware of her. She opened the door, backed noiselessly into the hall and closed the door after her.

"Dr. Bowen? Dr. Bowen?" the man pleaded into the telephone, "Is that you, Dr. Bowen?"

The next afternoon wore sunnily on toward dark as had the afternoon before. The room was a shadowy green again and the lamps and the tole boxes of philodendron over the gray-brick fireplace took on their deeper red. The River beyond the wide window was a clouded blue silver and the dusk again sifted in over it from the east.

The telephone rang. It stopped and rang again. On its second ringing a little gray lady in black and lace came out of the hall from the rear of the apartment.

She answered the telephone. "Yes? No. This is Mrs. Lemoyne, Mrs. Williams' mother. Oh, yes, Mr. Brownlee. Just a minute. I'll see."

She put down the telephone and went back down the hall. In a few seconds she returned to the living room.

"No, she isn't here right now, Mr. Brownlee," the little lady said into the telephone. "No, I wouldn't call later if I were you. Perhaps she will call you. Yes. Thank you."

She neatly replaced the telephone and went back down the hall again.

The room was still a long misty moment. Then, there came the sound of voices from the hall and presently the tall man appeared and with him a slender, graceful woman and an elfin, small man with a black professional bag.

"You're sure, Doctor?" the woman asked as they came full into the room.

"As sure as you can be of anything in my business, Mrs. Williams," the doctor answered in a voice that was quite deep for one so slight. "She'll have a long sleep, as I said last night, and that's about all there'll be to it." He picked up his dark gray felt hat from the table by the sofa and continued on toward the door. "Don't be worried if she drowses through another twenty-four hours or so." He stopped at the vestibule, carefully put on his hat. "We can thank our lucky stars those pills she's been mumbling about weren't up to snuff."

"We can first thank our lucky stars," the woman said softly, "that you, Doctor, got here when you did last night."

The man moved toward the vestibule after the doctor. His voice was low when he spoke as if he did not want anyone else to hear. "Doctor, are you going to have to report this—this to the—"

His voice trailed away.

The doctor delicately stuck the thumb of his left hand into his own left side. "It was the heart," he said.

"But—" the man lowered his voice even further, "but what about those—those pills?"

"It's still the heart," the elfin little doctor said. He turned. "I'll be back the first thing in the morning," he called back over his shoulder as he went out through the door.

Now, the shadowy green room was still again. The man went quietly to join the woman at the window. Lights began to star the evening beyond the window. After a moment, the man turned to the window. Then, the woman turned and together, side by side, in silence they watched the lights multiply and the dark deepen.

The telephone rang. They both turned slowly, looked at the telephone but made no move to answer it.

After a moment, the little gray lady came out from the hall and turned toward the telephone.

But the man stopped her. "No. Please, Mrs. Lemoyne, don't answer it."

The little lady stood and looked at the man and woman, almost shadows now against the window. The telephone continued to ring.

"Let it ring, Mother," the woman said.

The little lady looked at them another moment, then went quietly to the desk. She opened a lower drawer of the desk and took out a stack of letter paper. She put it on top of the desk.

"This is a letter your dear darling wrote to you. You didn't see it in the excitement. I read it this morning and wasn't quite sure when you should read it." She looked at the silhouettes against the window. "I've changed my mind. I think perhaps it might be wise to read it now."

The little lady turned, glided back through the shadow to the hall and disappeared.

The man and woman stood at the window, their silhouettes close together now. The telephone continued to ring.

❋

Seminary Hill

I had no use for Hugo from the first moment I laid eyes on him but my first impressions have been so often wrong, and my good wife so often right, I let her talk me out of my opinion, or, at least, out of acting on it. I must say I did not acquiesce too readily, my dislike of Hugo being as deep as it was immediate, and if it had not been for Father Andrews' devotion to him, I doubt if I ever would have acquiesced at all. It turned out it might have been better for all of us if I had stood boldly by my first impressions.

I live a good rifle's shot from the seminary, though it might be said it is nearer than that, for my home is on a small knoll while the seminary is on a high hill across a ravine from me, and looks almost directly down on me. Perhaps I should say I look up to it, for it dominates the whole country here, standing solitary and large and impressive against the sky. The fact that this is farm country and houses are few and quite far apart and Seminary Hill is by far the highest land hereabout gives the seminary even more aloneness and largeness and impressiveness.

The seminary is very much one huge building built around a quadrangle, one side of which is a cloister walk. Ordinarily, in the realistic light of a noonday, it is rather an ugly building in the hit-or-miss, red-brick Tudor style of much ecclesiastical architecture of half a century ago. But in the dusk or at night or in the fog that often comes in from the ocean some eight miles away it is something else again. The red of the brick is gone, the building seems to grow in size, and the turrets and oriels and gables give the dark pile antiquity and even mystery. My house, a frame house once white, is the nearest house to Seminary Hill and thus might be especially described as living in the shadow of its impressiveness, or of its mystery, as the mood might be. From a short distance, indeed, our knoll appears to be a part of the Hill, like a humble footstool for it. My house is a farmhouse though I am not a farmer, and my three weed-matted acres are, I'm sure, a blot on the farm-checkered landscape to those who can look down on them. I teach History in the high school in town twelve miles away and moved out here a little over two years ago so I could have quiet for writing in my spare time. I had quiet enough up till Hugo's arrival, and wrote enough, but none of it has seen print and my wife, Frances, is of the opinion I could do just as well (or just as badly) in the heart of town. Don't misunderstand Frances. She is the perfect mate for me and loves me dearly, I'm sure, but she has no great hope for my ambition to be a writer. I have no real sense of reality, she declares, and incline to escapism. The modern world is scientific, realistic, she maintains, and I belong to the past. As a writer, she means. I must say, looking down on my desk here at the stack of rejection slips from publications great and small, I have to admit there is much to be said for her point of view. On the other hand, this record I am now writing will, I feel sure, do much to help bolster my point of view, a point of view that can be simply and flatly stated by saying there is more to life than meets the eye.

Father Andrews brought Hugo into my life. Father Andrews was Spiritual Director at the seminary and a saint and a hard man to refuse anything. He was a slight man, a little less than tall, with gray hair that had once been blonde and blue eyes as level and as clear as any, I'm sure, ever possessed by man. He had a way of smiling his requests at you, saying, "I have the most wonderful idea," so that he made you feel he was doing you a very special kindness. He regarded all of his requests as opportunities. You might be amused at him but you could never be annoyed for whatever he asked for he asked for someone else. He gave of himself and his possessions to everybody for miles around the seminary, regardless of belief, station or repute. He was loved by everybody. Even Freemanson, the agnostic Swedish farmer up the road, always bicycled up to the seminary with his first best flowers for Father Andrews' altar.

I can see him now as he drove into the yard that September Saturday morning to tell me I was to have the opportunity of taking in Hugo. I was up here at the window on the second floor bedroom, writing as I am now, when I heard an automobile banging and bumping up the narrow road to my knoll. I expected from the racket it would be Father Andrews, for he was a very bad driver and his ever driving safely from one place to another could be taken, if one was so minded, as an illustration of that divine providence of which he so often spoke. In a moment, the seminary pickup truck, battered and muddy, reeled around the last curve, slid quaking to the far side of the gravel road, as if it would go down into the ravine, then, at the last instant, righted itself and, as the brakes were jammed on, skidded into the yard. Father Andrews, bareheaded and in his black cassock (with two or three top buttons missing as usual) stepped serenely out of the truck. I went down to meet him in the yard.

"I have the most wonderful idea," he began with his smile, and straightaway I knew I was in for it.

Father Andrews, even when excited with an idea as he was then, spoke very slowly, carefully choosing and measuring his words as if he felt they had some special importance and he was being held accountable for every single word he uttered. I suppose he actually did feel so, for he had an extraordinary sense of the importance of little things and seemed to see everything, as the ancient phrase has it, under the arc of eternity. He would stare in astonishment on the discovery of the most ordinary flower or would stop abruptly, surprised and immensely pleased, at the sudden sound of laughter and say carefully and distantly, "We have so much to be responsible for."

The wonderful idea he had for me was, as I have said, Hugo. Hugo was a refugee, a fugitive from Eastern Poland who had made his way through Czechoslovakia into Austria and thence into Italy and had now at last arrived, to use Father Andrews' words, in the land of his life-long dreams. He was a farmer, a peasant, the stuff, as Father Andrews put it, out of which civilizations are built, and uncultured though he was, his sufferings had given him a wisdom that was greater than any education. We were truly fortunate, Father Andrews declared, in having been chosen to give the heroic Hugo a home.

He waved eloquently to my three weedy acres. Hugo would turn my ground into a paradise of fresh vegetables and beautiful flowers. He suggested we could fix up the room and bath over the garage for living quarters for him—his wants were few and primitive—and we could give him a few dollars a week for spending money and we would have in turn an investment in accomplishment and loyalty far more pleasant and profitable than any money could buy. Everything was completely simple to Father Andrews. In his innocence and spirituality there were no such things as material problems, none, certainly, that could not be dismissed by a smile and an act of faith.

Hugo was not to be my only good fortune, it appeared as Father Andrews went on. Hugo had a nephew, Felix, also a fugitive from persecution, who had come to this country with him and had been accepted as a student at the seminary. His studies in Europe had been interrupted by the persecution and now he was to resume them here. His uncle, Hugo, was all he had left in the world and it would be a source of great consolation to have him so close by the seminary. Felix was a youth of great sanctity, Father Andrews said, and we would be blessed by his nearness and his prayers.

All this was in the way of a shock to me. The room over the garage was our storage room and it was piled high with trunks, suitcases, books and spare furniture,

and was completely disorderly with the discarded bric-a-
brac and odds and ends of ten years of married life. But
beyond that, I had no desire to have a stranger around
the place for no matter how self-effacing he might be, his
simple presence would, I was sure, ruffle the quiet I had
so carefully cultivated for my writing.

I avoided Father Andrews' eyes as I said, "I'll talk it
over with Frances and phone you later, Father."

"Fine, fine," he smiled. "They're coming to the seminary tomorrow afternoon and after I get Felix settled, the
three of us will ride down here to you." Then he added,
"You and Frances will be deeply rewarded for your charity—rewarded, I'm sure, beyond the benefits Hugo will
bring you."

He got into the pickup truck, backed it away in a
crazy arc, abruptly changed gears and went banging out
of the court yard and disappeared around the first curve
with the rear of the truck almost skidding off the gravel
road.

The rest of the day and most of the night, Frances
and I spent clearing and cleaning the room over the
garage. We had a two-car garage but only one car so we
arranged the spare space for storage. Frances did not feel
nearly as put upon as I did. For one thing, she had been
itching to get her hands on the surplusage in that room,
and I knew in a short time most of it would be on its way
to charitable institutions. But beyond that she liked the
idea of the flowers and fresh vegetables, not sharing at
all my profound belief that undisturbed quiet was necessary for my success as a writing man. In fact, I have a

suspicion that she looked upon Hugo's coming as a possible beneficial intrusion into what she considered my dream world.

Well, into my world, dream or otherwise, Hugo came. Late Sunday afternoon, at the beginning of dusk, Father Andrews arrived with him and Felix. Father Andrews, with Felix as a passenger, came in the truck in his usual miraculous fashion. Hugo followed in an ancient but by no means dilapidated Ford which he drove slowly and with care.

Father Andrews introduced Hugo and Felix with formality and pride. He was especially impressed with how sturdily they had endured the privations and persecutions of their past. Felix was a moderately tall blonde youth of about nineteen who carried himself with an erect military bearing as if he had had army training. He smiled as he acknowledged the introductions in only slightly accented English and then drew severely back a pace to leave the stage to his uncle, Hugo, whom he treated with obvious deference.

Hugo was the sort of man that anyone, relative or no, would be inclined to treat with deference. He was a short powerful man with a large, slightly protruding head. His forehead was high, especially at the temples, as in the case of many musicians, and his cheek bones were almost abnormally prominent, and from them his face was slanted sharply down to a narrow but powerful jaw. But it was his eyes that interested me most. They were black, large eyes that bulged slightly, and at whatever they looked, they stared, as if they were lidless, which they were not. There was a bold penetration to their stare which struck me, at least, as insolent. But insolent or not, it was a distorted, disconcerting stare.

Then, there were his hands. His arms were extremely short, and the hands including the wrist that showed under his coat sleeves were extremely long. The hands were soft and very white with abnormally long fingers, tapering slightly toward the tips. That these were the hands and fingers of a peasant and a farmer I could not believe.

Later in the evening when Frances and I were alone, and I could see from our living room the shadow of Hugo moving about in the room above the garage, I remarked he was a curious sort of character and I felt uneasy about him. I had purposely put my feeling very mildly. After Father Andrews and Felix had gone that evening, we asked Hugo to have supper with us. He accepted with a nod as if it was something he had expected. Frances really put herself out, heating over for herself and me the pot roast we had had the night before but cooking up a small steak for him, but he made no comment, taking it apparently as his due. He wasn't deliberately ungracious. Rather he acted with a cool and complete indifference to our feelings, as if there had been some sort of agreement that we were to administer to him, and our satisfaction in doing so was to be our thanks and reward. It was to me impudence and presumption of the first order. But not to Frances. He was amusing, she said, he was such a character.

Later, after supper, without invitation he sat down at the piano and played. He played one long, sustained strange composition that sounded to me like a solemn dirge that had been quickened to a fierce martial tempo.

I had never heard it before. I don't know too much about
music and Frances knows less so it may well have been
some quite well known modern creation. Hugo played
it powerfully with a controlled intensity, and he played it
for himself alone. It was obvious that this man, however
ungracious, was certainly no uncultured peasant.

Then, finished at the piano and indifferent to our loud
praise, he indicated he would like to go to his quarters.
He spoke almost, always in monosyllables, sometimes little more than grunts, but managed very successfully to
make himself understood. We took him across the yard
to the garage and up the outside stairs to his room. We
had put a great deal of effort into fixing up the room and
were quite proud of our work and expected at least an
expression of gratitude on his part. But there was none.
He complained about the overhead light being too distant and asked for a desk lamp for a table we had taken
from our sitting room and put against one of the windows. Frances hurried back to the house to get the desk
lamp from my writing table in the upstairs bedroom.
While she was gone, Hugo moved about meticulously
checking the windows, the bureau drawers, the bath and
almost every detail in the room. He said no single word
to me and acted as if he were unaware of my presence. He
matter-of-factly accepted the lamp when Frances, out of
breath in her hurry, brought it and he coolly and carefully
set it up as he wished it.

I was annoyed no end. But Frances, on the way back
to the house, apologized for him, saying that he had no
way of knowing all the work we had hurriedly put into
the room and that therefore I was a little too demanding

in expecting any expression of gratitude from him. I said nothing more at the time. But later, as I say, when I was in our living room watching his shadow moving about in the room above the garage, I had to tell her my feeling of uneasiness.

"He's eccentric, I agree with you there," Frances said, "but I think we should remember how amazing it is, as Father Andrews pointed out, he has not been more warped by the suffering he has undergone. The poor man has been through so much. And he does play the piano beautifully."

"Especially for a gardener," I retorted, putting such sarcasm into the words as I was able to muster.

Typically Frances, she said, "Darling, do you see him as one of your ogres? Have you put him into one of your stories already?"

"You may be right," I answered. "It may be all in my imagination. But still I could do very nicely without him."

Frances came to the window and drew down the shade to shut off my gaze. "You just wait till we have our garden and our vegetables and flowers."

"*You* wait," I suggested.

Frances threw her arms around me. "Darling, if you were one whit different I wouldn't love you."

I bowed, for the time at least, to her affection.

So Hugo came to stay. If he had any experience as a gardener or any inclination toward such work I was never able to discover any sign of it. He made no least pretense of it, permitting, even, the hanging geraniums Frances had put in his room to wither and die.

Frances, her naive faith in mankind challenged to greater trust by my dislike of Hugo, defended him. "What planting could I expect in September and October, she rightly asked. But when I replied he could at least help me rake up the October leaves, she retorted with sound feminine logic that raking leaves was no job for a fine gardener. In any event, I learned very soon that I had taken on a guest and not a gardener.

Frances and he, strangely enough to me, got along well together. I am a vacillating and too often bewildered person and, I suppose, the sight for her of this stranger in a strange land possessing such clear decisiveness and self-reliance made an impression on her. I was kind enough, I may say for myself now, never to have pointed out to her that his sort of independence comes easy when someone is paying for it, as I was. In any event he had not been there a week before she was making waffles for his breakfast and cooking all sorts of very highly seasoned casserole dishes for his dinner.

There were several times in those first days when I, in town in school, had disturbing thoughts about this stranger in my house. For I felt deeply then that there was a quality of evil and ruin about him though I could not have even hazarded a guess as to how it might show itself. He played the piano often at his own whim and completely for himself, as he had that first evening, and on each occasion the performance affected me profoundly. At the piano, with his huge head bent to those fierce and distorted solemnities he always played, he seemed like some perverse and malevolent Beethoven. And by that I mean he seemed capable of greatness—but of greatness in evil. His presence in that moderately pastoral farm country would ordinarily have seemed darkly out of place. Yet, when I looked up at the seminary, especially in an autumn mist or a winter dusk, I felt there might be some strange justification of his presence. For the seminary, which dominated the countryside and my knoll particularly, dealt as I saw it, with absolutes: God and Satan, good and evil, death and the judgment, heaven and hell. Hugo belonged in my mind with the absolutes.

Whenever I spoke such thoughts as these to Frances, which was not often now, she invariably chided me. I was in my world of fantasies. Hugo, she continued to maintain, was a poor, homeless creature seeking to hide the hurt that life had inflicted on him in the deep privacy of himself. He was not conventional, she agreed. His piano playing was proof of that. But because he was different, it did not follow he was wicked.

Father Andrews likewise continued to see Hugo as a heroic martyr and a victim of barbarism, and, saintlike, he loved him. Two or three nights a week, Father Andrews would come over in the pickup truck and sit with us, sometimes for only fifteen or twenty minutes, sometimes for the evening. Hugo acted with the devoted Father Andrews about the way he acted with us, listening in a sort of cool neutrality as long as it pleased him, then departing abruptly. Father Andrews was not in anyway discontented by this incivility on Hugo's part. He ascribed it to the fact that Hugo had now become busy with a great work. He was making, he said, a study of seminary life in the United States. It was to be a searching study, one that would bring glory to all of us.

How it happened that Hugo, the erstwhile wonderful peasant gardener, had suddenly become the searching scholar, he did not explain, nor did I raise the point. Father Andrews was much too devoted to Hugo for me to permit myself the utterance of even one small suspicion in his presence. There was no question Hugo was deep in a project whatever it was. When I was going to bed at night I would look across to the room above the garage and invariably I would see his great head bowed at the writing table in the diffused light of my desk lamp.

Winter came and snow and Christmas, and Hugo, though still aloof and strange, became a part of the routine of our lives. Little by little, softened by Father Andrew's unwavering affection and admiration for him and, to a lesser extent, by Frances' gentle chiding, I began to think that my suspicion of some deep malevolence in this strange character might possibly have been one of what Frances called my fantasies. Logic and the facts were, it seemed, against me.

But, if Hugo seemed gradually to cease to be the malevolent influence I had first imagined him to be, Felix, who had been hardly known to us in the beginning, just as gradually grew to be a personality and a problem in our lives.

On certain appointed afternoons the seminarians went for recreational walks through the countryside. It was the rule that they should walk in groups or in twos but not singly. They always looked, by the way, very picturesque and old-worldly in their black suits and leisureliness when you came across them on the highway or on the country roads. At first Felix would stop by our house on these walks and always he would have a companion. He would go up to the room over the garage to visit Hugo, leaving the companion to while away his time below. This visiting of relatives was not ordinarily permitted the seminarians on their walks but an exception was made for Felix who was so far from his home and homeland.

After a time we noted he came on these walks without a companion. And it was at this time he began to undergo a radical change in his appearance. He grew nervous in his walking, tense in his behavior. His erect military carriage slowly left him. He lost his well-fed, bland look and became quite thin and almost angular.

One holiday, Washington's birthday I think it was, I was home and happened to meet him face to face. It was midafternoon and I was crossing the yard to the storage space in the garage when I became aware of him coming in from the road. He was by himself. I was shocked at the change in him. We exchanged a few routine words and then, reluctantly I thought, he continued on to the garage stairs to visit Hugo. For the moment, I reverted to my deep dislike of Hugo and I felt a sudden sympathy for the boy.

A few moments later when I was in the garage loafing through the books stored there, I heard the rumble of Hugo's and Felix' voices in quarrel upstairs. Curiously, they were speaking English which struck me as strange. It seemed to me, being uncle and nephew, they would have a common native language, though it was, of course, possible they came from different countries. They spoke with intense feeling but as they kept their voices low, guardedly so I thought, I could make out very little of what was being said. I heard mention of Father Andrews several times and the words "duty" and "discipline."

That afternoon when Frances and I were shifting furniture about in the living room—when spring was in the air Frances had to move furniture about—I mentioned the quarrel I had overheard and commented on the change in Felix. "He seems to be tortured about something," I said.

I might have known what she was going to say. "'Tortured,' really, darling?"

I was a little annoyed. "The word may be a strong one but the looks of the boy call for it. I have eyes in my head, haven't I?"

Contrite, she came to me. "I'm sorry I—I thought maybe you had an idea Hugo was sticking pins in him or something like that."

"I wouldn't put it past him," I blurted out. "Something is happening to that boy."

Frances assumed her air of gentle wisdom, an air I love in her, not for the wisdom which I'm not too sure about but for the gentleness which is so much a part of her.

"I wasn't going to tell you," she began, "but Felix has been dropping in here quite often on his walks and I've got to know him quite well. I don't think you have any reason to be deeply concerned about him."

She supposed this announcement would relieve me of my concern but it had an altogether different effect. Frances is a compellingly attractive young woman, and this, I hasten to say, is not an exaggeration prompted by husbandly pride. She is about as far from the conventional concept of the housewife as it is possible to be. (This conventional concept of the housewife as a prosaic and dull person is anyway, in my observation, a great libel on housewives, certainly a libel on the housewives I have met.) I had no doubts about Frances but in the circumstances I naturally felt uneasy. I am possessive, for one thing, especially of her and I begrudged her company to any man. But more serious than that, I was well aware of the attraction an alluring woman could have for a lonely, young man, and the almost invariably unhappy consequences of such an infatuation. And on top of that, there was the seminary. The boy was studying to be a priest.

"It's no good, Frances, having that young man here around the house," I said bluntly. "It's against the seminary rules, for one thing."

She shrugged. "All the poor boy does is sit in the kitchen. He hardly ever talks but when he does it's mostly about Father Andrews. Sometimes he is hungry and I give him something to eat."

"Nothing but the best, I'm sure," I said coldly.

"Dear, dear," she sighed reproachfully. "Sometimes, good husband, you are impossible."

She turned away sharply and went into the kitchen.

The truth is, of course, that I was upset and my feelings were running away with me. It had been bad enough for me with the egomaniacal Hugo making free of my house and now here was the troubled Felix. They were strangers, no matter how one looked at it. And Felix was definitely breaking the seminary rules, and without, I was sure, the knowledge of Father Andrews.

I followed Frances into the kitchen. I asked her what Felix had to say when he spoke to her of Father Andrews.

She thought a moment. "This change you've noticed in him—I sort of have the feeling Father Andrews is the reason for it."

I asked her what on earth gave her that feeling.

She thought another moment. "I have an idea from little remarks he makes he's afraid of Father Andrews."

"Afraid of Father Andrews?" I was naturally astonished. "Father Andrews is the gentlest, kindest man on earth. He's a saint. And he's been father and friend to that boy. Why on earth should he be afraid of him?"

"Perhaps it's because Father Andrews is a saint that he's afraid of him," she said.

This was a rather profound, if puzzling, thought for my dear Frances and it silenced me.

"Now, darling," she went on, "don't go thinking up any dreadful ideas and getting yourself all in a bother. I'm sure all young men in seminaries have their little crises. Perhaps the boy wants to be a saint too, and is just beginning to see what a job it is. I'm sorry now I ever mentioned his coming here."

I looked at her sane and beautiful face and I could not keep from smiling. Confronted with such excellent evidence of the normality in the world, I asked myself again if it could ever be that my imagination was truly addicted to phantasms and distortions.

"What we both need," she said, "is a good cup of coffee."

Later, sipping the freshly made coffee, the world began to look like a good, wholesome world after all. But my new mood, it turned out, was not to last long.

On Sundays and holidays I always leave the car in the yard, and at dark, if we do not plan to use it, I usually put it in the garage for the night. This evening when I went out into the yard to put the car away, I found Hugo's Ford parked in the garage where there was only one space now because the other was being used for storage. This he had never done before and it struck me as a real impertinence.

Hugo always took extraordinary care of the old car. Time and again I came upon him in the yard working on the motor and it struck me he knew what he was about. Indeed, everything under the hood was extraordinarily spick and span for so ancient a model. In stormy weather he always carefully covered the car with an old tarpaulin I had given him. But never before had he parked it in the garage. The weather was clear and I was annoyed. I decided to back the car out without ado.

There was no key but the ignition was unlocked, the car having been made in days before it was necessary to lock the ignition in order to withdraw the key. I stepped on the starter but the motor was cold and sputtered so I pulled out the choke to give it a richer mixture. Almost immediately the motor began to backfire in a startling, rapid series of sharp explosions. It was not the normal backfire sound and seemed to be produced by design, as if by one of those devices with which boys sometimes equip the exhausts on their jalopies. Whatever the cause, the effect, as I say, was startling.

Hardly had I backed the car out into the yard when I saw Hugo come rushing down the stairs from the room above. He came fiercely, bulkily toward me, striding into the light of the headlights, his huge head thrust forward, his distorted eyes blazing with anger. I'm normally no fighter but the sight of his anger riled me. What I had done I certainly had a right to do. I jumped out of the car, faced him.

"What's eating you?" I practically shouted at him, my emotion getting the better of me. "This happens to be my home, and this happens to be my garage!"

He stopped in his tracks, obviously surprised at my sudden exhibition of strength. He glared at me, and in that glare I saw there was hate as well as anger. He stood indecisively for a brief moment, then abruptly he turned and strode out of the light into the darkness and back up the stairs to the room above. He had not said a word.

My anger left me as quickly as it had come. I was suddenly a little limp. Then slowly a feeling of exhilaration came over me. I felt quite proud of myself, as if I had won some great victory.

I drove my car into the garage, making for the ears I knew were listening overhead as much triumphant noise as I could. It was childish I know but I could not resist it.

Later, when I had closed the garage doors and was returning to the house and this childishness had left me, I looked back up at Hugo's lighted window and the strangeness of his extraordinary show of rage struck me with new force. What had driven him to such a fury? Merely my driving his precious car? Or my removing it from the garage, which I had all the right in the world to do? And could it be that the sharp series of sounds from the backfire were designed as a possible warning to him if anyone moved his car? And if so, why?

I did not mention that incident nor my feelings about it to Frances. I did not want to be argued against any more. In my feelings there were now facts enough and logic enough for me. I may be an escapist but I can see a shadow lengthening as well if not better than the next. I determined I would tell Father Andrews the next time he came that Hugo had to go.

Lent came and for weeks we did not see either Felix or Father Andrews. Hugo, of course, we had always with us. But now, it seemed to me, his ungraciousness was more intentional, and his cold indifference more insulting. Frances, I am sure, observed the change in him. She began to apologize for his rudeness, and I had the feeling that in apologizing for him she was vaguely trying to apologize to me for her heretofore high opinion of him.

I thought perhaps it was Father Andrews' Lenten duties that kept him from us and I had about decided I would drive up to the seminary to see him when unexpectedly he turned up himself on the knoll. It was Laetare Sunday, the mid-Sunday of Lent and a day set to mark with reasonable joyousness the passing of half of the penitential season, and a brilliantly sunny, windy spring day. I heard the pickup truck clattering crazily up the road and I knew it was he.

I went out into the yard to meet him but he did not stop by the house. He drove on to the garage and went on up the outside stairs to visit Hugo. He was bareheaded and in his cassock, and I noticed as he ascended the stairs his smile was gone. Never had I seen him without his smile. Indeed, his whole demeanor was unlike him. He who always belonged to the sunniest day now seemed as if he carried darkness with him. The man I saw mount the steps was not the Father Andrews you would expect to see in the joyousness of Laetare Sunday. Could it ever be, I asked myself, that the shadow, whatever it was, had lengthened to include him, the most innocent and saintliest of men?

It was a good hour later before I heard him at the kitchen door of our house. Frances, admitting him, was struck, as I had been, at the change in him. She went to make him coffee as she usually did but he would have none of it. There were some uncomfortable minutes of small talk, then an even more uncomfortable silence.

Finally, he spoke. He was telling us what he was telling us, he said, only because we were so deeply and, as he put it, so nobly involved. Felix had about decided he had no vocation and was planning to leave the seminary. It was a great blow to him, he said, because he had such high hopes for Felix, and it was a great blow to his uncle, Hugo.

"Hugo is truly a good man," Father Andrews said. "I've just been over with him trying to prepare him for the worst if the worst should finally happen. He is distraught, the poor soul, his heart has been so set on his nephew becoming a servant at God's altar, and I hope you can be even kinder to him than you have been. You will never, I feel sure, have a greater opportunity for your charity."

The idea of greater kindness to Hugo did not set very well with me. I made no comment, however. Instead I asked Father Andrews what made him so sure Felix had a vocation.

"I didn't say I was sure," Father Andrews gently corrected me. "The boy's vocation is not for me to decide. It is between himself and God. But I do have hopes for him, and I cannot help but feel that he is making a mistake in thinking of leaving the seminary. I have asked him to hold his decision until Easter. You have no idea of the great graces that can come to one during Lent." He meditated a moment and then went on, "Felix is a great soul, and he is now engaged in a great struggle. He knows darkness as well as light, despair as well as hope. His is the struggle that, if he wins, can well lead to sainthood. The greater the man, the greater the struggle, and the greater thus the victory." He got to his feet. "Pray for him," he pleaded, and his voice trembled with emotion, "pray for the poor boy, pray that the victory be his."

Frances murmured, "Yes, Father," but I could not bring myself to speak. I was too deeply moved, not by Felix' problem so much as by the extraordinary simplicity and sincerity—primitive simplicity and sincerity, I might call it—of the man who stood before me. I know very little of sainthood or grace or God but I had the feeling listening to Father Andrews that I was in the presence of something magnificently fundamental—in the presence of what I call, as I've said, the absolute.

He went to the door, turned with his hand on the knob. "And pray for Hugo, too. Pray hard for him. He has made great sacrifices for the boy. Pray that, whatever happens, they will not have been made in vain."

He opened the door and went out. Frances and I sat in silence and listened to the pickup truck as it tore across the yard and went banging down the road. I realized, and

I must confess I was not very happy about it, that now it would be out of the question for me to ask Hugo to leave.

"Poor Felix," Frances murmured into the silence.

She was truly moved. A thought came to me. I chose my words very carefully. "Could you ever, darling, by any chance, have let that boy fall in love with you—I mean unintentionally, of course?"

"Please!" She looked at me in unbelief.

"It would, of course, help to explain what has come over him—what makes him want to leave the seminary—you realize that, don't you?" I tried to be very casual.

"A woman knows when a man is in love with her!" She was firm. "You may be sure of that!"

Again I tried to be casual. "Even when the man is much younger—and a stranger and very much on the taciturn side?"

"Then, most of all. Felix is certainly not in love with me!"

Frances was vigorous in her belief. But I, aware of her charm, and remembering his coming to sit in her kitchen in his loneliness, was not so sure.

Easter Sunday began brightly enough with clear skies and a friendly sun, and the chimes, ringing down from the seminary chapel and echoing across the countryside, seemed to score the perfection of the day. But, in the early afternoon, a mist began to drift in from the sea some miles away and, creeping across the farmlands, succeeded before nightfall, in darkening and dampening the wide landscape that is dominated by Seminary Hill. The seminary itself, as seen from below, became a shadowy mirage blurred with lights, afloat in the foggy sky. When the vespers chimes sounded in the late afternoon they were eerie and muffled and seemed to come from a great distance.

Frances and I had gone for a ride up the coast after our late noonday dinner and when we returned the fog had already reached our knoll. Driving up the road to the house, we overtook Hugo in his Ford. He drove slowly, carefully as he always did.

We followed Hugo into the yard and when he stopped we saw Felix get out of the car with him. Felix carried a suitcase. The two, without speaking, went up the stairs to the room above the garage. They were rather shadowy figures in the fog, although it was not as deep then as it was to be later, and their silence seemed to have some strange burden to it.

Frances and I knew from the suitcase that Felix had made his decision. He had left the seminary. I could feel her choking up but she did not say anything beyond an exclamation at the first sight of the suitcase and neither did I. I knew she felt very unhappy about it for all involved, Hugo and Father Andrews as well as Felix. I shared her unhappiness though I must confess in my case it was mostly for Father Andrews. We sat there for about a minute and then I let her out and drove on into the garage.

I parked the car and was about to pull down the overhead door against the fog when I became aware of Hugo's voice above raised in sudden rage. In his emotion he mixed his blunt, crude English with explosive passages from his native tongue which I took to be Polish. A number of English words and phrases caught my ear, and so startling were they that I stopped in the act of closing the door and stood there with my arms raised above my head and my hands holding the door and listened.

I heard Hugo roar, "Idiot!—Idiot!—I should kill you!"

Then, Felix' voice, slightly high-pitched but in no way uncertain, rose in answer. "You are the idiot! Father Andrews will never tell! Never!"

"We are ruined!" Hugo's voice rumbled. "I should kill you."

Felix' voice rose again, "He will never tell. He will never break the seal of confession. Never!"

There was a sudden silence. Then I heard the window above me being abruptly opened. I looked up, saw Hugo's great head jutting out into the fog. I lowered the door as matter-of-factly as I could and turned toward the house, trying to the best of my ability to walk as if I did not know I had been seen and was unaware of Hugo's eyes still on me. I had not gone eight or ten steps when I heard the window being closed slowly and as noiselessly as possible. I guessed by this that Hugo was confident I had not heard him and Felix.

After I had entered the house, I locked the door behind me. Frances, leaving the den where she had put her coat and hat, saw me lock the door. In answer to her questioning stare, I told her what I had heard.

"It's the disgrace," she murmured, going unhappily into the living room to the window that faced the garage. "I have heard that families take it very hard when a member leaves the seminary. Why did you lock the door?"

"It was sort of mechanical," I said. "I'm kind of on edge, if you want to know the truth."

I turned out the lights she had turned on when she entered the house, and joined her at the window. The dark, abetted by the fog, had come on quickly. Already the garage was losing its silhouette and the lighted window was beginning to be blurred.

I took Frances' hand. It was an involuntary action and I could feel her eyes searching my face in the now deep shadow of the room.

After a moment she spoke and her voice, in key with the foggy dark outside, was little more than a whisper. "Honest, darling, my letting the boy come into the house had nothing to do with his leaving the seminary. Most of the time I don't think he knew I was on earth." Then, after a pause, she added. "Is that what's troubling you?"

"No—it's no one thing in particular." I remember speaking in a low voice as if afraid of being overheard. "It's—I have the oddest feeling that some sort of strange drama is drawing to its close." I hesitated a moment before I added, "Why should Hugo, or anyone else for that matter, be so worried about Father Andrews breaking the seal of confession?"

If her usual words of deprecation at my seeing significances where she was sure none existed were on her lips she did not this time speak them. I had a feeling she was being considerate of the intensity of my mood.

We stood at the window and watched the fog deepen and the night darken. Presently, where the garage had been there was only a vague shadow and the lighted window had become a washed yellow stain.

The fog and the noiseless dark eventually acted like sedatives on me. I turned away from the window.

"I don't know why I should be upset," I said with as much resolution as I could. "Whatever the problem is, it certainly isn't mine." I abruptly snapped on the wall lights. "It's Easter. We should be in an Easter mood. Let's have a highball."

This made good sense to Frances. She drew the shades, turned on the table and piano lamps and went to the kitchen to get the soda, ice cubes and glasses. I, in turn, went into the den to get the Scotch.

I was unlocking the liquor cabinet when I heard Hugo's Ford start in the yard. I straightened, listened. The car began quietly to move. Then, I heard the sound of running feet and Felix' voice cry out above the sound of the car, "No, Hugo! No! Stop! Stop!"

Then, abruptly, the staccato sound of the Ford's back-fire rose above Felix' voice. It was the same sharp fusillade of explosions that had startled me the night I was in the Ford and pulled the choke. The sound ceased as abruptly as it had begun. I could hear the car continue to move out of the yard and onto the road.

The picture of Hugo striding into the headlights that night, his huge head thrust angrily forward, his eyes on fire with rage, came back to me and stayed with me as I stood in the den, listening to the sound of the car fading down the road and dying away in the night. A sudden thought seized me, a wild suspicion, more out of my subconscious than out of my reason, but therefore more compelling, more terrifying.

Frances came to the doorway to the den. She studied me a moment, "You think they've gone off without saying good-by?"

I heard her but distantly and, looking at her, I hardly saw her. I went out from the den into the hall.

"You've forgotten the Scotch," she said.

Again I heard her only distantly. I went to the rear door and unlocked and opened it. The fog was so thick it was almost immediately wet on my face. I switched on the back porch light but it made only the feeblest of impressions on the foggy dark.

I went out from the house into the back yard.

"What's the matter, darling?" I heard Frances concerned voice call behind me but it seemed as if she were a mile away.

I moved across the yard to the driveway. I followed the driveway out along the house searching the dark as I went. Then I turned and followed the driveway back toward the garage. The rear porch light was, as I said, feeble against the night and I could hardly see two strides in front of me.

I had almost reached the garage when I heard a moan. It came from the yard a distance away from the driveway. I ran toward it. My mind may be escapist but my suspicion of the purpose of the strange backfire on Hugo's car had been realistic and right. Felix had been shot. He was on his knees on the ground, moaning, struggling to get to his feet.

I grabbed his arm, helped him up, steadied him. I told him not to worry. I'd get him into the house and get a doctor and everything would be all right. He had, I discovered from the blood stains later, been trying to make his way to the rear door, getting to his feet, stumbling and falling, then getting to his feet and stumbling and falling again. He had little strength left. I could feel the back of my hand wet against his coat.

Frances was still standing in the doorway and I called to her. She came, directed by my voice, and took Felix' other arm. She sobbed a little, and kept saying over and over, "What's happened? Dear God, what's happened?" but did not go into hysterics and proved a great help.

Felix tried to speak. There was something he wanted to tell us but it was not until we were on the rear porch that he had even the momentary strength for words. Then, with a hand against the door to brace himself, he said in a choked, almost inaudible voice, "Hugo—he's gone to kill Father Andrews. I—I tried to stop him—"

His hand slipped from the door and he lurched forward and it took all of Frances' and my strength to hold him up.

Now, I was even more stunned. Hugo gone to kill Father Andrews. Why, I didn't know, but I knew it was true. My first impulse was to run to my car and go after Hugo. Then I realized he had too much of a start. The telephone was my only hope.

We helped Felix into the house and put him on the sofa in the den and I left Frances to make him as comfortable as she could while I rushed to the telephone and called the seminary for Father Andrews.

Father Andrews was not in his room. The priest who answered the telephone thought he might be out in the cloister walk. I became frenzied and screamed out the whole story, pleading wildly with the priest to rush out and save Father Andrews' life. The priest thought I was mad. I had to put Frances on the telephone to make him realize the truth and the need for instant action.

The moment Frances hung up I hurried back to the telephone and called the police. I told them the facts and the emergency as sanely as I could and begged them to send a doctor and an ambulance, and to come immediately.

Felix, apparently in less pain now he was stretched out on the sofa, listened to what was being said. His eyes were wide open and sensitive to what was going on. Frances had opened his shirt collar and was keeping his face cool with cold towels. She had also, rightly or wrongly, given him a small glass of brandy. I could see a dark, irregular stain on the breast of the coat of his black, seminary suit.

Those minutes were almost beyond bearing. Hugo was well on his way up Seminary Hill, and there was nothing I could do to stop him. And here was this boy on the sofa before me while we waited for the doctor and ambulance to come from town twelve miles away. I kept calling the seminary but could get no answer.

Felix had not said a word, nor had he tried to, since on the rear porch he told me of Hugo. But after a while, helped, I supposed, by the brandy, he began to talk. His mind was reasonably clear when he began but toward the end he became hazy and it was not always immediately understandable just what he was trying to say.

"I am going to die," he began in a whisper, "I must talk to you before I die—"

I should have tried to stop him, I suppose, but so harassed was I by the tragic madness of the events of the night, I made no effort to do so. I told him the doctor was on his way and assured him he was not going to die.

I doubt much if I could have stopped him from talking if I had wanted to.

"I am ashamed," he whispered. "I must speak before I die—I have deceived you." He turned his face toward Frances. "You have been friends—I have deceived you in a great deceit—you—your country—I have lived a great evil—I must speak before I die."

He held still for a moment, then, he whispered, "Hugo is my superior—not my uncle. We came to your country as enemies—to destroy your church from within—we came as saboteurs."

It was dumbfounding, this revelation, and was made immediately believable only by the even more dumbfounding fact that Hugo was at that moment on his way to kill the saintly Father Andrews and that before my eyes lay this boy, possibly dying.

Little by little, brokenly, Felix told the whole story. He and Hugo and others, in the service of the Soviet, had come to this country to infiltrate the ministry and the priesthood here, dedicated to the ultimate subversion of the church and thus, eventually, of the people.

"I would have gone on—I was a soldier—under orders," he went on, choking, speaking with difficulty, "but—but something happened—I began to hate Father Andrews as I had never hated a man before—I thought I would have to kill him." He paused a moment for strength and then, turning his face toward Frances, almost inaudibly whispered, "The more I hated Father Andrews—the more he loved me. I could not endure it."

When he had said this, he closed his eyes as if he had said all. But after a while he began to talk again. It became clear that in the seminary—in the classroom, at the altar, in the persons of Hugo and Father Andrews—the two radically antagonistic faiths and philosophies had met head on, had met as they could meet nowhere else. The feeling that some strange and tragic drama had been unfolding here in the shadow of Seminary Hill I, as I have written, had long entertained, but never had I any suspicion of a drama so strange and tragic as this.

I remember Felix, his eyes closed, saying, "It was snowing—I went from the altar and spat the host out on the snow."

A little while after that, he whispered, "I hated Father Andrews—like I hated Christ."

Then, later, his eyes opened, he said, "Good Friday—that was my worst day. I crucified myself. I could not go on."

So went the tortured story. That morning—Easter Sunday morning—in chapel he had seen Father Andrews enter the confessional and on a sudden impulse he had gone in.

"Not to be absolved—I didn't go in for that—not to be converted—not for that." His voice faltered, and it was a moment before he could go on. "It was the torment—my hating him—his affection for me—I could not endure it longer. I had to tell him the truth before I left. I knew he could never betray me."

That afternoon, when Hugo ordered Felix to return to the seminary, he told Hugo he could never return—he told him he had confessed all to Father Andrews—and it was then he and Hugo had their deadly quarrel, a few words of which I had overheard shortly before when putting the car in the garage.

Hugo was maniacal with the belief that Father Andrews would never keep the seal of confession, that he would go straightway to the authorities. He immediately had gone to kill Father Andrews. Felix had leaped into the car to stop him. Then, Hugo had shot him.

"Poor Hugo," he whispered, "he cannot harm Father Andrews—he can kill him but he cannot harm him."

Those were about the last words he said to me.

I tried to telephone the seminary but again there was no answer.

Felix' mind was fading. "Christ, are you here?" he kept moaning. "Are you true, Christ? Are you here?"

I realized from the boy's words then that his struggle with himself had by no means ended with his visit to the confessional.

Then, over Felix' moaning, I heard a car drive slowly along the house into the yard in back. It continued on to the garage. I was sure it was Hugo.

I rushed in panic to lock the door.

But it was not Hugo. It was Father Andrews. His voice called out in the fog to me as he approached the house. I had not believed I would see him alive again.

He was hatless and his face and gray-blonde hair were shining wet from the fog. His eyes were solemn and his mouth was drawn, and it was clear he had had his day of torment, too. I saw the billowing thickness of the fog behind him as he entered the house and realized then why he had driven in so slowly. The priest who had answered the telephone had warned him of the peril of Hugo's coming but Father Andrews had rushed down to see Felix. He had taken the first car he could find, the rector's car which had been parked by the seminary entrance.

He had passed a Ford crawling up Seminary Hill in the fog and that could have been Hugo, he said quietly in answer to my worried question as we went to the den. He was obviously not concerned about Hugo or himself. He had only Felix on his mind.

As we entered the den, Felix raised his head with great effort and looked up at Father Andrews. His eyes were vague, cloudy.

"Christ, are you here?" he whispered as he had been whispering. "Are you true, Christ? Are you here?"

Father Andrews sat quickly down on the sofa beside the boy. I left, closing the door behind me.

Frances was seated in the living room, her head in her hands, sobbing her heart out. I put my arm around her. There was nothing I could say that would help at that moment so I said nothing,

It was because of Frances' sobbing that I did not hear the back door open.

When I first discovered Hugo he was already in the hall moving toward the front of the house. He had left the Ford at the foot of the hill, I found out later, undoubtedly so that there would be no tell-tale sound of his approach. I had heard his footsteps in the hall and imagining them to be Father Andrews' had hurried out of the living room. It was then I saw him in the hall.

He wore a black felt hat, high on his high forehead, and walked with a short, nervous step, throwing around him, as he went, the quick, taut looks of a man on a frantic search.

He saw me. He stopped, thrust his huge head forward. "Where is he?" he demanded grimly, his bulging eyes fixing mine.

My main feeling at that instant was not fear but fury at myself. Why had I not relocked the door? I should have known this madman would return. My concern for Father Andrews forced me to get a grip on myself.

"The police are on their way," I said with as much authority as I could command. "They'll be here in seconds. If you have any sense you'll get out of here."

"Why do *you* warn me of the police?" He had instantly seen through my poor strategy and his words were cold with contempt. "Where is Felix?"

I realized then he had no idea Father Andrews was in the house. He had evidently not associated the rector's car in the yard with the priest—if, in the fog, he had seen the car at all. It was news of Felix he wanted. I suspected from his clothes, soaking wet from the fog, he had been groping around out in the yard before coming to the house.

"Where is his body—that's what you mean, isn't it?" I grew suddenly bold, knowing now the cause of his hurry and uneasiness.

At that moment, Frances, coming out of the living room and discovering him, screamed. It was a long, piercing scream such as I had never heard in my life before, the scream of one whose nerves had finally reached the breaking point.

At the scream, Hugo whipped a black, snub-barrelled automatic out of the inside pocket of his coat. The scream had shaken him. He held the revolver tightly against his body to steady his hand.

We were at the moment not more than a foot apart and he stepped abruptly forward closing the gap. I could feel the automatic against my stomach.

"I will kill you!" he shouted. "Where is Felix?"

He might well have killed me there and then, had not the door of the den opened and Father Andrews come out.

Father Andrews had heard Hugo's last words and, as he came through the door, he said quietly, "If it's Felix you want, Hugo, you have come several seconds too late."

Hugo, startled, spun around. The hand holding the revolver dropped. He was astounded at discovering Father Andrews calmly approaching him.

Father Andrews came openly toward him. "But if it's me you want, Hugo," he went on as quietly as before, "here I am. I have just seen a martyr go to his magnificent reward. He is even now, it could be, in the presence of his smiling Lord. I shall consider it a privilege to be able to follow him."

Hugo drew the automatic back against his body as if again to steady his hand to fire. But he did not fire. He was unnerved, off balance.

Father Andrews stopped before him. "You seem ill at ease, Hugo," he said. "You were sure I was on my way to the police, weren't you?" Then he added sadly, "How little you know, Hugo—how little of me—how little of Him whose poor servant I am."

Suddenly, the siren of the police ambulance rose from the road in the distance. It rose and fell, its whine taking on an eerie tone in the heavy fog.

Hugo's head snapped back, fiercely alert. He was no longer the searcher. He was the hunted. Slowly, with a catlike caution, he backed away down the hall toward the rear door.

Father Andrews did not take his eyes off him.

Hugo reached the door which was still open as he had left it when he made his surreptitious entrance. He backed into the doorway, the dark fog swirling thick as smoke behind him. He stood there and slowly levelled the revolver at Father Andrews.

Father Andrews looked down at the revolver. In an even voice, he said, "It is only martyrs who can destroy the evil you stand for, Hugo."

Hugo's hand and the revolver began to shake. It was as if Hugo, facing Father Andrews, was facing a reality so completely outside of his experience that he was bewildered before it.

The silence became deep, harrowing.

Then, into the silence, the siren, nearer, again rose and fell. Hugo grew taut. Abruptly, as if something in him had snapped, he wheeled around and rushed wildly out into the fog and dark.

The tension broke. I was in a cold sweat. I felt as if I was going to reel and fall. But Father Andrews grabbed my arm with a strong, firm hand and turned me and led me back into the living room.

"I'm afraid our Frances has fainted," he said quietly.

Hugo made his way some thirty miles up the coast highway before running into a police road block that had been set for him. But Hugo, as always, had his own ideas. He drove the Ford in full speed off the road and down a steep embankment into the ocean.

The Ford was found, wrecked, in shallow water at low tide the next day. But, now after five weeks, no trace of Hugo's body has been found.

It is, I think, this last curious circumstance as much as any other that has finally persuaded my dear Frances to agree, in some measure at least, with my simple and commonplace belief that there is more to life than meets the eye.

❋

The Big Red House
on Hope Street

"How about bumping somebody off?"

The skinny youth, sitting behind the wheel of his hopped-up coupe, fondled the .32, flipping it from the palm of one hand to the other.

"It ought to be a kick." He turned to two girls on the seat beside him. He was casual. "How about it, kiddies?"

The car, with the motor running, was parked in the dark of a cheap residential street. There was enough light from house windows to illumine the faces in the car.

One of the girls was blonde, one brunette, and both were pretty in a bold, physical way. Their coloring was markedly different but they could have been sisters so close was the resemblance of the expressions on their faces. Both sets of eyes had a cool drowsiness in them, and both sets of lips had a spoiled, I-want-it look that was only a slight degree short of a sustained pout.

Babs, the brunette, who sat near the door, looked over at the revolver. "Count me out, Duke," she said to the youth. "Six months in the bandbox was enough for me."

"Chicken?" His lips curled slightly. But otherwise his

thin face was bland with its washed blue eyes. "Or maybe you don't go for me any more?"

"Please, Duke," the girl, her composure suddenly gone, pleaded, "anything but shooting, anything but that."

"What can we do for a kick? We've done everything else." He felt under his T-shirt for a money-belt strapped beneath his ribs, took out of it a red plastic cigarette case. "Here, punk, have a puff." He snapped the case open, held it out. "Give you some guts."

Babs reached for a cigarette, changed her mind, pulled back. "Not till you get rid of the gun, Duke."

"Yellow!" He spit the word at her and then, suddenly, leaned over and slapped her face, slapped it hard. "Get out, you little tramp! Get out of here!" He flung the door open. "Scram!"

He pushed her out the door.

"No, Duke. No." Babs, now frantic, grabbed the handle of the door. "I'll do anything you say! Anything!"

He snapped the door lock. "Beat it, you bum! I don't want no more of what you got to offer!"

He yanked the car into gear and it leaped away. Babs who held to the door handle was jerked forward, almost thrown to the street.

Duke drove two blocks, turned a corner and pulled up to a stop by a deserted, dimly lit playground.

He took a cigarette out of the red plastic case, lighted it, inhaled deeply. He closed his eyes, waited for the inhalation to take effect. After a moment, a small, pleased smile moved on his lips.

He held the cigarette out for the blonde. "Take a drag, kiddy, and dream."

The girl stared at the burning cigarette, hesitated. "I don't want to go all out, Duke," she said.

"Why?" His amiability faded. "Mike?"

She nodded slowly. "Uh huh."

"You specializing now?" He took another puff of the cigarette. "When did you give up making the rounds?"

The girl moved uncomfortably on the seat. "He's crazy about me, Duke, and I'm trying to give him a fair shake."

"You in love with him?"

She looked straight ahead into the darkness. "What's love?"

He laughed. "You're all right, Vinnie," he said, holding up the cigarette. "I figure this love stuff is like the weed. You buy it and smoke it up. Sure you won't have a drag?"

"I told you, Duke, I don't want to go all the way."

He shook his head in disgust. "Saving up for a lousy marine. They're the pigeons of all time, kiddy. Marines are. Patsies. And this time, 'specially. They're throwing them away."

"You mean it, Duke?" her eyes were bothered.

"Sure. They're heroes, ain't they? They got the big build up after the last war and now they can't let themselves down. They got to go out and get killed." He put an arm around her. "I wouldn't figure on Mike coming back from this one. The best you can hope for is a wheel chair."

She looked at the smouldering cigarette. "He's the only guy that ever treated me fair, Duke."

Duke drew his arm more closely around her. "I'll treat you fair, kiddy. You know me."

"I don't mean it like that," the girl said. "You pay for what you get, I know that, Duke. But Mike, he never even tried to move in. He used to kiss me good night like I was a choir girl."

Duke laughed. "The sap. He belongs in the marines."

"I used to think so at first." She spoke matter-of-factly, without emotion. "But after a while he got under my skin. I began to feel like maybe I'd learned to count wrong somewhere along the line."

He smoked a moment. "Nobody ever told him about the gang?"

"Why should they?"

"He musta known about your vacation up at the Reform School, kiddy."

She shook her head slowly. "He never mentioned it. He moved into the neighborhood after I came back. Maybe he never heard of it."

Duke moved his head close to hers, spoke softly, purring now in the relaxation of the drug. "Like those clothes Babs had on, sweetie? Notice that skirt? Real suede. Like it?"

"You bought it for her?" Her cool drowsy gaze searched his baby blue eyes.

"I didn't exactly buy it. I got it for her. That sweater, I bought that for her, though. Like it?"

"Dreamy. Yeh." Then, still searching his eyes, she said, "With all that investment, why did you give her the scram?"

He took another drag of the cigarette, smiled his

smug smile. "Vibrations, kiddy. You were sitting right next to me, close, and I could feel you all over. That's for me, I said, and that was curtains for her." He purred again. "You like nice clothes, don't you sweetie?"

Her drowsy eyes left his face, went again to the cigarette butt smouldering in the dark.

He spoke softly into her ear. "Nice clothes and Duke, the dream lover. Right here, too. Right on hand. Why save up for a wheelchair?"

She continued to stare at the smouldering cigarette butt.

His skinny jaw line tightened. His washed blue eyes grew cold. "Sore, are you?" There was no purr in his voice now. "Sore because I wanted to be nice to you, huh? Sorry. Beg pardon." He pulled away. "Who the hell do you think you are, anyway?"

She smiled a lazy little smile, moved closer to him as he pulled away.

"Get away! You're just another little bum!"

She picked the cigarette butt out of his hand, took a long drag on it, sucking the light down almost to her fingertips. Then, she put her head back on the top of the car seat, closed her eyes.

"Let's dream," she whispered, hardly moving her lips.

He watched her a moment, his small thin smile triumphant on his lips. Then, abruptly, he grabbed her, pulled her fiercely to him, pressing his mouth against hers.

A little over an hour later, the hopped-up coupe pulled up to the curb a short distance from the entrance to Carricola's liquor store.

The store was one of a dozen small stores on a neighborhood business strip but the others, with the exception of the drug store on the corner, were dark, because of the lateness of the hour. Carricola's was a narrow shop, blazing with light, gleaming with bottles.

Vinnie was now behind the wheel. Duke sat in the seat beside her. Their eyes were abnormally bright, bright as the glittering window of Carricola's liquor store.

"Keep her in second," Duke gave her a last briefing. "And remember, I'll back out of the store. When you see me coming, creep up. When I start to run for it, throw the door open. Turn the first corner easy, the second fast. I'll take it from there. Nervous?"

"Me?" She laughed softly. "Stop it, will you?"

"You're my baby." He felt the slight bulge at his left arm pit. "Three minutes top'll do it. Kiss me, kiddy."

She kissed him and he got out of the car. He sauntered toward the liquor store.

Carricola, swarthy, stubby, slag-bellied, was in his shirt sleeves shifting bottles from the counter to the shelves. His back was to the door when Duke entered.

"How about some ginger ale, George?" Duke was off-hand.

Carricola turned. "How many an' the name ain't George."

Swiftly, Duke pulled the revolver. "This is a stick-up!" He shot the words through his teeth. "Gimme all the bills in the till and keep your hands up over the counter!"

"You dirty little stinker!" Carricola's jaw jutted out.

"An' fast!" Duke held the revolver close to his body so it could not be seen from the street. "I'm hopped up and I'm trigger happy and you better be in a hurry!"

Duke lowered the revolver so it was aimed directly at Carricola's belly. Carricola, almost blind though he was with fury, could see the madness in the youth's eyes. He turned to the cash register, rang it open, scooped up the paper money and angrily flung it on the counter before Duke.

Duke hastily, fiercely, stuffed the bills in the side pocket of his coat with his free hand. Immediately, he backed toward the door, still keeping the revolver close to his body.

Carricola, his eyes on fire with his fury, watched the youth's every move.

Duke, backing away, reached the door, fumbled behind him for the door knob. At that instant, Carricola, unable to contain himself longer, grabbed up a wine bottle from the counter, hurled it at Duke. The bottle missed the youth, smashed through the glass of the door.

The crash of the glass cracked Duke's nerve. He stumbled, fell to one knee on the floor. At the same time, he started shooting. One, two, three. Three fast shots.

Carricola fell forward against the counter, holding his belly. He slumped, slid and fell out of sight to the floor.

Duke flung open the door, ran for the car. Vinnie was at the curb with the car door open. Duke dived into the car, pulling the door shut behind him.

Vinnie moved quickly away in second gear, shifted smoothly into high, and took the first corner easy.

As the car disappeared around the corner, the siren of a police car screamed suddenly out in the darkness.

There was a wild chase.

It ended abruptly when Vinnie, unnerved by shots from the police car, crashed the hopped-up coupe into the wooden guard-rail at the end of a dead-end street. A half hour after the shooting Duke and Vinnie were in jail. Neither Duke nor Vinnie knew that Babs, wild with jealousy, had telephoned the police to be on the watch for a sandy-haired boy with a blonde girl and a gun.

But Duke and Vinnie were lucky. Carricola did not die. He should have but he would not. He hung on by a thread for a week, and then fought his way back. Pale and groggy, he was up and around for the trial two months later.

Duke, in confinement, was abusive, insolent. Vinnie was stubborn, spiteful. But Gallagher, their lawyer, made them over for the trial. Gallagher was a smart, shrewd court lawyer who had been an assistant district attorney. Duke's aunt, with whom Duke lived, had mortgaged her two-family house to hire him.

Gallagher packed the jury with women, ten out of twelve, and made the trial an open holiday for the sob sisters. Vinnie, well rehearsed by Gallagher, wept through the days in court. Duke played a helpless, innocent youth. On the stand he, with a well-acted manfulness, confessed to the attempted hold-up. He was hungry, he said. He had no idea of shooting anybody. He had never fired a gun before in his life.

He got scared, he said, when Carricola threw the bottle, and as he stumbled and fell the revolver went off. It was all an accident.

The key point of the defense was that the shooting was accidental and the attempted robbery was little more than kid stuff. The prosecution depended on Carricola's testimony to establish Duke as a cold-blooded, would-be killer.

The night before Carricola took the stand, he received a telephone call at his home. It was "The Gang" calling, a young voice said. If he didn't testify the shooting was accidental, he was told, he'd be bumped off in a week. If he reported the telephone call, he could kiss his wife and kids goodbye. "We'll get you sure next time." The young voice was cold, mean, brief.

Carricola at the telephone in the hall looked into the living room, saw his wife seated under a standing lamp, reading to his three children. He knew the reputation of The Gang in the neighborhood. He wiped the sweat off his face with a shaking hand.

The next day on the stand, weak, trembling, he agreed with Gallagher that the shooting could have been accidental.

Duke got five years, Vinnie one.

It was a triumph for Gallagher. He went to Duke before they led him off to jail.

"Five years!" Duke, cold, insolent again, greeted him. "You're a bum, Gallagher."

"Better than ten to twenty, kid," Gallagher said easily.

"If you take money for this," Duke sneered, "I'll get you when I get out!"

Gallagher shook his head sadly. "Still think you're in a comic strip, huh? What a jerk."

He turned away in contempt.

A matron led Vinnie past. There were no tears now. "I'll be waiting for you, Duke," she said boldly.

"You won't be waiting long!" Duke shot the words' after her.

The big red house on Hope Street rose placidly and pleasantly in the dusk. The big red house was what the people in the neighborhood called it but actually it was a brick-walled monastery occupying a whole block in the heart of the city. Beyond the high walls, nuns, their white habits gleaming in the long shadows, strolled in recreation through the gardens.

In her little office, just off the entrance vestibule of the monastery, Sister Mary Paula waited patiently. She wore a black habit with a white coif, for she was an outside sister, the contact between the cloistered sisters in white and the outside world. Now and then she would go to the front door, look down the driveway, and then return to her desk.

"I wish they'd all come in the morning, Mother," she said, addressing a small statue on her desk. "The evening seems such a poor time to begin anything."

The statue was made in the likeness of St. Mary Euphrasia, the foundress of the Order that maintained the monastery, and Sister Mary Paula addressed it as if she believed the Mother Foundress were there in the room, which she did. The Sister's face was round, old with wisdom, young with innocence. Her facial coloring was reddish as if once long ago she might have had red hair, and she spoke with a slight Irish lilt in her voice.

She went back to the door and this time her visit was rewarded by the sight of a new black sedan coming to a stop at the stairs before the entrance.

She went back to the office, called Sister Laurentia,

the Directress of the training school, and returned to open the front door. Miss Jenkins, the Probation Officer, entered, followed by Vinnie who in turn was followed by a police matron. Miss Jenkins was young, looking very much like a college graduate a few years out, which she was, but her face was grave and troubled with the seriousness of her responsibility. It was her first visit to the convent and the newness of the experience gave her an air of nervous uncertainty. The police matron was soft, bulky and could have been the mother of ten.

Vinnie entered slowly, her pouting face sullen with antagonism, but warily with the wariness of those who have been in jail. Her senses were obviously all alert, her eyes especially. In one glance, she took in Sister Mary Paula and her childlike smile, the severely clean vestibule with its polished parquetry, the shining oak staircase ascending to the second floor, the religious paintings on the walls, and the statue of St. Michael slaying the serpent, an obvious but nonetheless dramatic piece that dominated the entrance.

"Mother will be right down," Sister Mary Paula addressed the three: Vinnie, the Probation Officer and the police matron. All sisters were Mothers to those sent to the school. Those confined, regardless of age, were known as children.

As Sister Mary Paula spoke, Sister Laurentia descended the stairs. She was tall, abnormally thin but very erect. Even as she descended the stairs, her eyes casually appraised the new girl, Vinnie, as they had appraised a thousand girls before her in her years as Directress of the Training School. She saw that Vinnie was harder, colder, more sure of herself than her sisters of other years. The years since the war had presented many new problems to Sister Laurentia.

"The sins are the same," she would say to Sister Mary Paula, "but the sinners are different."

She greeted Miss Jenkins, the police matron and Vinnie as if they were there to pay a conventional social visit, greeting each one in the same gently patrician manner, in no way distinguishing Vinnie from the rest. Then, Miss Jenkins and she retired to Sister Mary Paula's little office. They sat at the desk.

Miss Jenkins produced the records on Vinnie, neatly typed and indexed. They gave a complete summary of the trial, of Vinnie's background, her home life, her parents, her entire past.

Miss Jenkins explained that the judge thought it a good idea to put Vinnie in the custody of the Sisters. There were too many of her intimate associates at the State Reformatory.

Miss Jenkins was anxious to discuss the case in detail. But Sister Laurentia merely glanced at the records. She seemed reluctant to go into Vinnie's past.

"I'll go over the records when I get a moment, Miss Jenkins," she said with a little smile. "Sometimes it happens the girls have come and gone before I get a chance to read them."

Miss Jenkins was taken back. "I should think it would be important, Sister, to know this girl's environment immediately. Her mother spends her days in cocktail bars and we are quite sure she spends her time in them soliciting. We have not been able to prove it as yet but she has no other apparent means of support. Regularly, she takes men home with her from the bars."

Sister Laurentia nodded quietly. "It is an old story, Miss Jenkins."

Miss Jenkins was disappointed that this dramatic revelation had no more effect on the cloistered nun. "The father has a long police record," she went on tensely, feeling certain this time her declaration would shock the Sister. "Right now he is wanted as a murder suspect in another state. The police are pretty sure he had something to do with the shooting of a bank clerk during a stick-up."

Sister Laurentia was no more moved than before. "Parents divorced?"

"I don't think they ever bothered about such a technicality, Sister. They just called the marriage off. It is particularly unfortunate in this case because the girl was quite devoted to her father. Her mother and she have little regard for each other. Their lives together are one constant quarrel."

Sister Laurentia got to her feet. "So much misfortune seems to start in the home, doesn't it, Miss Jenkins?" She put the records back in their envelope. "Well, what happened to the girl in the past is not so important. It is what happens from now on. Let us pray hard for her."

Miss Jenkins felt a little ill at ease. She had a vague impression that Sister Laurentia was hardly scientific in her approach. "A complete knowledge and study of every detail of the inmate's past are of tremendous importance, Sister," she said. "Your psychiatrist and social workers will bear me out, I'm sure."

"I'm sure they will," Sister Laurentia agreed with a smile. Sister Laurentia led the way back to the vestibule.

Sister Mary Paula withdrew, and after a moment Miss Jenkins and the police matron left, and Sister Laurentia and Vinnie were alone. There was a moment's silence.

"Well?" Vinnie, surly, challenged.

"Suppose we go and see if we can't find you a little supper." The nun spoke easily.

"I don't want any supper!" Vinnie spat out the words. "And I don't want any of your Holy Mary business, either!"

Sister Laurentia was unruffled. "I understand. It is a little hard in a strange place at first. Suppose, then, we go and get settled."

Vinnie stiffened with hostility. "I'm not going to wear any of your long stockings and prison uniforms, I can tell you that right now! I'll rip them off if you put them on me!"

Sister Laurentia stood tall and serene, her arms folded, her hands buried in the wide sleeves of her habit. "You don't wear uniforms here, child. Tomorrow, I would like you to wear another dress, though. The rather daring one you have on might make some of our other children look plain and possibly make them jealous. I don't think that would be fair, do you? You may wear short socks if you wish."

Suspicious, Vinnie tried to find signs of deceit in the nun's face. "I've heard about you Good Shepherds," she sneered. She nodded at the hands in the wide sleeves. "That's where you hide your gun, isn't it? You didn't fool me."

Sister Laurentia shook her head ever so slightly. "I don't carry a gun. I'm not a policeman. Indeed, I have never laid eyes on a gun in my life." She unfolded her arms, let her hands and sleeves drop to her sides. "Come, my dear. It is getting late."

The nun turned toward a passageway that led to a door that opened on the convent proper.

Vinnie did not move. "I'm not going!" She screamed the words. "And you're not going to make me, either!"

Sister Laurentia turned back to her. She was as serene as before. "It *is* getting late," she said.

Vinnie jumped away as the nun returned. "Don't you touch me!" she cried. "I'll tear you apart!"

Still the nun did not change. "I'm not going to touch you, my child. We don't use force here. Please do not be afraid."

Sister Laurentia's serenity unnerved Vinnie. She was suddenly hysterical, her face distorted with the viciousness of her frustration. She leaped at the tall, delicate nun, slapped her face, slapped it fiercely, slapped it once, twice, three times.

Sister Laurentia moved slightly back before the force of the girl's blows and at each blow her face grew taut with pain, but otherwise she was unchanged. She kept her arms at her sides.

Then, abruptly, Vinnie went to pieces. She began to sob, crumpled to a chair. The fury of her hysteria ebbed.

Sister Laurentia, her usually pale face faintly pink from the blows, her white starched coif slightly rumpled, folded her arms again, her hands hidden in the wide sleeves of her habit. She looked down on the sobbing girl for a moment.

When she spoke, she spoke in exactly the same quiet

voice she had used before. "Suppose we go now, my dear, and get settled," she said.

She turned toward the passageway. Vinnie, weak, shaking after her strange experience, rose limply from the chair, mechanically followed the nun.

The infirmary was a pleasant room with six prettily canopied beds and many muslin-curtained windows. The color scheme was rose and white, almost in nursery fashion. It was not merely cheerful, it was young, almost childlike, and obviously purposely so.

Vinnie woke up in the infirmary with bright sunlight in her eyes. She also woke up with hate in her heart. Her shifting insolence and fury of the night before had now become a cold, steady animosity. She had hated religion and all its trappings, had hated piety with a perverse passion. Now, this morning as she awoke, she felt deeply and fiercely that Sister Laurentia by not fighting back had made a fool of her. She felt she had been defeated by Sister Laurentia, abjectly defeated.

She looked around the pleasant room and, in her frustration, hated its prettiness. She hated the fringed canopies, the frilled curtains, the rose and white decor. She especially hated the slender black crucifix above her bed and the religious pictures on the walls. She even hated the sunlight that was bright in her eyes.

Vinnie got up, put her feet into, slippers that had been set by her bed, and went to a window. She noted in the direct sunlight that the pyjamas that had been issued her were gaily colored and even modish, and she hated them, too. They were, she felt, also part of the conspiracy against her.

The window looked down on a large playground with a softball diamond, a basketball court and many picnic tables and benches. In one corner was a small, whitewashed stone grotto with a faded blue statue of the Madonna. Beyond the wall of the playground was the street.

Vinnie's eyes lighted up as she studied the wall. It was high but there were no barbed wires on its top, no spikes. For the moment, her passionate hatred gave way to an equally passionate hope.

She saw the picnic benches were movable, that one lifted against the wall at the right angle would provide an easy ramp to the top of the wall and freedom. There were problems, of course. It would take three, possibly four girls to lift the heavy bench. More serious was the problem of getting into the playground when no one was there and, at the same time, being sure no one was observing from the windows. It looked too easy not to have been thought of and guarded against. She knew that. But it was an idea, a hope. She would work on it.

A neatly dressed girl entered the infirmary with a breakfast tray.

"I'm Eileen," she said. "Mother Laurentia has asked me to do what I can to make you comfortable."

Eileen was about twenty-six, a senior girl known in the school as an auxiliary, a girl who, after her term had been served, stayed on in the convent. There were many auxiliaries in the convent, some of them very old. They were neither nuns nor inmates. They were free to leave when they chose. But they chose not to leave. They were devoted to the Sisters and dedicated to the life of the convent.

Eileen had been sent to the school for soliciting. She was hardly more than sixteen at the time. Her home was a brothel run by her mother and sister. When she went back after her time was up, they wanted to put her on the streets again. But her year at the training school had changed her. The life she had once found gay and glittering seemed tawdry and dull.

Late one night, fearful, after a long battle with herself, she rang the door bell of the convent and asked to be taken back. She had been in the convent ever since.

Vinnie coolly looked her over. She was thin, she saw, and, except for her deeply quiet, brown eyes, homely.

"What's the joker?" Vinnie asked her. "Why should that dame want to make me comfortable?"

"Mother Laurentia?" Eileen was matter-of-fact, at ease with the poise of one who knew both sides of the fence. She put the tray down on the wide arm of an easy chair. "Mother has an idea that happy people usually find it easier to be good."

Vinnie laughed contemptuously. "Tell her not to waste her happy goo on me, Susie."

Eileen lifted the napkin covering the tray. "I hope you like your breakfast," she said evenly.

Vinnie approached her. "Tell me—what is your racket?"

The homely, thin, narrow-faced girl faced the pretty, boldly physical Vinnie. "This is my home," she said.

"This joint?" Vinnie studied her. "Haven't you ever seen the big, beautiful world outside?"

"Uh huh. I've seen it." Eileen answered quietly.

Just as quietly she explained to Vinnie the routine of the first days at the school. Vinnie, like all new entrants to the training school, had been sent first to the infirmary. There would be no confinement as such. Meals would be brought to her but doors were wide open.

Here, in the infirmary, she would bathe, receive her new clothes. Here the visiting physician would examine her. Here the psychiatrist would interview her. Here she would make her first close contact with the life she was to live.

Here she would be given a new name, a name unlike her own, a name of her own choosing if she wished. No one in the convent except the Directress and the Mother Superior would ever know her right name. Nor would anyone ever know the crime committed or the wrong done or any detail of her past. Even those Sisters who taught her, watched over her intimately during her stay would never know.

"You can be very happy here—if you want to be." Eileen finished very casually and turned to the door. "I'll go and get your new clothes."

Vinnie whirled around, noticed for the first time that her clothes were gone from the chair where she had laid them. "My cigarettes! Where're my cigarettes?" she cried out in panic.

Eileen stopped at the door. "We don't use cigarettes around here," she said and continued on out.

Vinnie's eyes blazed in anger. Life without cigarettes was a horror she had not anticipated. She ran to the chair, searched it and the floor about it in the hope that one cigarette at least might have fallen from the package.

"I'll die," she moaned. "I'll die."

There were no cigarettes. Then, she discovered on the

floor, a little distance under the bed, the cardboard folder of matches that had been with the cigarettes. It had obviously dropped there unnoticed. She picked it up, turned it over in her fingers. She read the legend on the cover:

RUBY'S
Cocktails—Liquors—Fine Foods
—DANCING—
No Cover Charge

She read it with moody, nostalgic eyes. It was a small but vivid link to the past.

Then suddenly, angrily she flung the folder into the flowered waste paper basket near the bed. Again, her hatred of all around her flamed. She went abruptly back to the window that looked down on the playground. Again, with desperate hope she studied the wall, the picnic benches. The idea of escape obsessed her more fiercely now.

Then, Eileen returned with the new clothes.

The next afternoon Vinnie met Sister Lucy.

Sister Lucy was a bright-eyed, slender, buoyant nun who seemed to see in everybody nothing but good.

Once, an older Sister speaking with the Mother Superior about Sister Lucy said, "She's in love with everybody, the dear."

Then, the Mother Superior had quietly remarked, "When you're in love with God, Sister, you can't avoid being in love with everybody else."

Sister Lucy came from a gentle, amiable family. Her

father was well to do, and the family had had the world's goods in sensible measure: a town house and a bright, practical summer home at the ocean; education at the best colleges; travel; friends; top ranking in the community; and, especially, much love and laughter.

After her graduation from college, she had gone to work in the advertising department of a swank women's magazine. It was one of "the things to do." Life was busy, gay and romantic. She was more than ordinarily gifted with good looks and had more than her share of suitors. But she began to be troubled. She felt she should try to pay somehow for the good and wonderful life she had been given. She decided she would dedicate herself in some way to the service of those who had been less fortunate than she. One Saturday afternoon, weekending at a friend's house, she came across a little book on the work of the Sisters of the Good Shepherd. That, abruptly and completely, was it.

"The book really fell from a top shelf and hit me on the head," Sister Lucy would explain, smiling.

Now she had been more than ten years in the convent. No one could tell it from looking at her. Her family on their visits observed her grow steadily younger and more childlike and amused themselves after each visit by setting the age she appeared to be. After their last visit, they had put her age at about eighteen.

Sister Laurentia and Sister Lucy came into the infirmary together.

"My, but you're pretty!' Sister Lucy exclaimed when first she saw Vinnie.

"In this jerk-water outfit?" Vinnie scornfully shook the somewhat conservative cotton print dress she was now wearing. "You kidding?"

"Perhaps we can find other dresses you'll like better," Sister Laurentia said, addressing her as if there had never been a bad moment between them. "Just now, I'd like you and Sister Lucy to have a little talk. We want you to consider your stay here not as a period of punishment but an opportunity for self-advancement. This is primarily a school and we have different courses here that might interest you. Sister Lucy will discuss them with you."

Sister Laurentia left the room.

Sister Lucy waited until she had gone, then whispered to Vinnie, "Tell me—what does jerk-water mean?"

"Yappy." Vinnie answered coldly.

Sister Lucy laughed softly. "Goodness, but I'm ignorant. Sometimes you girls talk such a wonderfully fresh and vivid language, you make the school reading seem very dull."

Then, she saw the girl's deepening hostility darken her face. She was immediately contrite.

"I'm sorry, my dear," she said genuinely. "I shouldn't be so gay and scatter-brained when your heart is so heavy. I know how hard being here is for you. For the first few days, especially. Forgive me, won't you?"

Vinnie kept a sullen silence.

Sister Lucy indicated a pair of chairs in the sunlight by the window. "Come. Let's sit over here and talk and see if we can't become friends."

Vinnie reluctantly followed her to the chairs. They sat facing each other; the nun, friendly, warmly eager to win Vinnie's affection; Vinnie, antagonistic, coldly determined to preserve her hate. They faced each other, two women who had come from such widely separate beginnings, who had travelled such widely different roads to meet in the rose-and-white infirmary. And as deep as was the gulf between their pasts, so deep was the resentment Vinnie bore the nun.

It was in some measure instinctive, this resentment. Her hatred of confinement, her obsession for escape were normal and general. But her resentment of Sister Lucy was personal and particular and psychotic as if she, victim of selfishness and neglect, product of a broken home turned loose in a shabby world, had read in the simplicity of the nun's face the history of her home and family, of her youth and growth in an environment of kindness and affection.

"First," Sister Lucy said, "we must find you a name, a new name for your new life here. Have you any favorite?"

Vinnie shrugged. "What difference does it make?"

"Well, if you had a saint's name it might help you. You could pray to her for success in your new work."

"Me? Pray?" The girl laughed derisively.

"Don't you ever?"

"Never—and I wouldn't if I knew how."

"Didn't your mother ever lean over your bed at night and have you say, 'Now, I lay me down to sleep.' ?"

"Most of the time, my bed was the back seat of the family sedan," Vinnie answered scornfully. "Outside of a cocktail bar. That's where my mother spent her nights."

"It's hardly your fault you're here then, is it?" Sister Lucy was moved.

"But I liked it," Vinnie said quickly, defiantly. "I liked the lights, and sometimes I could hear the juke boxes."

Sister Lucy pondered this mystery but could not penetrate it. After a moment, she said, "Teresa would be a nice name for you, I think."

Vinnie shrugged her indifference.

"Little Teresa not Big Teresa," Sister Lucy went on. "They're both wonderful. Big Teresa lived a long while ago while Little Teresa died only a few years ago. She was young, too, when she died. Twenty-four. I have a feeling you and she could become wonderful friends."

"The dame is dead—and we're going to be friends?" Vinnie stared into the nun's guileless eyes in startled disbelief.

"She's dead, but she's very much alive," Sister Lucy explained gently. "When she was dying, she promised she would spend her heaven helping people on earth."

"You kidding?"

"Oh, no, my dear. That's exactly what she said," the nun replied.

Vinnie began to laugh crazily and got to her feet. "Where've they sent me? To a nut house?" she asked when she had recovered. "I don't have to take this, do I?"

Sister Lucy was very serene. "I think that will be a wonderful name for you. Teresa." She got to her feet. "I like it. Teresa. I just *feel* it."

"Call me anything you like," Vinnie replied, "but listen. Once I had to go down to the city morgue and identify a souse who used to rent the room over our garage, and I saw a lot of stiffs. All kinds. Shot, burnt-up, poisoned, smashed-up, all kinds, and they had them all on a lot of slabs filed away in a big ice box like it was a filing cabinet, and in some cases all they had of them was a leg or an arm or a head. And they were all dead, awful dead. That's when I got hep and made up my mind I was going to go in for plenty of living. When you're dead, sister, you're dead, like the song says. So skip the malarkey, will you? All I want is to get out of this joint."

Sister Lucy listened quietly, her eyes never leaving Vinnie's face. "You and I are going to be good friends, my dear," she said, gently. "You have spirit."

Vinnie was surprised. "You didn't get me right," she said quickly, defensively.

The nun smiled. "I think I did—Teresa."

Vinnie's aggressiveness was gone for the moment. "Well, I don't get you," she mumbled.

Sister Lucy laughed softly. "Come. Let's go and look around a bit. It may not be so dreadful as you think."

Sister Lucy glided to the door, Vinnie, annoyed and ill at ease, slowly followed her.

Sister Lucy led Vinnie through long, shining corridors. They passed wide, unbarred windows, looking down on orchards and gardens. They passed little shrines with flowers before the statues.

They stopped now and then to peer through doors, here into the quiet, shadowy library, there into the vast assembly hall with its theatre stage, and its motion picture screen and projector. They looked into the long dining room, saw the dental clinic as they passed, noted the long dormitories with their gleaming lavatories, glimpsed, in passing, the many classrooms.

Sister Lucy took Vinnie into the beauty parlor. It was a large establishment equipped to give anything from a pedicure to a finger wave. Operators were brought in from outside to give the girls beauty treatments, Sister Lucy explained, and several professional operators held regular classes. For practice, the girls worked on one another.

"The prettier a girl looks," Sister Lucy said, "the less grateful she has to be for small favors. That's what Mother Laurentia says."

Vinnie was not interested.

They passed white-habited nuns as they went through the corridors, and now and then Sister Lucy stopped to chat with auxiliaries, one of whom was very old, wizened and stooped but with eyes still bright with amusement and love of life. No girls were seen. They were all at recreation in another building.

"We'll meet them all presently," Sister Lucy said.

She led Vinnie into one suite of rooms with obvious pleasure. This was a modern apartment with living room, dining room, library alcove, kitchen, bedroom and bath, all completely and smartly furnished. Here, Sister Lucy told Vinnie, girls taking home management courses were taught to arrange furniture, were given lessons in cooking, serving and general housekeeping.

"Sometimes," Sister Lucy confided, her eyes twinkling, "especially in the spring, I slip in here by myself and shift the furniture around just for the fun of it."

"I hate housework!" Vinnie was bitter, perverse.

Sister Lucy spoke softly. "Doing housework is a small price to pay for having a home, I think."

They left the apartment and moved down a corridor to the secretarial school. They stopped in a long room with desks and typewriters.

Vinnie's eyes showed interest for the first time. The room looked immediately down on the playground Vinnie had seen from the infirmary.

Sister Lucy misread the interest. "Have you had secretarial training, Teresa?" she asked.

"Uh-uh," Vinnie shook her head.

A secretarial job was a good job, Sister Lucy said, and could be an important job. At the school, they tried to teach girls so they could get jobs in which they could support themselves and thus be independent.

Vinnie's eyes were on the wall beyond the playground. "It might not be so bad," she said flatly.

Sister Lucy was pleased at what she considered progress.

Now, Sister Lucy took Vinnie into the chapel. Here for the first time she appeared to lose her almost contemptuous poise. It was a towering place, rich in marble, built in the design of a Greek cross with a marble-canopied altar set in the heart of the cross under a lofty dome, many stories high. Onyx and gold mingled with the marble in the soft, delicately colored light from many tall stained-glass windows.

The chapel was really four chapels in one, for each arm of the cruciform chapel was separate from the others. The Sisters' section faced the front of the tabernacle; on their left was the senior girls' section; directly on the other side of the altar from the sisters was a junior girls' section; and to the right was the section of the Magdalen

Sisters, an order of nuns within the order of the Good Shepherd.

Several of the Magdalens in their dark brown habits with white coifs showing under black veils moved distantly in the shadows of their section of the chapel. Sister Lucy directed Vinnie's attention toward them.

The Magdalens, she explained, were women who had once been committed to the care of the Good Shepherd nuns but, unlike the auxiliaries whose vocation it was to serve as lay workers, had decided to follow a religious life of their own, a strictly cloistered, contemplative life dedicated to work, prayer and penance.

Vinnie, the first awe at the chapel having faded, was bored again.

Their last stop was at the gymnasium. Here were most of the senior girls at recreation, watching a basketball game between two teams chosen from their numbers. Benches on both sides of the floor were crowded with cheering partisans. Spectators and participants alike wore gym suits. A nun, whistle in hand, was referee.

Sister Lucy led Vinnie into the gymnasium. She found her a seat on a bench near the door.

This was an important moment—the new girl's meeting with those who were to be her companions. But Sister Lucy purposely was very casual. "Sit here, my dear," she said, "and I'll be back when the game is over."

Sister Lucy went back into the corridor.

The girl on Vinnie's right was too intent on the game to notice her. But the girl on her left turned to her. Both girls gave little screams, unheard in the cheering, as they recognized each other.

The other girl was Babs.

Babs had been committed for shoplifting a little more than a month before.

Duke had been slick at lifting, though he considered it kid stuff, and had introduced Babs to his technique. A bottle, brought to the store for the purpose, would be dropped and crashed to the floor by Duke as if by accident and, in the subsequent commotion, the accomplice would quickly work a counter.

In those first days, when Duke and Vinnie were held without bail while the Law, dangling a murder charge over their heads, waited for Carricola to die, Babs, who lived to dress, began to crave new clothes.

She and a member of The Gang known as Hot Rod went to the town's leading department store to lift some scarves she fancied, but Hot Rod, after crashing the bottle, lost his nerve and ran for the street. A store detective, immediately wise, picked off Babs with the stuff on her the moment she cleared the door.

The two girls talked in low voices, being careful not to look at each other. Vinnie told Babs about the trial and Duke's five year sentence.

"He'll never take it," Babs whispered. "He won't stay locked up. Not Duke."

"I'm not going to take it here, either," Vinnie whispered back, her eyes apparently intent on the basketball game.

Babs gave her a quick, startled look then stared ahead again.

"All it means is more trouble, Vinnie. There's only a chance in a million."

"It's a chance I've got to take."

Vinnie questioned Babs about the playground. As she expected, there were always monitors there during recreation, nuns and auxiliaries. And the door to the playground was locked when recreation was ended.

But this knowledge did not diminish Vinnie's resolution. "I've got to make a break," she declared, raising her voice. "I can't take this pious stuff. I'll go nuts."

"Shh," Babs warned her, looking sharply at the girl on Vinnie's right. "You got to be careful, Vinnie. Some of these dames here think the nuns hung the moon. They'd snitch on you in a minute."

Vinnie was silent for a while. They appeared to watch the basketball game.

Finally, Vinnie leaned over, whispered to Babs. "You're in with me on this, aren't you?"

Babs stiffened, looked fearfully around her. "I—I don't mind it here so much, Vinnie."

"Chicken!" Vinnie's eyes flashed with contempt. "Duke had you right, didn't he?"

Then, the game ended and Sister Lucy appeared. She glided buoyantly to the bench.

Babs, as taught, got to her feet in respect.

"Hello, Martha," the nun, smiling, addressed her. Then, turning to Vinnie, she said, "Enjoy the game, Teresa?"

Vinnie sat, not moving. "Yeh," she said through her teeth. "It was just beautiful."

The nun seemed not to notice the discourtesy or the sarcasm. "Come, then, my dear. We have just time for you to see your dormitory before supper."

Sister Lucy and Vinnie went off together, Vinnie going reluctantly.

Babs, unhappy, a little frightened, watched Vinnie go.

Vinnie, nursing both her passion for escape and her resentment of Sister Lucy, moved stubbornly into the routine of the school.

The day began with chapel at seven o'clock. Vinnie was required to attend chapel but not being a Catholic, was not required to participate in the services. After chapel came breakfast, and after that recreation, either inside or outside of the building, and after that school.

School began at nine o'clock and continued until noon. From twelve to one were lunch and recreation, and then school again until three. After three, there were special classes of varying durations in music, homemaking, sewing and the like. Vinnie, who had a good ear and voice, took music. After the special classes there was recreation again, and after that, supper. Then, a last recreation—a motion picture, a school play, a musical recital, television—and then, evening prayers. Vinnie was not required to join in the prayers but she was asked to respect the devotion of those who did. The day ended with lights out in the dormitory and all of the girls calling to the sister in charge, "Good night, Mother." Then, silence.

An auxiliary presided over the dormitory proper, sleeping there. A sister had an adjoining room. Agatha, a serene young woman, was the auxiliary in Vinnie's dormitory. Sister Lucy was the sister who slept in the adjoining room.

At first, Vinnie had little trouble sustaining her antagonism to the convent and its sisters, and especially

Sister Lucy. She had chosen to go to secretarial school but, in and out of the classroom, she maintained her attitude of cool hostility. And so far as the new experiences of each day were concerned, she appeared untouched by them and, usually, unaware of them. Her main concern was her plan for escape.

She carefully studied her companions for possible accomplices. But the more she studied them, the less confident in them she became. The nuns and the place appeared to have changed many of those committed there. While they were there, at any rate. She was not certain of Babs, for example. It was clear something was happening to her.

Vinnie thus turned her interest to newcomers. She watched them shrewdly. Finally, she became sure of two. One, Cecelia, was a little older than she; the other, Rose, younger. Both were hard, aggressive, bitter. They became her accomplices.

It was Cecelia, evidently with some experience in the matter, who urged that a diversion was essential to any plan of escape. Excitement was needed to distract attention from the getaway. It was, Vinnie remembered, the technique Duke used in his shoplifting operations.

Cecelia suggested a riot. A riot, she said, always raised havoc with routine. But Vinnie felt it would take too much time to organize a riot. She was not going to stay in the place that long. Also, it was a precarious venture. One squealer could spoil the whole undertaking.

Vinnie then hit upon the idea of a fire. A real fire, she said, a conflagration. It would be fine with her, she announced, if the whole place burned to the ground.

Babs, who at this stage was still a part of the conspiracy, protested against the idea of a fire. There was a danger that girls and sisters might be burned to death, she said.

Vinnie was annoyed. "Let the girls make a run for it, the way I'm going to," she declared, "and as far as your nuns are concerned, if they get killed, so what? That's that martyrdom they're always talking about, isn't it? If they're on the level, they ought to be crazy about the idea, shouldn't they?"

Babs was shocked and did not disguise it. From that time on, Vinnie gradually dropped her from her plans. Babs was relieved to be out of them.

The idea of a fire was easier to invent than to execute. Vinnie grew troubled, impatient as she tried to figure out how to manage it. The fire would have to burst suddenly, spread quickly. There were too many watchful eyes in the buildings and too many precautions taken for her to put her hope in any ordinary fire. It would be detected in no time.

Then, unexpectedly one day, she found exactly what was needed.

Not far from the dormitory was a large linen room. Here were stocked the clean sheets, pillowcases, towels and wash cloths waiting their turn in the dormitory. Vinnie, passing the room, had noted its contents often but it was not until one evening, going there with Agatha, the auxiliary, to get some spare sheets that she discovered the room's closet. The door to the closet heretofore had been closed and locked. But today it was open, and in the closet Vinnie observed mops, brooms, stacks of cakes of soap—and a gallon jar of cleaning fluid. The red-lettered word on the jar leaped out of the dusk of the closet at her. The word was: INFLAMMABLE.

That was it, then. The linen and the cleaning fluid provided the perfect conflagration. Thenceforth, the broad outline of the plan was clear. Agatha kept the closet keys in her desk but she rarely locked her desk. It would be an easy trick to lift them in the evening before bedtime. Then, later, with lights out, she would tip toe to the linen room, start a fire. A conflagration would be immediate and sure and, in the subsequent panic, she and her companions would make their way swiftly to the secretarial class room, lower themselves to the playground by a rope or knotted sheets, climb the wall using a tilted bench as a ramp, drop to the other side to the street and be off to freedom.

Vinnie glowed happily as she anticipated the hour. Escape! Liberty! She dreamed of another life somewhere, perhaps in Canada, of Duke joining her, of cocktails and juke boxes and dancing, and clothes, clothes!

She was determined she would tell no one of her plan until the last minute, not even Cecelia or Rose. It was too happy a secret to risk with anyone. She would not even tell them the date. It was to be the night of St. Mary Magdalen's feast day, July 22nd, when, she had learned, there were to be much excitement and festivity in the school and convent. On that day, the Magdalen sisters repeated their solemn vows. On that day, the regular routine was suspended and all in the place were festive. The sisters usually waited on the girls for dinner. And there was much music and singing and general joy. That night bodies and spirits would be tired and slumber deep.

July 22nd was but a few weeks away. There were some details to be worked out such as arranging for a getaway car to be waiting beyond the walls but they would be worked out easily, leisurely. A few weeks....

Vinnie, coolly at ease now, began to count off the days. Her plans made, she became the side-line sitter, the observer. Sister Lucy, now believing she saw in Vinnie a sign of adjustment, was grateful, and told her gratitude fervently in her prayers.

Vinnie began to notice the sisters more, seeing them for the first time not as ogres but as rather conventional enemies. She could afford this new tolerance. Wouldn't she, in a brief while, be free?

She felt, in watching the sisters, in noting the lights and shadows of the life at school, she was simply giving the place a last look. But the last look, as she thought it, was really the first, and, in spite of herself, it did something to her.

Chapel gradually ceased to be merely an early morning scheming period, and recreation merely a time for sullenness. She slowly became aware of the solemnity of the early morning Mass. The reverence of the communicants, the sincerity of their prayer, the tranquil grandeur of the chapel hour began to make a series of small impressions on her. There was a sublimity that transformed the characters of even the drabbest of the girls, changing them more deeply than the candle glow and stained-glass window light changed their faces. It was pretty much theatrical to Vinnie and affected her as several films in her life had affected her. But theatrical or not, it affected her.

There were the sisters themselves. Mother Superior, for example. Mother Superior was responsible for the management of the convent and school, for the lives of hundreds, but she was so frail, it was a wonder to Vinnie she was able to carry the weight of her habit. It was only when Vinnie first permitted herself a look into the steady brightness of the Mother's eyes that she saw her inner strength. It was hard for Vinnie to look into those eyes for long.

There was Sister Bernardine who taught her music. Sister had a sly sense of humor and now Vinnie found herself smiling at her jokes. Now, too, when Sister Bernardine praised Vinnie's aptitude for music and urged her to make the most of it, saying that she might very well become a fine musician, Vinnie found herself listening. The sister's efforts to inspire her didn't seem quite so contrived as they had only a few days before. Vinnie felt that no longer were they all in conspiracy against her. How could they be? Wasn't she, she told herself, in successful conspiracy against *them*?

Then, there was Sister Lucy. She felt it especially wise to be tolerant of Sister Lucy. For Sister Lucy knew her better than anyone else. An air of mild amiability would divert any suspicion, should any have arisen. Also, she felt condescending in this new attitude. It was pleasant to be condescending.

Now, again, something happened to her. She found, in spite of herself, her deep, instinctive resentment of the simple spirited nun diminishing. As she sought to tolerate her, she began to understand her. She began to see that Sister Lucy's belief in her fundamental goodness was real, that her belief in everybody's fundamental goodness was real.

Once, in the first days, Vinnie surlily got to her feet as Sister Lucy approached her in the dormitory.

Immediately, Sister Lucy was glowing. "Teresa," she said, "you are one of the most naturally courteous girls I have ever known."

At that time, Vinnie had coldly dismissed the remark as what she called the malarkey. "This is a come-on," she told herself. "She figures if she tells me that often enough, I'll believe it."

But now, in her new tolerance, she began to see that the nun genuinely believed the praises she gave. It was foolish to believe them, Vinnie said to herself, but believe them she did.

Sister Lucy taught typing and shorthand in the secretarial school. Romanticising everything as she did, it was no dull, matter-of-fact class that she conducted. Many of the typing exercises were poetry, and Vinnie soon saw that each poem was chosen with some little point to it. The girls were subtly led to believe that the study of typing and shorthand was a preparation for a dedicated life and had almost a sublimity to it. Certainly, it began to appear as something far more idealistically significant than the utilitarian study it actually was.

So, Vinnie, the relaxed observer now, began to see life in the school and convent more as it was and less as she imagined it to be.

One morning, after Vinnie had counted off the eighth day, Sister Laurentia came for Vinnie. She was in the beauty parlor. Babs, under instruction, had just finished

giving her a shampoo and a wave. Vinnie looked pert and
new, and Sister Laurentia was pleased with what she saw.

Sister Laurentia told Vinnie that there was a visitor
for her in a front parlor, her mother. It was a very special visit, she intimated to Vinnie, as they walked across
from the senior building. Indeed, she would find it to be
something of a surprise, she was sure. Mother Superior
had agreed to the special visit only because of the good
reports Sister Lucy had given her. All were happy, Sister
Laurentia told her, that she was at last getting into the
spirit of the school. All held out great hopes for her.

Vinnie concealed her cynical smile under her hand.
It was good to be making fools of them, she told herself.

Vinnie, entering the visitors' parlor, saw her mother
first. Then, behind her, she discovered Mike. He was on
crutches. He wore his marine uniform with a corporal's
chevrons on his sleeve. Her first impulse was to turn and
run.

But he was grinning amiably at her as if this were
some sort of lark, and he was in on it. "Hi, kid," he said.

She smiled gratefully at him, appreciative of his non-
chalance. He was a tall, thin, dark youngster, abnormally
thin at the moment.

One glance at her mother's flushed face and shining
bright eyes told Vinnie her mother had been drinking.

"He's home on sick leave and he's got to have an
operation on his leg," Vinnie's mother piped up in a high
voice, artificially gay as if she were announcing some
happy news. "He got himself wounded and he's got to
go to the hospital tomorrow. The docs are going to try to
save his leg."

She giggled and looked sillily around from one face to another.

Vinnie's mother was a peroxide blonde, chubby woman with full features that seemed healthy for all her dissipation. She obviously had the feeling, common to self-indulgent people, that she was a lovable creature loved by everybody and that she, in her amiability, could never say the wrong word or do the wrong thing. Vinnie felt ashamed of her, ashamed for herself. Her mother had always drunk beer in the morning but beer had always made her dull and torpid. Now, she was in almost hysterical high spirits. Gin, probably, Vinnie thought. Gin, her mother's favorite drink.

"Don't worry about Mike, sweetie," her mother babbled. "He knows all about you. He saw the clippings of the trial but he still loves you. He really does. He's glad you're here with the sisters, too." She turned to Sister Laurentia with a vapid, patronizing smile. "He thinks you sisters are wonderful." Then she grabbed Mike's arm, almost upsetting his crutches. "You're wonderful, too, Mike, wonderful." She turned back to Sister Laurentia, giggled. "If all men were like Mike, there wouldn't be so many bad women in the world, would there, Sister?"

Sister Laurentia sat quietly silent. Vinnie's pleasure at seeing Mike overcame her embarrassment at her mother. They talked inconsequential things and soon Vinnie had the curious feeling that there was, no barrier at all between Mike and her.

After fifteen minutes, Sister Laurentia announced the visit was ended. Mike was boyishly grateful for the sight of Vinnie and managed to say so. Vinnie's mother babbled away, unaware of reality, and Vinnie could still hear her piping, almost hysterical voice when she was already out of sight.

On the way back to the senior building Vinnie was silent, moody. Sister Laurentia noticed her lack of spirit but said nothing until they had reached the beauty parlor.

"Didn't you enjoy your visit, Teresa?" she asked Vinnie, watching her face carefully.

"No."

"No?"

Vinnie turned her eyes away. "I'm sorry I saw Mike again."

"But he seemed a good, likeable boy." Sister Laurentia tried to understand the girl's dejection and defensive mood.

"I just wish I hadn't seen him." That was all Vinnie said.

Vinnie returned to the beauty parlor and Sister Laurentia, puzzled, meditative, went about her work.

Now, Vinnie's new ease left her. The approach of July 22nd, Saint Mary Magdalen's day, began to trouble her. She began to doubt the wisdom of her planned escape. She kept purposely away from Cecelia, and Rose, her sister conspirators. She lost confidence in her strength. She was at battle with herself.

Then, suddenly, the past, which had slowly been letting go its grip on her, struck through the monastery walls, seized her, stunned her.

First came the news of Duke's break from jail.

Babs' mother had come to the visitors' parlor to see her on a routine visit. The mother, a giggly, addlebrained woman who worked in a beauty parlor, dropped the dramatic news along with a litter of other items ranging from Babs' little sister having the measles to the people next door having a television set. Sister Laurentia was displeased that the mother should have told Babs of Duke's escape. But the news, coming in the gibble-gabble as it did, was out before she could interpose a restraining word.

Duke, who had been transferred to a prison farm, had overpowered the driver of one of the farm's pickup trucks and, driving it in crazy desperation, had run down the nearest of the guards. Before the other guards could get in cars to follow him, he had reached a river about an eighth of a mile away. He abandoned the truck and leaped into the river. The guards, reaching the river soon after his leap, fixed at him. The guards believed he had been hit but no sign of him or his body had been discovered. That had been ten days before. There was an all-points search being made for him.

Babs was stunned. Sister Laurentia quickly made a point of the folly of such conduct and changed the subject.

Later, when Sister Laurentia and Babs were on their way back to the senior building, the nun, sensing Babs' excitement, warned her that she be careful about concern with the past. Duke had no place in her present, and any association with him even in memory could do nothing but harm.

Babs protested that just because she was excited, didn't mean she was anxious about Duke or, even, very much interested.

"I used to think he was quite a character, Mother," she said, "but now I've come to the conclusion he is just a punk. I don't care what happens to him."

Sister Laurentia stopped abruptly. "Goodness, child, that is no attitude to have. Pray for him, pray for the poor boy. God help him."

Babs was puzzled. "But I thought you meant I should forget him, Mother?"

Sister Laurentia smiled. "Except in your charity, my dear. Pray hard for him."

They moved on toward the senior building.

Babs found Vinnie practicing the piano in the music room. She made sure they were alone, then told of Duke's escape.

Vinnie was suddenly limp, pale. "He'll come here," she whispered. "He'll do something crazy."

Babs shrugged. "He can't touch us here."

But Vinnie was not quieted. "I feel it," she said. "I'm frightened. I don't know why but I am."

Thus, Duke, came back into Vinnie's life. He troubled her days and kept her awake nights while all the other girls in the dormitory slept.

Sister Lucy noticed the change in her. Vinnie returned to her old reticence if not hostility. Her interest in her music and her marks in school fell off.

Graduation time for senior class at the school was only a few days away, and Sister Lucy was busy making favors and decorations for what always was a great event. Now, purposely, she made it a practice of calling Vinnie in to her room to help her. She watched the sombre Vinnie carefully but, except for one occasion, made no comment.

That once was when Vinnie, taking an aversion to the ribbons, paper lace and colored cards with which they were working, pushed them away from her exclaiming suddenly, "I'm sick of this baby stuff!"

Sister Lucy stared in surprise. "You're not discouraged, are you, Teresa?"

Then, the old Vinnie flared. "I can't stand the preachy stuff around here. It's getting on my nerves."

Sister Lucy smiled. "It gets on my nerves sometimes, too." Then she added quietly. "You have no idea how hard it is for me to try to be good."

"Yeh. I know." Vinnie said sarcastically.

Sister Lucy managed her little smile. "I'm glad to see you have not lost your spirit, Teresa," she said.

But it was the second blow from the world outside the walls that brought back all of Vinnie's hostility and bitterness and fiercely revived her plans for escape.

Sister Laurentia had had the news for several days. It posed a critical problem. Sister Laurentia consulted with the Mother Superior. If they told Vinnie, they were sure the effect on her would not be good. If they did not tell her, they would, they felt, be denying her an essential right.

In the afternoon, Sister Laurentia, as casually as possible, led Vinnie into the garden for a walk. There was a shrine to Saint Teresa in the garden. They stopped before it. A weather-beaten cement figure of the Saint, clad in the brown and black of the Carmelites, held in its arms a spray of cement roses. A dozen real roses were in a vase before the statue.

"This is your saint, isn't it?" Sister Laurentia was very offhand.

Vinnie stared up at the serene figure of the saint, looking down from its tall pedestal, said nothing.

"There was another girl who was called Teresa here a few years ago," Sister Laurentia went on. "She had a very hard time of it. It seemed as if always her former life was reaching in here after her, pulling her back. But finally she won out. She is happily married now and comes back to the reunion here each year." She pointed at the roses in the vase. "Now and then she sends roses for the shrine. Roses are Saint Teresa's special flower."

Still, Vinnie made no comment. She was not sullen but indifferent.

Then, in the sunlight by the statue, Sister Laurentia told her what she had brought her there to tell her. Vinnie's father had been found guilty of murder in another state some time before. He was to be executed for the crime that night. Sometime after eleven o'clock the electrocution would take place, sometime between eleven and twelve.

There was an instant's stunned silence, then Vinnie cried out wildly. "No! No! They can't kill my father! No! No! Pop is just a slob, a good slob who never meant to hurt anybody! They can't kill him!"

Sister Laurentia sought gently to calm the girl. "Pray, my dear, and put your trust in the Lord. He orders all things for the best though we may not see the wisdom of His ways right now."

"The hell with that Lord stuff!" Vinnie screamed. "I prayed to Him the other day for the first time in my life and—" She pointed up to the statue. "—and I prayed to her too. And this is what they've done to me!"

"Hush, my dear." Sister Laurentia's voice was firm. "You must not blaspheme. Nor must you despair. They are great sins."

Vinnie began to sob. "They're going to kill my pop. Poor pop. Nobody ever gave him a chance." Then, suddenly, her chin stiffened. "The bastards!"

"Hush!" Sister Laurentia spoke sharply. "You must not talk that way! You are only embroiling your own soul."

Abruptly, Vinnie began to laugh, to laugh shrilly and hysterically. "My soul! Who thought that one up! My soul, yeh! and Pop's soul, yeh! What a lot of boloney that is! I wish he'd killed a hundred people! I wish I could kill them! Who's got any soul? The cops, huh? The judges, huh? The dirty stinkers!"

"Stop it!" Sister Laurentia was stern, authoritative. "Stop this viciousness! It will devour you!"

Vinnie slowly got a grip on herself. Not to please the nun but because her old hatred had suddenly returned to her. That hatred, fiercer now than before, gripped her, made her strong. She dried her eyes with the knuckles of her hands, stood tensely erect.

"That's a good girl," Sister Laurentia said, misreading her resolution. "And pray. We shall all pray for your father. The whole community will pray. Not the courts but God is the final judge."

The dormitory that night was very quiet. Lights were out but nobody slept. All lay awake awaiting eleven o'clock. For all knew of Vinnie and her father.

Vinnie had told Babs. And from Babs the news had spread to all, even to Agatha, the auxiliary in charge.

Agatha finally, fearful of facing the critical hours of the dark alone, had told Sister Lucy.

After lights out, the dormitory had, with Vinnie's tragedy in mind, said the Rosary with Sister Lucy leading, marking off decade after decade on the beads that hung by her side.

The nun called out the ancient words into the darkness of the dormitory, called them out evenly but fervently:

> Hail Mary, Full Of Grace,
> The Lord Is With Thee,
> Blessed Art Thou Among Women
> And Blessed Is The Fruit Of Thy Womb, Jesus

And from the dark the girls responded with the ancient response:

> Holy Mary, Mother of God
> Pray For Us Sinners
> Now And At The Hour Of Our Death, Amen.

Thus was the death watch kept for Vinnie's father. But Vinnie did not join in the prayers, nor did she give any sign she was aware of them. She lay flat back on the pillow, her hands folded behind her head. Through lowered lids, her eyes were fixed on the dormitory clock which could be shadowily seen in the vaguest of light. She watched the hands move, and as they moved her hatred of the world, inside and out, grew coldly, steadily.

When the prayers were finished, there was silence for

a moment. Then, one of the younger girls sobbed. Then, a second.

Soon, it seemed as if the whole dormitory, caught up in mass emotion, was sobbing.

But Vinnie did not sob. She lay awake as before, seemingly oblivious of the sobbing, thinking out her hatred, thinking it out to the bitter end.

Sister Lucy, concerned lest the sobbing lead to hysteria and to Vinnie's going to pieces, went down the dark of the dormitory to Vinnie's bed. She stood by the bed a moment before Vinnie became aware of her presence.

Vinnie raised her head. The clock said eleven.

"Teresa, I'm going to the chapel," Sister Lucy whispered. "Would you like to come?"

"No."

The sobbing in the dormitory increased.

"It might be easier for you there, my dear," the nun said.

Vinnie sat abruptly up. "Maybe you're right."

Sister Lucy got her robe and slippers.

"These poor punks here, they mean all right," Vinnie went on coldly as she got into her robe, "but they'll drive me nuts!"

Sister Lucy and Vinnie went silently out of the dark of the dormitory into the dusk of the corridor while all heads on the pillows turned to watch.

The chapel was dark except for the small red light of the sanctuary lamp before the tabernacle. Sister Lucy and Vinnie went into the senior girls' section of the chapel, made their way down through the vast darkness to the first pew. Sister Lucy knelt down. Vinnie sat a little distance from her.

Now and then, the red sanctuary lamp would suddenly flicker, sending a brief ripple of shadows across the altar. But that was the only stir in the great chapel, and it would disappear quickly. Other than that there was no sign of life of any sort, no movement or sound. The marble altar rose palely, massively into the towering shadows. High above, the great dome of the chapel could be dimly seen.

Vinnie sat erectly with arms folded, stared directly ahead. The nun knelt with face slightly tilted toward the tabernacle.

It was long after midnight when they returned to the dormitory.

The next day was graduation day, a day of great excitement and festivity.

The ceremonies were elaborate and extremely formal. The graduating class wore white caps and gowns in the manner of a college graduation. The school orchestra played. The class sang. There were addresses, poems. The chaplain gave a little speech of farewell.

After the ceremonies, there was a reception. All the senior girls attended. The graduates were given their presents, mostly personal things such as bags, costume jewelry, gloves. Each girl was given the same number of gifts and, with slight variations of color and size, the same gifts.

The senior girls came up to see the gifts and to say goodbye to the graduates.

Vinnie went up with the others. But her face and manner in no way reflected the gladness of the occasion. She went quietly, almost indifferently. She seemed interested only in the summer pocketbooks the graduates received.

They were brightly colored pocketbooks of different hues, and each had a neckerchief to match. Vinnie opened one, opened it quite casually as if out of routine curiosity.

Then, swiftly, with a glance around to see that no one observed her, she slipped an addressed envelope into the pocketbook. It was addressed to a member of The Gang. Pinned to it was a note saying, "Please mail this outside. Its important. Please!"

Vinnie snapped the pocketbook closed, and went on to examine other presents.

July 22nd, and the feast of Mary Magdalen came. The day broke sunny and quiet, and the stained glass windows in the chapel shone in the level golden light when the solemn services for the Magdalens renewing their vows were held.

Breakfast was gay, with Sister Laurentia saying a few words after Grace, telling the profound significance of the feast of Mary Magdalen, the sinner, whom Christ forgave because she had loved so much.

The day was almost entirely a day of recreation. The big noonday dinner was served in the playground on the picnic tables, set out in banquet array. The sisters waited on table for the girls.

Vinnie, Cecelia and Rose sat together at one table. They kept to themselves. Their gayety was strained. After dinner, when the picnic tables and benches were being returned to their original places, the three girls were busy helping. It was as if by accident that one of the benches happened to be set near the wall.

Sunset came, and with the growing shadows Vinnie's tension grew. Not for a waking minute since the night of her father's death, had Vinnie given herself to anything but her resolve to escape and her desire for revenge. Now the hour was near.

Sister Lucy, aware that Vinnie had changed since the tragic night, had tried every possible way to penetrate her cold and sullen front. Vinnie had not fought the nun's efforts. She simply ignored them. Her personal hostility was lost in her deeper purpose.

Sister Lucy was sorely troubled though she hid her concern behind her smile. She increased her kindnesses to the girl. She sought her out, gave her little tasks to do that brought her more closely into her company. She had hoped for flashes of her old antagonism, flares of her old spirit. But Vinnie was cold and impenetrable.

Sister Lucy now was completely at a loss. All she could do was increase her prayers and mortifications for the girl.

After sunset, the quiet of the day was blown away in a wind that began easily but grew in force until with dark it was blowing a gale. It was unusual for July, everybody remarked. Loose windows flapped and the trees in the garden, protected though they were by the high walls, swayed and whined in the blasts.

After lights out in the dormitory, all, weary and content, were soon asleep—all but Vinnie, Cecelia and Rose.

They stayed tensely awake. The gale, moaning through the arches and eaves of the buildings, supplied a doleful accompaniment to their enterprise. It frightened Rose, and she signalled to Vinnie she was losing her nerve. But Vinnie grimly would not accept any withdrawal.

Ten o'clock came. The three girls rose noiselessly, dressed without sound. Cecelia and Rose then returned to bed to stay there until Vinnie's part was done. Cecelia was white with apprehension. Rose shook in fear. But Vinnie, cold, sure of herself, fiercely determined, tiptoed out of the dormitory. She carried her shoes, and such slight sound as she made could not be heard above the whining and moaning of the gale.

Vinnie had the linen room keys, taken from Agatha's desk just before bedtime. She had a folder of matches lifted from the purse of an operator in the beauty parlor. She moved quickly down the dimly lighted corridor. In the corridor, the sound of the gale came as a muffled lament.

Vinnie stopped at the linen room, quickly unlocked the door. It was too dark in the room for her to see the keyhole to the closet at the end of the room. She closed the door behind her and turned on the light.

Suddenly, above the wind, there was the sound of a sudden crash, like the shattering of a tree or the tumbling of a lamp post.

Vinnie, startled, alarmed, stood rigid an instant. Then, with frantic speed, she flew to the closet at the end of the room.

Sister Lucy, despite the toil and excitement of the day, had not slept soundly.

Carefully, but without Vinnie suspecting it, she had watched the girl during the long day and she had been more and more disturbed by her cold aloofness. On another day, it might not have disturbed her so deeply, but that Vinnie had kept apart from the spirit of this most festive of feasts was of critical and immediate concern.

Sister Lucy had watched too many girls in her years at the convent not to know when trouble was stirring. The insolent, the hostile Vinnie of other days had not bothered her so greatly. Then, she was giving vent to her ill feeling. But now, and especially with the coming of dark, it seemed as if her recent weeks of moody detachment were approaching a climax. It was something strange the nun felt rather than knew. The feast of Mary Magdalen, she thought, had always had a climactic feeling for her.

Thus, the sudden crash, splitting the wail of the wind, had awakened her.

Swiftly, following her first impulse, she hurried to the door to the dormitory, looked in. All seemed placid and undisturbed. Bed after bed stood whitely in their appointed places, and, in the shadowy light, head after head could be seen motionless against their pillows. Vinnie had pulled her blanket up and curled a corner of it against her pillow. Sister Lucy's eyes rested there only a moment. In the darkness and distance the illusion was flawless.

Sister Lucy turned away from the dormitory. She was on her way back to her room when a sudden and dramatic rising moan of the gale frightened her, stopped her. In that moment, standing stock still, she discovered the door to the linen room was edged with light. She moved swiftly down the corridor to the room.

Sister Lucy opened the door noiselessly. It was a long moment before the absorbed Vinnie, busy opening the jar of cleaning fluid, became aware of her.

She spun around and faced the nun.

There was a long, tense silence.

Sister Lucy saw that the girl was fully dressed except for her shoes. She saw the shoes on a stack of sheets beside her. She saw the matches. She saw the cleaning fluid. She saw, instantly, the fire and its possible tragic consequences. She saw the desperate and ruthless plan of escape.

The nun's youth ebbed from her. Her buoyancy was gone.

She went to the stunned girl, took her hand. She led her from the room.

"Thank God," she finally whispered. Her words seemed to come from a long distance.

Vinnie, in sullen silence, sat in Sister Lucy's little office. The gale had diminished and now it was a quiet wind that troubled the night.

It was some minutes after they reached the room before Sister Lucy had been able to talk. The enormity of the peril in the projected escape had frightened her. At first she prayed, prayed silently for charity and patience. She kept telling herself that this was the day that commemorated Christ's forgiveness of Mary Magdalen and she must try to forgive.

But it was hard to forgive one who did not ask for forgiveness, who was not penitent, whose only emotions seemed to be hatred and the anger of frustration.

Sister Lucy, when finally she had command of herself, spoke softly into the silence. She had been so fond of her, she told Vinnie. She had liked her spirit, even the openness of her defiance. She had liked the bravery with which she had endured the shock of her father's death. She was sure one day she was going to be proud of her.

She had prayed constantly for her. She was confident her prayers would be answered. And now....

"I prayed!" Vinnie fiercely broke her silence. "I even prayed to that Teresa of yours! The next day they told me my father was going to be executed." She sneered the words, "That's what prayers did!"

Sister Lucy spoke quietly. "Do you think your father's tragedy was a result of your prayers, Teresa?"

The girl returned to her silence and did not answer.

The nun tried to draw her out again. She asked her if she realized the catastrophe that might have occurred if the fire had been set. She pointed out to her the futility of her escape had she achieved it A man might hide for a while but not a girl. A girl could never lose herself in the land of shadows. She asked her if she felt sorry, if she could say anything that might lighten the burden of her guilt.

But Vinnie did not stir from her sullen silence.

Sister Lucy could no longer conceal the depth of her dejection. The tragedy was, she said, that Vinnie would now be sent away. She could no longer stay at the school. No girl who was so great a danger to the others could be permitted to remain.

A look of surprise quickened Vinnie's sullen face. This was something Vinnie, who thought she had considered everything, had not considered. The look faded almost as quickly as it had come.

It was a rule of the school, the nun unhappily went on, a rule final and complete.'

"Good!" Vinnie flared. "Any place'll be better than this joint!"

Then, even as Vinnie spoke, there rose out of the darkness beyond the window the cry of the siren of a police car. It screamed and died away.

Vinnie, pale, got slowly to her feet, stared in terror at the window.

Sister Lucy, puzzled, got to her feet after her. The sound of a police siren was common enough in the neighborhood.

Then, the siren cried out again but abruptly its screaming was cut to shreds by a fusilade of shots.

The fusilade hammered the dark in a rapid, angry staccato, then stopped abruptly. The siren's cry faded to a whisper, died.

There was silence again, complete, empty.

"It's Duke, it's the cops," Vinnie monotoned. "I'm finished, I'm finished good now." She turned slowly from the window. "I told him not to come. I begged him not to come, the dirty—"

Then, she broke. She threw herself face down on the narrow sofa in the office, began to sob.

The sullenness, the defiance, the hate, fiercely sustained for weeks, ebbed from her. She grew limp, weak, became very much another young derelict, lost and frightened.

Sister Lucy, moved beyond words, stood in silence over her. The sobbing, choked futilely into the bedspread, rose and fell, rose and fell, then stopped.

After a while, Vinnie, like one making a confession, began to talk. She talked at first into the sofa with her face still down, and her words, almost inarticulate with emotion, were hardly intelligible. But after a moment, as her confession eased her terror, her speech became clearer.

She told Sister Lucy the story of her past, of her home, of her life with her crowd, of The Gang, of Mike, the marine, of Duke, of the shooting, of the trial and the judgment. The nun tried to stop her at first, not wanting to know what she wanted to tell. Then, realizing that this was a burden the girl had to deliver herself of, she ceased to oppose her and listened.

Vinnie told of her plans to escape, of the letter sent to the outside. Duke had come with the others in the getaway car, she was sure. She was afraid he would come if he could, and she had begged them not to let him. She had a feeling his coming would bring only misfortune.

She talked on and on and then, finally, her soul confessed, could talk no more. She slipped down into complete exhaustion and then into sleep. Sister Lucy covered her where she lay.

It seemed to Sister Lucy that the confession that drained the girl's strength had also drained from her the last drops of her perversity and bitterness, as if her final, anguished realization of the futility of her life had exorcised her of malice.

Daybreak found Vinnie still sleeping. Sister Lucy sat in her chair, silhouetted against the pale light of the window, wide awake, saying her beads, praying for courage to face the decision of the day.

Sergeant Elkart, who looked like a conservatively dressed manager of a branch bank but was a police inspector, sat in Mother Superior's office. Across from him sat Mother Superior and Sister Laurentia. The morning sun was still so early that its light came almost levelly through the window.

Mother Superior's bright eyes shone gratefully in her thin, delicate face. "Thank God, Sergeant," she said, "we had no trouble here last night. There was no commotion among the girls. None that I know of, certainly."

The inspector got to his feet. "Good enough," he said. "The report I got made it look pretty sure there was some tie-up between The Gang and your kids inside here. We figured there might have been an attempted break." He turned to go, creased his felt hat. "Course, these jerks nowadays don't have to have any reason to make trouble. They like trouble. They'll start shooting just for the hell of it." He grinned. "Excuse me, Sister, but you know what I mean."

Mother Superior and Sister Laurentia, on their feet now, nodded gravely.

Mother Superior went to the door with the inspector. "This boy—the boy they call Duke—will he die?"

Elkart shook his head. "No such luck. He's tough as nails, the so-and-so. They've cut the slugs out of him and he'll be walking around in a couple of weeks. But he won't be walking very far. He nearly killed a guard he ran over up at the farm when he escaped. He's going to have plenty of extra time to recuperate." He waved a hand. "Good morning. Thanks."

After the door closed on the inspector, the two nuns looked into each other's eyes with deep concern. Despite their years of experience with wickedness they had never been able to be at ease before the mystery of iniquity.

Meanwhile, Sister Lucy had put Vinnie to bed in the infirmary and now, fearful, was hurrying down the long corridors to Mother Superior's office.

Mother Superior and Sister Laurentia, grim-faced, listened to Sister Lucy's account of the night before.

She told them of her premonition, of the strange crash that had awakened her, of finding Vinnie in the linen closet, of the police-car siren and the shooting in the streets, of Vinnie's collapse.

"Why didn't you come and wake us?" Sister Laurentia asked. "Or why didn't you come to us the first thing this morning?"

"I couldn't," Sister Lucy answered. "I felt I couldn't leave the child alone a moment, not for a moment, and I couldn't trust anyone with her. She was in such a despair. Her anguish was especially deep because some time ago she had learned to pray—she had even prayed to her patroness, little Saint Teresa—and all she could see come from it was misfortune and more misfortune. She had a dreadful time of it last night, had really dark hours of suffering."

There was quiet a long moment.

"What was the strange crash you heard?" Mother Superior finally asked. "Was that any part of the plan to escape, do you think?"

"I have no idea, Mother," Sister Lucy answered. "It could have been some loose slates from the roof."

"Yes, we must have the roof fixed," Mother Superior said.

Then Mother Superior told Sister Lucy of the police inspector's visit. "We will have to turn Teresa back to the police," she ended quietly. "It's our duty, Sister."

Life ebbed from the young nun's face. "I'm sorry they had any idea our children were involved," she whispered. "I was going to ask that Teresa be permitted to remain here. It's a great pity."

Sister Laurentia was very grave. "Do you think it would be wise, Sister, to permit a girl like that to remain here? Too often there's a next time. She is, I'm afraid, in need of sterner measures and stronger confinement than we are able to provide."

"God only knows what would become of her if she left here," Sister Lucy said.

Mother Superior was distressed. "I wish we could keep the child," she said. "But we have all of our other children to think of, and their souls to save. It is our most solemn duty in God's eyes."

Sister Lucy, suddenly intense, began to plead for Vinnie. She told in detail of the girl's breakdown and confession. "She is changed!" Sister Lucy cried out. "I know! I saw her heart torn up by the roots!"

Mother Superior and Sister Laurentia were deeply moved.

"You deserve great credit for your wisdom and alertness, Sister," Mother Superior said.

There was a finality to Mother Superior's words. No one spoke. After a moment, Sister Lucy, with a humbly obedient bow of acceptance, withdrew.

Now, silence lay between the two older nuns. It was restless, uncomfortable silence.

After a moment, Sister Laurentia rose from her chair, began to move in gentle disquiet about the room.

Mother Superior finally spoke. "Sister Lucy is a true Sister of the Good Shepherd. She loves all of her lambs, and is guided only by her love of them."

"It was hard not to give in to her wish that Teresa be permitted to stay," Sister Laurentia murmured.

"Very hard," Mother Superior sighed. "Sister Lucy has the simple wisdom of a child, the wisdom without which we cannot enter into the kingdom of heaven. It is difficult to oppose it."

"Still, it was a terrible tragedy this child could have wrought," Sister Laurentia continued to move abstractedly about the room.

Mother Superior bowed her head. "Especially for those who are not ready to meet their Maker."

There was silence again. Sister Laurentia came to a stop before the window. Something she saw beyond the window had caught her gaze.

It was a moment before Sister Laurentia spoke. Mother Superior was surprised to detect in the Sister's gentle, long-disciplined voice a quaver of emotion.

"I think, Mother," she said, and her efforts to keep her words controlled were obvious, "that perhaps we should have another talk with Sister Lucy."

Mother Superior was surprised at this change in Sister Laurentia. She studied her back against the window, saw it was tensely erect.

"Would you come here, Mother?" Sister Laurentia said, not turning.

Mother Superior went to the window.

Sister Laurentia nodded down to the garden. "See. Do you suppose that could have been the crash that Sister Lucy heard?"

It was a moment before Mother Superior spoke. "It could well have been," she said quietly.

On the grass in the garden lay what once had been the statue of Saint Teresa. It lay tumbled from its shrine, shattered into many pieces. The two nuns at the window continued to look down into the garden in silence.

Finally, Mother Superior said, "It was the high wind last night that caused the crash, I'm sure."

"Yes, Mother," Sister Laurentia nodded her agreement. "It was the high wind."

"It was unquestionably the high wind," Mother Superior said in her quiet voice.

Sister Laurentia said nothing more. There was a long silence.

Mother Superior turned away from the window to her desk. "It may be that you are right, Sister," she said. "It might be wise to have another talk with Sister Lucy."

Mother Superior lifted the telephone to send for Sister Lucy. Sister Laurentia, at the window, continued to look down into the garden.

And so it came about that Vinnie was allowed to stay in the big red house on Hope Street.

Notes for the Reader

ON THE REASON FOR ANN & OTHER STORIES

The following abbreviations are used in the notes:

*CE*All references to the *Catholic Encyclopedia* are to the original edition published from 1907–1912 in New York by Robert Appleton Company in fifteen volumes. This comprehensive reference work is available online at New Advent (www.newadvent.org/cathen).

*CW*G. K. Chesterton, *The Collected Works*, 37 vols. (San Francisco: Ignatius Press, 1986–2012).

[*DR*]All Bible references are to the Douay-Rheims 1899 American edition, unless otherwise noted.

*OED*Oxford *English Dictionary Online*, Oxford University Press, March 2019.

"The Reason for Ann"

3: "Some entries…in red, some in black"

Connolly's imagery evokes the text of a Roman Missal or Sacramentary, ordinarily printed in red and black; thus, the popular instruction to priests: say the black; do the red. See the next note for an explicit reference.

8: "An ancient illuminated missal"

See the previous note for the significance of the colors of the text in a Roman Missal. Illuminated texts like *The Book of Kells* were exquisitely decorated; many are considered fine works of art in and of themselves.

8: "Stern and almost scientific"

Though Basil is far from a villain in the story, Connolly warns against an excessive scientism, a reduction of the human person to "numerals, dates and computations." By giving Basil a central place in the story, however, Connolly acknowledges the importance of such data; it cannot be overlooked or ignored. He was nonetheless concerned about the rise of scientific materialism: in his 1950 novel *The Bump on Brannigan's Head*, a cold and austere scientist is a prominent antagonist.

9: "Precise, well-behaved columns"

This line echoes Walt Whitman's famous "When I Heard the Learn'd Astronomer," a thematically though not necessarily theologically sympathetic text.

10: "The darkness was deeper"

That is, both literally and spiritually: in escaping the consequences of his actions, O'Sullivan's soul is now even more at risk.

11: "The last of his mother's prayers"

Connolly invokes St. Monica, who prayed incessantly for Augustine's conversion. See this volume's introduction for a discussion of how Connolly uses the necessity of prayer as a literary device in the story.

11: "Sticker"

A sticking point; something difficult to figure out or get beyond.

13: "Physical beauty...man's desire"

Basil's response is designed to counter Gerald's overly Romantic view of beauty. Indeed, O'Sullivan has a bit of the Byronic Hero in him. Basil references the Platonic or idealist concept of beauty as a function of desire or longing.

13: "Unangelic wings"

The angels' discussion here will doubtless remind many readers of Capra's film *It's a Wonderful Life* (1947), on which Connolly worked, though to what extent is unclear.

The innovation for Connolly here, however, is that he has proposed that earthly wings—i.e., quite literally becoming a pilot—has paved the way for O'Sullivan to earn his angelic wings, so to speak.

23: "Lush or highfalutin"

"Lush" is slang for drunk here; "highfalutin" means pretentious or over-the-top, especially in one's speech.

23: "The more she gave, the more she was herself"

This line encapsulates Connolly's spiritual emphasis: one gains life and finds oneself, as it were, by giving oneself away completely for Christ, following Christ's explicit teaching of the same (e.g., Luke 9:23–24). This teaching is sometimes called "the law of the gift," following again one of Christ's explicit words on the matter: what you give away is what will be given to you (e.g., Luke 6:38).

27: "Heaven is the end of all dreams"

The first function of this line is humorous suspense. Basil means "end" as "no more," that is, heaven is where there will be no more dreamy romanticizations, for what purpose could they have in the beatific vision? But by the end of the story, we realize that "end" can mean "final cause," that is, in heaven all of humanity's most noble dreams are fulfilled. Heaven is humanity's proper end or *telos*, in other words, and Connolly's line puns on "end" to help the reader experience the joy of the story's surprise ending.

The second function is to make an abstruse but ultimately rewarding allusion. Connolly was a lifelong fan of Chesterton: he referenced him and his ideas frequently in his fiction, and he worked with him when Connolly edited *Columbia*, the international journal of the Knights of Columbus. Chesterton appreciated the art of the famous poet Charles Swinburne but frequently rebutted his ideas; Swinburne's quasi-mystical, neo-pagan spiritual vision could not have been more different from Chesterton's. In his column "Surviving the Swinburne Epoch," for instance, Chesterton references Eliot, Wilde, and others in warning his readers about the inevitable collapse of "Swinburnian" love.[1]

What Connolly is doing in this line, therefore, is joining in that debate about the "end" of love and dreams. Basil means that Swinburnian Romanticism has no place in heaven, and while Chesterton might agree, he would be the first to figure the Christian journey as an adventure. As he argues in "The Romance of Orthodoxy"—a chapter of *Orthodoxy* in which he quotes Swinburne and refutes many of his ideas—"you cannot finish a sum how you like. But you can finish a story how you like."[2] Basil and Gerald, and Connolly's story itself, seem to be born from this line.

Connolly may also have been aware of Ezra Pound's odd appreciation of Swinburne, captured memorably in the iconoclastically titled poem "Salve O Pontifex!" (1908).[3] Strangely enough, another Pound poem about Swinburne, titled simply "Swinburne: A Critique," contains the line "the end of all dreams."[4] The poem, however, remained unpublished until 1976.[5]

28: "Casuistry"

Basil means a kind of theological finagling by which one wrangles one's way into heaven despite the certainty of

---

1.   *CW*, Vol. 35, pp. 487–91.

2.   *CW*, Vol. 1, p. 342.

3.   Michael John King, ed., *Collected Early Poems of Ezra Pound* (London: Faber and Faber, 1976), p. 40.

4.   Ibid., p. 261, line 13.

5.   Ibid., p. vii.

facts. Such laxity is not casuistry proper, but in Connolly's time the word had become synonymous with its abuses. See *CE*, "Casuistry," for a detailed history.

30: "Old Russian DB-Three"

Ilyushin DB-3s were Soviet long-range bombers active during World War II. Continuously developed and improved, they were effectively replaced by the Ilyushin Il-4 in the early-to-mid-1940s. A DB-3 in the Korean War would have been a very rare sight: none are officially recorded to have been in service.

31: "Yaks"

Yakovlev Yak-9s were Soviet fighter planes used by the North Koreans.

"Love, Tomi"

47: "Bert Mellowes having a telephone bill…"

In *Mr. Blue*, Connolly used numerous details—many of them word for word[6]—from Fitzgerald's *The Great Gatsby* to present a very different American dream: the beauty of total self-offering in joyful service of God and neighbor. Here, Connolly is drawing on one of the biggest clues to Gatsby's clandestine, national counterfeiting network: his constant, mysterious phone calls from shady characters. While that detail remains dramatic irony in *Gatsby*—even Nick seems not to figure it out until the end—Connolly uses it here

---

6.   See my introduction and notes in the annotated edition of *Mr. Blue* (Tacoma, WA: Cluny Media, 2015).

both to help the reader suspect Bert's villainy and to invest the postman Jim Grady with heightened perception ("some sort of racket"). Given Connolly's love of Chesterton, this show of great yet unrecognized humanity in the postman—"nobody would listen to Jim"—is likely a reference to the well-known Father Brown story "The Invisible Man."

48: "Away out of date"

A common expression at the time that has now been replaced by "way out of date."

49: "Annapolis"

The location of the United States Naval Academy. Connolly served in the Navy in World War I.

52: "Lugo"

Perhaps a reference to Lugo, Spain, the Galician city famous for its ancient Roman walls and its contributions to Galician wine.

55: "C.A.'s"

"Ca." is a common abbreviation in medical journals for cancer.

60: "And maybe we…your idea of us."

This fundamental expression of *metanoia*—a change of life flowing from a dilated soul occasioned by a spiritual person's seeing the best in you—is at the heart of Connolly's fiction. The concept is the driving force, for instance, behind the characterization of the title character in Connolly's 1951 novel *Dan England and the Noonday Devil*.

68: "Blue Jacket's Manual"

A massive handbook—up to 800 pages in some editions—introducing the basic concepts of seamanship to those entering the United States Navy.

68: "No one could…on paper."

Father Anthony's advice to Tomi is something more than feel-good sentimentalism or pop psychology. Indeed, the priest is portrayed as "strict and stern." For a fuller discussion, see the introduction in this volume.

69: "God is a father…Pop."

By ending the story on this association between Tomi's biological father and God the Father, Connolly opens up the entire narrative as a spiritual colloquy. The letter Tomi has written is as much to God the Father as it is to his birth father. For a fuller discussion, see the introduction in this volume.

"The Pigeon from St. Bartholomew's"

73: "Impersonal world"

Connolly will repeat this characterization later in the story when Mr. Somerset admires a statue of Atlas and "the rhythmic impersonality of his firmament" (83). Connolly portrays the protagonist in this way precisely to undermine or invert that very view: the world for Connolly is deeply personal, suffused with the grandeur of the Incarnation.

74: "Homburg"

A formal dress hat similar to a fedora but more proper or staid.

76: "Toss-pot"

A depreciative if not urbane expression to describe a drunkard.

77: "*That'll* be my church today"

As Connolly pointedly did in his third novel *Dan England*, he sharply criticizes secular humanism as a wholly inadequate substitute for God. Here, the secular project is represented by the United Nations, which had been established in 1945, less than a decade ago before the publication of this story. (The U.N.'s predecessor, the League of Nations, had been established in 1920.)

79: "Sapience"

This keen wordplay by Connolly works on many levels. Literally, Mr. Somerset believes himself intellectually better than the church-goers: they are "foolish," but he is wise and knowing: sapient. Given the multi-generational insistence on genetics in the sentence, Mr. Somerset is quite literally identifying himself as *homo sapiens*, the evolved man free of the dumbing-down effects of religion, as he sees it. Yet Connolly, always deeply invested in the Catholic tradition, points to the irony of his protagonist's use of the word. *O Sapientia*, one of the "O Antiphons" of the Advent season, identifies Christ Himself as Wisdom Incarnate. The true wisdom Mr. Somerset desires—and indeed believes he already possesses—comes not through secular humanism, Connolly implies, but through Christ's presence in His Church.

80: "Happiness Through The Conquest Of Desire"

No book by this name existed in Connolly's time, nor has

one in this name been published as of early 2019. Given the pious context, the title may be Connolly's nod to the strain in Catholic spirituality that emphasizes radical detachment, even from one's own desires. Take the well-known quotation of St. Louise de Marillac, for instance: "No desires, no resolutions. The grace of my God will accomplish in me whatever he wills."[7]

However, Connolly is up to something more, as Mr. Somerset's further comments make clear. The protagonist, though an avowed agnostic, is exactly right when criticizing religion as pragmatism: praying in order to "grow thin" is not prayer at all but self-fulfillment at best and deluded self-worship at worst. For Connolly, piety must not become navel-gazing.

There may also be a prophetic function to the book's title. In popular spiritual movements, the "conquest of desire" refers to an Eastern mystical tradition: the path to enlightenment, to non-duality and oblivion, and the like. Such ideas were commonplace in the United States in the 1950s[8] and would become very popular in both secular and Catholic America in the next two decades, thanks to books like Thomas Merton's *Mystics and Zen Masters* (1967) and *Zen and the Birds of Appetite* (1968), and Robert Pirsig's *Zen and the Art of Motorcycle Maintenance* (1974). Given Connolly's

7.   Alban Butler, *Butler's Lives of the Saints*, New Full Edition, vol. 11 (Collegeville, MN: Liturgical Press, 1999), p. 155.

8.   "The United States by 1950 had become better acquainted with traditions well beyond the confines of Judaism and Christianity... The buds of an ever-broadening religious pluralism became evident to all, and these burst into full bloom after 1965." Edwin Gaustad and Leigh Schmidt, *The Religious History of America: The Heart of the American Story from Colonial Times to Today*, rev. ed. (New York: HarperOne, 2002), pp. 288, 291.

constant emphasis in his work on the power of redemptive suffering found only in substance in the Catholic Church, his invention of this title seems like a warning against what he saw as dangerous spiritual trends.

81: "Genii"

Plural of both genie and genius, though most often used in the sense of the former (*OED*).

82: "Vulgus"

"The common people; the ordinary ruck [crowd]" (*OED*).

82: "Bedizened"

"To dress out, especially in a vulgar or gaudy fashion" (*OED*).

83: "Maori"

The indigenous peoples of New Zealand, the Maori experienced rapid growth in the 1950s and began to integrate more fully into cities: "In the early 1950s, Māori-run institutions were strengthened or created to meet the needs of urban-based Māori, such as the Māori Women's Welfare League, the volunteer Māori wardens, and the urban committees."[9]

85: "Holmes, the American jurist"

The famous quotation is by Supreme Court Justice

9.   Natacha Gagné, *Being Māori in the City: Indigenous Everyday Life in Auckland* (Toronto: University of Toronto Press, 2013), p. 31.

Oliver Wendell Holmes, Jr., from his article "Natural Law," which appeared in *The Harvard Law Review* in 1918.

87: "Viscid"

A word used almost always to describe sticky food textures or, in ecology, glue-like attributes of plant parts, Mr. Somerset's application of it here to human beings is very much out of place in terms of common usage—but very much of the materialist mindset Connolly wishes to portray in his protagonist.

87: "Adductive"

Like his use of the word "embolus" at the end of *Mr. Blue*, Connolly here uses a word with a clear literal meaning that also draws the reader deeply into the theological mystery of the story. Literally, adductive here means the power to draw a part into its greater whole: Mr. Somerset, along with the crowd, is pulled into St. Patrick's, the Catholic church in the story. However, adductive also refers to a long-standing debate about the Eucharist and transubstantiation. See the introduction in this volume for a fuller discussion.

88: "Golden ciborium"

The more common name for this canopy is a "baldacchino," though in a Catholic architectural context it is roughly synonymous with "ciborium." A ciborium also refers to the sacred dish in which hosts are reserved in the tabernacle or used to serve the faithful. See the introduction in this volume for a fuller discussion.

92: "Mr. Somerset was buried"

The title of the story now makes more sense. The pigeon that inadvertently killed Mr. Somerset was apparently from St. Patrick's, the Catholic church; the title can refer to that bird only obliquely. The title more fully refers to Mr. Somerset himself: a "pigeon," in the common parlance of the times, is someone naïve or foolish, a scapegoat. See the introduction in this volume for further details.

92: "The Future of Marriage"

One can hardly miss the irony here: Mr. Somerset's wife cannot attend her own husband's funeral because "the future of marriage" is more important.

92: "One pigeon…made off with the largest piece"

This line echoes a passage in the first book of Samuel: "The well-fed hire themselves out for bread, while the hungry batten on spoil."[10] See the introduction of this volume for a fuller discussion.

"Natural Causes"

97: "Tole"

"Tin-plated sheet-iron which is first varnished and then ornamented by decorative painting" (*OED*).

99: "Highboy"

Synonymous with "tallboy," a tall "chest of drawers or a bureau standing on a dressing-table" (*OED*).

---

10.   1 Samuel 2:5, NAB translation.

100: "In his cups"

"The drinking of intoxicating liquor…drunken revelry" (*OED*).

100: "Organdie"

"A fine but stiff, translucent kind of muslin" (*OED*).

114: "In youth…"

The verses cited are the last four lines of the sixteen-line poem "Gold Leaves" by Chesterton. It appears in *The Wild Knight*, a very early collection of his poems.[11] Chesterton himself jokes that "many of them [are] juvenile."[12]

123: "Jalopy"

"A battered old motor vehicle" (*OED*).

128: "Black and lace"

An outfit traditionally associated with death and mourning. Connolly sets up a false foreshadowing here so that Betsy's survival will be a surprise.

"Seminary Hill"

136: "Oriels"

"A large polygonal recess with a window, projecting from a building" (*OED*).

---

11. G. K. Chesterton, *The Wild Knight*, 4th ed. with additional poems (London: J. M. Dent & Sons, 1914), pp. 25–26.

12. Ibid., p. vi.

140: "Surplusage"

Synonymous with surplus (*OED*).

145: "Stranger in a strange land"

The now-famous Robert Heinlein novel of the same name would not come out until 1961, almost a decade after Connolly's story. The phrase as Connolly uses it here was a commonplace, likely popularized by the King James translation of Exodus 2:22: "I have been a stranger in a strange land."

154: "Laetare Sunday"

The fourth Sunday of Lent looks forward to the Resurrection of Easter in a special way. "The contrast between Laetare and the other Sundays [of Lent]…is emblematical of the joys of this life, restrained rejoicing mingled with a certain amount of sadness."[13]

157: "Score"

"To compose or arrange for orchestral performance;" to make a musical score (*OED*).

159: "The seal of confession"

One of the most serious matters in all Church law, the seal of confession is absolute: "Regarding the sins revealed to him in sacramental confession, the priest is bound to inviolable secrecy."[14] The penalties for breaking it are severe; at one point in the Church's history, the penalty was the

---

13. *CE*, "Laetare Sunday."

14. *CE*, "The Sacrament of Penance."

defrocking of the priest and a lifetime of penance in a monastery.[15] See also *CE*, "The Seal of Confession."

161: "Fusillade"

"A simultaneous discharge of firearms; a wholesale execution by this means" (*OED*).

"The Big Red House on Hope Street"

179: "Pigeons…patsies"

A pigeon here means "a naïve or gullible person; a fool or simpleton," while a patsy is "a person who is easily taken advantage of, esp. by being deceived, cheated, or blamed for something" (*OED*).

182: "Slag-bellied"

A regional variant, derivative, or confusion of "swag-bellied": to have a "pendulous paunch" (*OED*).

182: "Till"

"A drawer, money-box, or similar receptacle under and behind the counter of a shop or bank" (*OED*).

186: "Coif"

"A close-fitting cap covering the top, back, and sides of the head" (*OED*). A religious sister might also attach a veil to the coif. Connolly's point, however, is that Sister Mary Paula's habit is a different color, which distinguishes her as the "outside sister," the one designated for interaction with the world.

---

15. Ibid.

186: "St. Mary Euphrasia"

Saint Mary Euphrasia Pelletier (1796–1868) founded the Congregation of Our Lady of Charity of the Good Shepherd. She was canonized in 1940, little more than a decade before Connolly published this story.

198: "Jerk-water…yappy"

Jerkwater is colloquial for a "small, insignificant, inferior" place; Vinnie means that the dress is the kind one would wear in such a location (*OED*). Her subsequent synonymous definition of "yappy" is unconventional and likely slang.

201: "Got hep"

Slang for "the fact or condition of being (or appearing to be) well-informed or in the know" (*OED*).

210: "INFLAMMABLE"

"Capable of being inflamed or set on fire" (*OED*). The antonym is nonflammable.

217: "Addlebrained"

"Lacking clear or rational thought; muddled; stupid" (*OED*).

232: "Saying her beads"

A common expression at the time for praying the Rosary.

Cluny Media

Designed by Fiona Cecile Clarke, the Cluny Media *logo
depicts a monk at work in the scriptorium,
with a cat sitting at his feet.*

*The monk represents our mission to emulate
the invaluable contributions of the monks
of Cluny in preserving the libraries of the West,
our strivings to know and love the truth.*

*The cat at the monk's feet is Pangur Bán, from the
eponymous Irish poem of the 9th century.
The anonymous poet compares his scholarly
pursuit of truth with the cat's happy hunting of mice.
The depiction of Pangur Bán is an homage to the work
of the monks of Irish monasteries and a sign
of the joy we at Cluny take in our trade.*

"Messe ocus Pangur Bán,
cechtar nathar fria saindan:
bíth a menmasam fri seilgg,
mu memna céin im saincheirdd."

Made in the USA
Middletown, DE
02 September 2021